*Steve
Wilson*

Red Sky
at
Morning

Published by White Feather Press. (www.whitefeatherpress.com)

ISBN 978-1-61808-035-6

Printed in the United States of America

Cover design created by Steve Wilson and Adam Wilson Design

This is a work of fiction. The characters and incidents are not to
be construed as real. Any resemblance to actual events or persons,
living or dead, is entirely coincidental. While some technology is
grounded in reality, certain liberties have been taken in the interests
of creating a compelling story.

Author photo courtesy of Betty Klepacki,
www.bettyrocksphotography.com

White Feather Press

Reaffirming Faith in God, Family, and Country!

For Sheila

Red Sky
at
Morning

Prologue ✶ Green Light

Bishkek, Northern Kyrgyzstan,
Former Soviet Union

FIRST LIEUTENANT MICHAEL NEILL, USMC, settled into the Humvee he rode in and watched as the snowy countryside rushed by. This vehicle wasn't heavily armored like those found in the war zones of Iraq or Afghanistan; its canvas-covered doorframes were drafty, and let in the cold, but the heater was working and the Marine was getting warmer. It helped that Neill wore a fleece liner beneath his Gore-Tex all-weather jacket. Outside, a front was moving south, dumping more flurries that promised to add another layer to the ice crystals already blanketing the frozen topsoil.

Neill turned his attention to the west. Night came quickly this time of year, but above the forest of leafless pistachio and walnut trees—in addition to a few white spruces, their branches unaffected by the weather—Michael could see the peaks of the perpetually snow-covered mountain range known as the Tian Shan, the Central Asian version of the Alps.

In the front seats of the lumbering vehicle were the driver and a Staff Sergeant from the Security Forces Squadron. Another Humvee followed behind, carrying more Security Forces personnel and a photographer from Public Affairs.

Next to Neill was the base commander, Colonel Mabry. Leaving the city of Bishkek—once known as Frunze during the Cold War—the Humvees passed the International Airport and made their way to the gated entry point of the Manas Transit Center, the sole American military base in this part of the former Soviet Union.

On the ramp, a variety of aircraft were parked; C-17s and C-130s—gray tails, as they were dubbed—the big cargo planes that were the mainstays of the U.S. war effort; commercially chartered rotators, used to transport American and coalition troops to Bagram and other bases in Afghanistan; and a few smaller aircraft; unmarked, save for a single emblem comically depicting the silhouette of a bushy tailed rodent holding an automatic weapon—the 'secret squirrel' insignia adopted by some in the Special Forces community. A few were preparing for departure, and ground crews were de-icing the wings in the face of the bitter winter weather.

Activated in 2001, the facility had been known by several names over the years and for a short time it was designated as an air base—but that was too militaristic for the Kyrgyz government. The Transit Center's primary role was to support U.S. and coalition military forces in Afghanistan, a two to three hour flight to the south, depending on the aircraft. Its current name sounded benign enough, but for many of the combat troops headed to forward operating bases near Pakistan or Helmand Province, it was simply known as the Gateway to Hell.

The U.S. servicemen in the Humvees had spent the better part of the day at two of the city's orphanages, delivering food, clothing, and school supplies. Public Affairs had tagged along to take a few pictures. It was part of an on-going effort to be involved with the local community, improving the lives of the citizens of Bishkek and, in turn, increasing the likelihood that an American presence would continue there for some time.

In the past, relations between the U.S. and the Kyrgyz population had soured; the shooting of a Bishkek citizen and rumors that the American base was mishandling toxic chemicals had led to an uneasy relationship. On top of that, the Kyrgyz parliament was feeling the pressure from Russia and China. Neither country appreciated having an American military presence embedded so close to their borders, and both wanted the base shuttered. Kyrgyzstan responded by raising the rent; and since that time, the United States had agreed to pay three times more each year for the use of the Transit Center's facilities. To the Department of Defense, it was a deal with the devil; but with the on-going war in Afghanistan, the agreement was crucial to moving troops in and out of the war zone.

Neill had arrived three months earlier, just as winter was setting in. He'd been assigned to Manas primarily because of his fluency in Russian; Michael had grown up in Ukraine, the son of missionaries. A congressman—the same one who had secured Neill's appointment to the Naval Academy—had suggested that maybe the young Lieutenant could give American and coalition forces in the republic a hand. The gambit had paid off.

It was time to get along, and in an effort to restore good will, the Transit Center personnel—operated for the most part by the Air Force—had embarked on a series of gestures designed to regain the hearts of the Kyrgyz people. At first these attempts were awkward. Then Neill suggested that the base open its gates to local hospitals and doctors. He knew, from first-hand experience, that clinics in the former Soviet republics were years behind their Western counterparts. And he was also painfully aware of the poor health conditions these people endured.

The experiment had been wildly successful. Mabry couldn't have been happier. The culture of the Air Force was big on 'bullets'—measurable achievements used to bolster careers—and this outreach to the community had added a big feather to the Colonel's cap. Neill's role as interpreter was crucial. The young Marine seemed at ease with the Kyrgyz people, and that was fine by Mabry. Soon the doctors of both nations had begun working side by side, with the American physicians providing training in procedures that were rarely—if ever—practiced in Kyrgyzstan. It was not without its share of problems in the beginning, but these proved to be minor. For one, the legal eagles were a little skittish about letting Kyrgyz physicians treat the Center's personnel—a legitimate concern, as it turned out—so the local docs were restricted to observing only.

The arrangement went both ways. On their days off, or when the Clinic's census was low, the Air Force medical personnel accepted invitations to visit the hospitals of Bishkek. What they found there was an eye-opener. The practice of re-using syringes was wide-spread. Antibiotics were in short supply. Many surgical procedures were behind the times and practiced under less than sterile conditions. The American doctors left shaking their heads—in spite of the media barrage back home, the quality of healthcare in the U.S. really *did* eclipse other countries.

Neill enjoyed trips like the one today. Of course, it had very little to do with his role as a Marine, but it was always gratifying to make a difference in people's lives, and that was something desperately needed in places like Bishkek. He'd spent enough time in Eastern Europe to remember the gypsy children there, encouraged at a young age to beg from strangers. He felt sympathy for anyone unfortunate enough to be born under those conditions in this part of the world.

To a cynic, there was no getting around the political motivations behind the military's interaction with the local community. It was damage control, pure and simple. But it was also much more. Today's humanitarian mission was also an attempt to calm ruffled feathers and tamp down tensions between former adversaries in an uneasy alliance. Neill was aware of all that, but shrugged it off. Helping people was virtuous, even if the motivations behind it weren't always so pure.

Now the lead Humvee was navigating the narrow roads running through the Transit Center, and that brought Neill's mind back to the present. The characteristically Soviet design of some of the older buildings, (big, boxy and unimaginative) leftover from the days of communist rule, gave way to newer structures set up by the U.S. or ISAF—the International Security Assistance Force. Big tents dotted the outer edges of the base, set up to house the thousands of transient service members that passed through Manas each week.

The lights were on now, positioned on high towers ringing the Transit Center's perimeter, illuminating the snow as it fell. More were glowing as they powered up along the few streets winding through the base. It was dinner time, and with chow being served, the troops—bundled up against the cold—were converging on the DFAC, or dining facility.

Neill was starving. The driver stopped the Humvee between the recreation center—Pete's Place, as it was known—and the DFAC to drop him off. Neill gave the base commander a crisp salute and then headed off for some food as the Air Force personnel continued on to the command post. The sudden chill of the evening air brought a shiver to the Marine. He adjusted the zipper of his jacket so the collar rested snugly under his chin.

The food at Manas was excellent, much better than some of the chow halls Neill was accustomed to. Fresh milk was always a big hit. The Transit Center seemed to have plenty of it this winter. The local cuisine was also occasionally featured, and most of that was quite good, too.

Neill blessed his food and dug right in, then indulged in a slice of apple pie with coffee for dessert. He considered heading over to the rec center to see what the evening's festivities might be, but then saw a familiar face heading his way. His roommate, an Air Force Captain named Sanderson, approached wearing a puzzled look.

"You lose your phone, Neill?" he asked. "I've been calling

you for an hour."

"Wow," Neill blinked. He pushed himself from the table and fished around in the breast pocket of his jacket. "I've had it turned off all afternoon. Whassup?"

Sanderson pulled up a chair. "The Wing Vice Commander's been lookin' for you. No worries, though," he smiled. "I told him you were out in town sight-seeing."

Michael nodded, switching on his cell phone. "Appreciate that. Did he say what he wanted, or do you zoomies communicate with each other?"

Sanderson shrugged and then seemed to pout. "Sounds like I'm losin' a roommate. I think those people you work for back in Washington—what do they call them again?"

"Marines, flyboy."

"Yeah, right. Them. Anyway, they wanna talk to you. Must have another assignment in the works." His eyes brightened. "Hey, wanna go get a beer at Pete's?"

The rec center was unusual in that they served alcohol—most bases in deployed locations didn't. There was a catch, though. Each service member was limited to only two beers per day. Pete's served a pretty potent Russian brand that seemed to be everybody's favorite.

"No thanks," Neill answered, looking at his phone's display. Sure enough, he had several messages waiting in his in-box—two from his command back in D.C. "I'm gonna make a few phone calls and see what this is about." He got up from the table and picked up his tray, then gave Sanderson a grin. "You can buy me one later, though."

"I can barely hear you." Sergeant Christina Arrens needed coffee. It was still early morning in Washington, D.C., at the office of International Operations and Intelligence, and the day had not started well. "You probably should have used the hard line at the command post."

Snow crunched underfoot as Neill exited the DFAC. "I thought it might be important," he replied. "Everything okay,

Sergeant? You sound a little stressed."

Arrens cradled the phone on her shoulder and picked up some paperwork from the top of her desk. "Things are just a little hectic here today," she answered. There was a slight delay as her words travelled halfway around the world. "Did you get my message?"

"Roger that." Neill passed the rec center on the way back to his quarters. In spite of the cold, an overflow crowd filled the patio at Pete's. "I haven't checked my email yet. What did you send me?"

"A pdf of your orders," Arrens said. "They were approved yesterday. Take a copy of them over to the pax terminal and see if you can get a flight out—shouldn't be too hard, the system is showing a rotator leaving in three days."

Finally, Neill thought. *A green light.* There was a pause as the news registered in his brain. "What's the timeline for all this?"

Arrens consulted a hard copy of Neill's orders. "You ship out from Andrews in three weeks. Had admin work it so you'd get back to D.C. long before that, though—I thought you might like a little time at home before leaving." *And it would be good to see you again*, she didn't say.

This was all a little sudden, but not unexpected. "Mabry's not gonna be happy about that," Neill said.

"Orders are orders," Arrens replied. "The State Department's been negotiating the details for months."

"You make it sound like a prison sentence," Neill said with a smile. Constant delays kept pushing the mission back. The diplomatic give and take between nations ensured that no set schedule would ever be followed. In fact, Neill had begun to wonder if it would ever be approved at all. "But three weeks should give me enough time to thaw out. You think I should do some laundry before I go?" It was one of Neill's rare attempts at humor.

Arrens laughed for the first time all morning. "Just get yourself back here, Lieutenant. I'll make sure you're squared away for your trip."

Neill ended the call. The news had distracted him. He completely forgot about that beer with Sanderson. He considered walking over to the pax terminal; but to be pre-selected for a flight he'd need his orders. Besides, it was getting late. He decided it could wait till morning. The next flight back to the States didn't leave for three days anyway, and at this time of year the weather had the final say in aircraft departures, so there was no need to rush. Besides that, he was bone tired and wanted to get some sleep.

Michael smiled to himself. It would have made more sense to fly directly to his next assignment, rather than return to the United States. If he traveled west, it would be on the way. But sometimes the dots just didn't get connected like that.

Neill reached the barracks that housed his quarters and savored the warmth of the hall. His room was even warmer. He let himself in, then pulled his sea bag from the wall locker and tossed it on his bunk. His seventy-two hour bag was next— he'd be living out of that for the trip back to the States.

After three rewarding months in Kyrgyzstan, Neill was going home, only to leave three weeks later for an assignment in Ukraine—*another* republic liberated from the old communist empire.

He started packing his rucksack. He had few personal belongings, so it didn't take long. By morning he'd checked in with the logistical planning office to determine his itinerary. Two days later, Kyrgyzstan was just a pleasant memory.

Chapter One ☆ Breakfast in Kiev

In the skies over Ukraine

IT WAS A SHORT FLIGHT, EXACTLY ONE HOUR BY the Colonel's watch. Andrei Ulyanov was thankful for that—the cramped cockpit of this particular fighter was far less comfortable than most he had piloted. That was a consideration he'd rarely been concerned with in the past, but he wasn't as spry as he used to be. To the east, a ribbon of scarlet and gold announced the dawn, and as he dropped to a lower altitude, the stiffness he felt reminded him that jockeying warplanes through the Ukrainian skies was a vocation left to much younger men.

Still, he welcomed the chance to log some time in the air. Flying released him from the drudgery of his present responsibilities, since most of the time he found himself parked behind a desk, but he still remembered what it was like to be a hotshot Lieutenant blazing through the sky at twice the speed of sound. The reality of that furrowed his brow; he'd always considered himself a line officer, not a rear echelon type, and certainly not a pencil pusher.

That reminded him of something. The thought brought a smile. What was it the Americans used to call them—before computers? Ah, yes, *Remington Raiders*; those staff officers softened by their air conditioned surroundings, and despised by their colleagues who embraced hardship in the field. The name was a reminder of the days when typewriters were common, a clumsy device now found rarely enough even in the backwater corners of the former Soviet Union. How things had changed, Andrei told himself. And how quickly. The Colonel truly disliked paperwork, but after all, who didn't?

Ulyanov dismissed these thoughts as Kiev came into view, and he concentrated on getting his aircraft on the ground. Far below him was a neatly laid-out pattern of farm land and fields, separated by an interconnecting network of roads and highways. The Colonel's eyes swept to the west. Zhulyany field was smaller than the Borispol International Airport, but was more commonly used by aircraft with domestic destinations. Locating it was no problem; the Colonel dialed in the appropriate frequency and requested permission to land. His radio crackled to life as the tower directed him to the primary runway that dominated the field, an approach that pointed him into the morning light spilling across the countryside.

Descending even lower, he sized up the landing site and the wind conditions, then checked the runway for moisture or debris, anything that might prove an obstacle to a safe touchdown. Ulyanov lowered his gear, then pulled back on the stick and adjusted his throttle as the wheels brushed across the well-worn asphalt.

Ulyanov taxied to the ramp and powered down the jet while the ground crew chocked his wheels. One began pulling a fuel line his way while another attached a metal ladder below the canopy. Looking beyond the scurrying figures Ulyanov expected to see an official vehicle of some sort, probably a Russian made sedan; more than one, most likely. He was correct on two counts. A pair of limousines were motoring slowly through the gate, but these were brand new Mercedes.

Ulyanov climbed out of the cockpit and was met by a member of the security detail that emerged from the second car. Handshakes and pleasantries were exchanged and then the

Colonel pulled a garment bag from the plane's storage compartment. The officer in charge proved to be very efficient, securing an empty office inside the terminal so that Ulyanov could change—the Colonel's friendship with the President was well known, but it wouldn't do for him to arrive wearing a flight suit. The security detail waited dutifully, of course, and minutes later, Ulyanov settled into the back seat of the first car and stretched his legs. Half an hour after landing he was on his way downtown.

Despite centuries of conflict and the ravages of war—no one had forgotten the Nazi occupation of the last century—the golden-domed city held on to its ancient splendor, nestled like a jewel on the banks of the Dnieper River, lush, green, and deeply forested, and one of the most beautiful parts of the Commonwealth.

Ulyanov rarely visited here, kept away mostly by the responsibilities of command, but each trip fostered an almost mystical connection with his homeland's capitol city. Much of Kiev had been destroyed in World War II. During the rebuilding many of the streets had been widened and lined with trees. On this brisk morning the boulevards were framed with the colors of winter, but the snowfall had been light. With a clear sky above, Ulyanov savored the view.

The early hour promised swift progress—and a low-key arrival—and within minutes the Colonel's driver was navigating downtown on a path toward the Pechersk District. A turn west, then east again. At the end of Kirova Street a perimeter of ornate fencing enclosed the Marinsky Palace. This had been the Tsar's playground in another era, but in more recent times it housed the functionaries and bureaucrats of the country's parliament. Built nearly 250 years earlier, it had burnt to the ground and been rebuilt more than once. And it was here that the Ukrainian President maintained a suite of offices for business that required discreet attention.

The guards on post waved the motorcade through the gate. Scaffolding had been erected on one side; evidently the old baroque structure was scheduled for another coat of paint. White semi-columns ran the length of the building, evenly spaced along the distinctive turquoise outer walls. The Presidential Standard flew in the courtyard, snapping in the breeze, announcing the presence of the country's chief executive. The cars maneuvered slowly past the steel framework to the western entrance where a smiling face waited to greet the Colonel as he arrived.

"*Dobre ootra*, Ilya." *Good morning*. Ulyanov emerged from the car and extended his hand, but found himself caught in a bear hug. Ilya Lebed served his president as executive assistant, a kind of chief of staff. The Colonel had always liked the man.

Ilya's smile widened. "You rouse me from my bed at an early hour, *tavarisch*."

Ulyanov shook his head. "Don't blame me, old friend. I could use more sleep myself. Or better yet, some tea and sausage."

Lebed laughed and waved him inside. "Sleep I can't help you with. But the President will join you for breakfast."

"And you?"

For the first time a frown replaced the smile. "Something light for me, I'm afraid." A large hand stroked his stomach. "Doctor's orders. My cholesterol is much too high."

"*Pah!*" It was the Colonel's turn to laugh. "You sound like an American now, Ilya." Both men were characteristically Slavic—which meant robust in girth—but Lebed's had migrated mostly to his waistline. Gravity and age were two forces of nature that were sadly beyond their control.

Ilya's grin returned. "And who can blame me for that? There are enough Westerners running around here." By now they had moved through the foyer and into the main hall. "You know we have a saying in Kiev these days, Andrei. When we hear our people using their mother tongue, we remind them that they are in Ukraine—"

"—and you tell them to speak English like everyone else." Ulyanov had heard it before and there was just an inkling of truth to it.

The building's ground level included a network of security checkpoints, sophisticated (and very Western) equipment that seemed to clash with the old world charm of the Palace. First came the metal detectors. Ulyanov passed through these without incident, Lebed in tow, and a guard issued him a visitor's badge. The grand staircase was next. The Colonel took the steps two at a time, forcing Ilya to double his stride just to keep up. On the second floor they were met by yet another guard who escorted them directly to the President's outer office, but at 6:45 it was still far too early to find his executive secretary on the job. Ilya tapped lightly on the door and a booming voice on the other side ordered them in.

The President's office occupied nearly one quarter of the entire second floor, but still wasn't as opulent as his official post elsewhere in the capitol. A row of windows along the south wall offered a spectacular view of Sovetsky Park, the well-groomed gardens that adjoined the palace. Closer to the door—and away from the windows—was a large desk where Ilya and the Colonel found President Alexander Pavlovsk reclining in a high-backed chair while poring over an open folder.

"Andrei, you must be starving." Pavlovsk rose quickly, not something he did for every guest. He crossed the floor and took Ulyanov's hand. "Would you care for a cup of tea?"

Pavlovsk was an open, engaging man. His drive and charisma had recently won him a second term as President. Ulyanov had served with him briefly when both men were young officers in the Air Defense Forces of the Soviet Union, long before the lumbering bureaucracy collapsed. But unlike Andrei, Pavlovsk had left the military to pursue politics. His instincts had served him well. In the chaos that followed the fall of the USSR, Pavlovsk kept his wits and looked for opportunity, finding it in his native Ukraine. He climbed the political ladder quickly but steadily, and his vigor and popularity with the people won him the presidency at a relatively young age. While other men had struggled to guide the post-communist nation, Pavlovsk had proven more than equal to the task, forging useful alliances with the West along the way, alliances never imagined in the days of Soviet rule.

Breakfast consisted of hot kasha, eggs served two ways, sliced cheese and sausage, black bread, and, of course, plenty of steaming tea. Ulyanov selected a variety of food from the serving cart and found a seat at the conference table next to the President. All three men were hungry, wolfing down the meal without saying much at all. The Colonel noted that, true to his word, Ilya was exercising great restraint.

"How are things in Nikolayev, Andrei?" Pavlovsk was the first to finish, smacking his lips and wiping his chin with a napkin. "Irina is well, I trust."

"Quite well, Mr. President. She frets about her garden and wishes for spring. I'm afraid my own duties leave me little time for such diversions."

Pavlovsk nodded his understanding. "Our country requires much from both of us, Andrei."

Which is why you've asked me here, Ulyanov didn't say. "Comrade President, you didn't invite me to Kiev just for breakfast. Is there some … matter that requires my attention?"

Alexander poured himself another cup of tea. "I need your advice on a matter of policy."

"Policy? I'm afraid politics is beyond my scope of expertise, Mr. President." Ulyanov was beginning to see where this meeting was going, but he knew that feigning ignorance would not excuse him from anything his friend might ask.

"Well, at some level, yes, it is a political matter. Right now I'm more concerned with its implications for national security."

The Colonel's eyes narrowed. The conversation had just

taken an interesting turn before it had even truly begun. Pavlovsk retrieved the folder he'd been reading before breakfast and handed it over to Ulyanov. Inside was a draft of only three pages, one of which was the cover sheet identifying the material as highly classified, but Ulyanov guessed as much. The Colonel pulled a pair of glasses from his jacket and began to read. No literary embellishments whatsoever, just a dry listing of facts, but those were enough to send a chill up the Colonel's spine.

Ulyanov finished the report and blinked. "*Bozhe Moi.*" *My God.* A flood of questions came to mind, but the Colonel hardly knew where to start.

"Thirty-six nuclear warheads," Pavlovsk confirmed. "C-type arrays once used on the Nyeva ICBMs. Crated. Do you understand my concern now, Andrei?"

"Thirty-six," Ulyanov repeated. By far, the largest number of unaccounted for weapons that he was personally aware of. The senior fighter pilot glanced again at the second page. "In Donetsk. A warehouse?"

A nod. "A French firm is gearing up to build an automotive plant there," the President explained. He disliked the French, but that was beside the point. "The warehouse was being renovated. A location once used by the Rocket Forces for storage purposes."

Storage indeed, Ulyanov thought. *As if they were a gross of canteens.* "How long had they been there? Have the serial numbers been run down?"

"We're not sure how long they were in Donetsk," Ilya spoke up. "They seemed to be … undisturbed. We ran the numbers, and they match those on a materiel manifest that was handed over to us in 1992."

"That long." Ulyanov shook his head. "This is inconceivable."

That assessment almost struck Pavlovsk as funny. "I'd hardly call it that, Andrei. You were a part of the machine. You remember how things were. The Soviet military was less than efficient at record-keeping."

The Colonel grunted. "Not the only legacy left to us, unfortunately. Where are these warheads now?"

"Secure for the moment," Lebed spoke again. "They've all been taken to the dismantling station in Odessa. We felt it safer to keep the lot intact—for the time being—rather than send them on to Moscow."

"So the situation is well in hand?" Ulyanov asked hopefully.

"Unfortunately, no." Pavlovsk handed the Colonel a separate sheet lying on his desk.

Ulyanov read the document slowly, noting the mention of a name he was all too familiar with. This time he wasn't surprised.

"Mayakovsky," he said, anger welling up in his voice.

Ulyanov silently cursed Mayakovsky. *How could a man in his position do such a thing?* The Colonel sat back in his chair, removed his glasses and rubbed a hand over his face. Major Vadim Mayakovsky had betrayed his country in the worst possible way, by endangering the lives of thousands of innocent people. Ulyanov tried to console himself with the fact that, according to the report, Vadim now sat in a military prison, but it was a small comfort.

Ulyanov had spent half his life in the Soviet military, but when the government collapsed, he returned to his beloved Ukraine. The Colonel had known Mayakovsky professionally; both men were commissioned officers, Andrei the dashing fighter pilot, risking life and limb in the Soviet Air Force; and Vadim, the stoic and resolute member of the Rocket Forces. Strangely enough, Ulyanov had never trusted Mayakovsky; he had a knack for reading people. Something about Vadim had always rubbed him the wrong way. Now Ulyanov knew what it was.

The man was a traitor.

Ulyanov handed the report back to the President. *How many of his countrymen knew of this?* He wondered about the rest of the republics. Could this happen there as well? Some of them handled their internal security with much less care than Ukraine.

And what of the Americans? News of this situation could be kept a secret for a brief time, but in just three short weeks—

"Does Moscow know these warheads have been located?"

Pavlovsk shook his head. "No one knows, Andrei. Not yet. But that will change. Once we begin disassembling them in Odessa, I will inform the Russian and American ambassadors."

Ulyanov considered how politically embarrassing this might be for his old friend. "So you intend to dismantle them here?"

"I would prefer to, yes—to demonstrate to our friends in NATO that we can be trusted to act responsibly."

Ulyanov quietly wondered if that might work. Too many of these weapons had been discovered in Ukraine of late—years after all of them had supposedly been returned to Russia.

"There's work to do, Andrei," Pavlovsk's voice brought the Colonel's mind back to the present. "And I need someone I can trust."

"I serve at your pleasure, Mr. President. What would you have me do?"

"I want you to assume command of the dismantling station in Odessa. Mayakovsky's co-conspirators are still at large." Pavlovsk looked his friend in the eye. "Clean this mess up, Andrei. A great deal is at stake."

"I must confess, this is outside of my experience. If you require—"

"Andrei, you have risen to the top of your career through leadership," the President began. He had neither the time nor patience for false modesty—even from Ulyanov. "I recognize this goes beyond your list of accomplishments. But as I said, I need someone I can trust. You may not know much about dismantling nuclear weapons, but you are a senior military officer who knows how to get a job done.

"*That* is your most important qualification."

Chapter Two ✭ Into the Storm

Aboard the U.S.S. George H.W. Bush
One week later
The Sea of Japan

THE RAIN HAD BECOME TORRENTIAL, AND A gusting north wind drove it almost horizontally against the windows of the big ship. By now visibility was reduced to only a few hundred feet.

From his position on the bridge, Admiral James LaSalle cursed the weather and lowered his binoculars. Somewhere out there was the rest of the battle group; a couple of guided missile cruisers, an anti-aircraft vessel and two anti-submarine frigates, patrolling in a wide perimeter around the carrier. But seeing anything was difficult now, and the glare from the overheads didn't help. LaSalle glanced up at them and then over at the Officer of the Deck, a perceptive young Lieutenant, who nodded his understanding, moved to the bulkhead control pad and adjusted the internal lighting. Instantly, the soft red, green and orange glow that came from the various instruments and equipment filled the quiet compartment.

It was the quiet that drew LaSalle to the bridge. Solitude was a rare thing aboard ship, and even more so in the top tier of leadership. This part of the vessel was much better suited for thinking than the Combat Information Center, or CIC, which was the vessel's nerve center. Right now the CIC was a hotbed of some very focused energy. A great deal of attention was directed on monitoring an aircraft that had launched just before the weather soured. LaSalle spent an hour in the CIC when the mission began, then climbed up through the ship's superstructure for a look at the sea. It was something he did often when he had a lot on his mind.

The Admiral looked down and to his left. Two generations of warplanes overlapped as they sat on the pitching, rain-swept deck. There were Marine Corps F-18 Super Hornets and Harriers and a squadron of Seahawk helicopters. These aircraft had been the workhorses of naval aviation from the Cold War, through both Gulf wars and right up through Afghanistan. But closer to the bow, LaSalle could see several Ospreys, the vertical take-off plane designed to replace the aging inventory of Marine Corps helicopters, their distinctive shapes barely visible through the rain.

The Admiral's favorite, of course, was the F-18. As a younger man he'd flown one in the first Gulf War. Early on he'd been jumped by an Iraqi MiG as he headed toward Baghdad. The Iraqi pilot was good enough to send a few rounds dangerously close before LaSalle managed to down him with a Sidewinder missile.

That war had proven, once again, the technological superiority of the United States, but the human element could not be ignored, either. American air and ground forces were the best trained in the world, and their determined efforts had won the day.

Times had changed, though. With that war over and the collapse of the Soviet Union, the Eastern bloc didn't look as threatening. The U.S. military was downsized; some of it was justified, but to cold warriors like Jim LaSalle reducing the nation's armament did more to invite disaster than to put it behind them. The so-called 'peace dividend' that many politicians expected never materialized. Then came 9/11; and after more than a decade of war, and the majority of troops had been withdrawn from Iraq and Afghanistan, the call to reduce America's armed forces was heard once again.

One thing hadn't changed, and that made the Admiral very happy. Despite the reductions in personnel and equipment, the U.S. Navy could still put to sea with the most formidable carrier battle group of any nation afloat. The aircraft carrier was still the heart of any naval operation that required an American presence. The might represented by a carrier and its support ships constituted not only a strategic military weapon but a political one as well; history had shown that more than a few diplomatic goals had been achieved through the show of force.

Of course, it was always the policy of the American government to negotiate solutions rather than inflict them. But when that policy was ignored by countries intent on aggression, the Big Stick—carrier battle groups like LaSalle's—would be nearby.

Intent on aggression.

The Admiral mulled that over. Was that the case here? If so, the stakes would be too high for the United States to remain in the dark about it.

Behind him, the Marine Corporal who served as the Admiral's orderly came to attention as the ship's commanding officer entered the bridge. Captain Paul Desouza walked to LaSalle's side, thermos in one hand and two mugs in the other. He was a tall, muscular man whose physical presence commanded just as much respect as the rank on his collar. One of the mugs, emblazoned with two stars, he handed to LaSalle.

"Figured I'd find you here." Desouza unscrewed the lid of the thermos and poured. "Coffee's hot, Admiral."

"Hotter the better, Paul," he said, taking a sip. "LONE WOLF reported in yet?"

"Yes, sir. Heading is due north." Desouza eyed the Admiral as both men sipped. "Storm's held them up a bit, so they're climbing to avoid it." When he spoke again his voice was much lower. "What's this all about, Jim?"

The Admiral winced, but at the same time he felt relief. He didn't like keeping secrets from his officers. Captain Desouza had been very patient, but now he wanted some answers. The Admiral was only too happy to give him some.

Without a word, LaSalle moved to the center of the bridge to a flat navigational console. A 25-inch monitor in the center of the console displayed the Japanese coastline to the east and the Asian land mass to the west. In the center of the display was a small green box with a thick white outline. This represented the carrier and her support ships.

"Ten days ago naval intelligence detected a major troop buildup on both sides of the Russian-Chinese border." LaSalle tapped a few keys on the console and the display changed to a full color map of Eastern Russia and Central Asia. "Nobody's sure, but we think the Russians started it."

Captain Desouza studied the map. Red dots placed on both sides of the border showed troop positions.

"Could be just an exercise."

LaSalle shrugged. "That's possible. Or it might be that the Russians are making a move to the south. Whatever it is, it's got the Chinese rattled." He sat his mug down and reached for the thermos. "Right now we just don't have enough information to make a good guess."

Desouza was beginning to understand now. "So that's what LONE WOLF is up to: electronic intelligence gathering."

The Admiral grunted. "That's right." He traced a finger across the screen. "Commander Taublin and his crew will fly along the coastline between China and Russia and intercept any transmissions they can. Once we've analyzed the data they collect, maybe we'll have some hard intelligence on what both sides are up to."

Captain Desouza frowned. "Using a drone would've been safer." He knew that wasn't the proper term, but the word had seeped into common usage. "I've got a brand new, shiny Navy variant on the hangar deck that my people have been itching to try."

LaSalle nodded "For any other mission I'd agree with you. Unfortunately, an unmanned vehicle is too small for all the specialized reconnaissance gear needed for this job." Besides, the Navy's UAV wasn't fully tested. LaSalle switched off the display. "They're up there for a look-see, Paul. They don't have to stick out their necks. Only their ears."

Captain Desouza nodded and finished his coffee. "Let's just hope they don't get 'em shot off, sir."

Chapter Three ✷ Lone Wolf, Dangerous Sky

COMMANDER TAUBLIN'S PLANE WAS AN ES-3A Viking—codenamed LONE WOLF for this mission—and had a crew of three for today's flight. His co-pilot was Lieutenant Walter Coats, and the sensor operator was Lieutenant Arturo Dante. The drone of the aircraft's twin jet engines and the hum of the instruments filled the cockpit as each man concentrated on his duties.

Lieutenant Dante sat behind Commander Taublin. It was his job to monitor all the electronics equipment being used for the mission. After running a final systems check, he selected a frequency normally used by the Russian military.

"Okay—electronic and signal gathering gear is functioning normally," he said, looking forward. Slipping on a pair of headphones, he noticed the storm was getting worse.

"We're intercepting some radio traffic, Commander. Sounds like Russian."

"Can you make out what they're saying, Dante?" Coats called over his shoulder, grinning. Walter Coats was an athletic young man who hoped to play professional baseball once he got out of the Navy.

"*No comprende, señor.* Here—you give it a listen." Dante started to hand him the headphones but Coats waved him off with a laugh.

"I don't speak it either. Knew a guy at the Academy that did, though. He grew up in Russia. In fact, he was born there."

"You knew a guy at the Academy that grew up in Russia?" Taublin asked.

"No, actually it was Ukraine. His parents were missionaries, went over after the Soviet Union broke up."

"Never been there myself." The turbulence was noticeably worse. "This guy's in our navy now?"

Coats shook his head. "Naw, he's a jarhead. Works for intelligence in D.C. *Whoa*—that was rough." Both Coats and Taublin reacted as the aircraft lurched to the right.

"You want to just fly the plane? I'm gonna lose my lunch back here," Dante said.

"Quit your whining. Storm's going to get worse before it gets better. Maybe we can alter course a little and avoid some of this mess," Taublin said, moving the control column that guided the plane.

Lieutenant Coats checked his instruments as they began to climb and turn in a north-westerly direction. "That'll take us closer to the coast, Commander," the black officer said.

Taublin nodded. "Storm's building to the northeast. I figure we can skirt around the western edge of it and return to base course before we get too close. I sure don't want to fly through much more of this."

* * * *

"Then it is definitely not one of our aircraft?"

"No, Captain."

The Lieutenant handed his superior officer a manifest that listed all of the day's authorized flights. As a radar operator at the ground station in Fushun, China, it was his job to monitor military air traffic in the region. "Shall we challenge them?"

The Captain studied the list. "No. Continue to maintain radio silence." Next he looked at the junior officer's radar screen. "How long have you been tracking this contact?"

"Fifteen minutes. It has been following a north-easterly course most of that time."

The Captain remembered something from his morning briefing and handed back the manifest. "An American battle group entered the Sea of Japan yesterday. Perhaps it is one of theirs." He stood and turned to face the younger man. "In any case, it is closer to the Russian mainland than it is to us. Continue to monitor its progress and report any changes in course to me."

* * * *

"Why do they call Marines 'jarheads,' anyway?" Lieutenant Dante said to no one in particular. Commander Taublin glanced over at Coats and grinned.

"Have you ever really looked at a Marine, Dante?" Commander Taublin's eyes swept ahead and saw the sun for the first time since they left the carrier. In spite of that, he frowned.

Something didn't feel right. He couldn't explain it, but his intuition told him something was wrong.

* * * *

Fifty kilometers away in Vladivostok, a Russian Corporal manning a mobile tracking station noticed a blip on his radar console. He alerted the officer in charge, a Major, and both men watched as the image moved closer and closer to Russia. Unlike the Chinese Captain in Fushun, the Major had no knowledge of any American ships nearby. He concluded that the plane had to be from China, considering the recent tension between the two countries and the fact that Russian aircraft were restricted from conducting operations in that sector. He picked up the phone and dialed the number for the airbase ten kilometers to the north.

The Major's call received immediate attention.

At the Russian air field near Vladivostok, an alarm klaxon sounded. The order to scramble the alert aircraft had been given.

Lieutenant Viktor Radischev raced to the flight line hangar and strapped himself into his fighter. The routine pre-flight checks came next.

The engines spun up to speed very quickly. Radischev double-checked his weapons system, then rolled the aircraft out of the high security hangar and taxied to the runway. It was a bumpy ride. The taxiway was in disrepair, as were most things in any part of the former Soviet empire.

Arriving at one end of the runway, he radioed the control tower and requested permission to take off. Within minutes the plane streaked into the sky. The ground crews watched as the sleek aircraft gained altitude and vanished to the south.

Squadron Commander Yuri Kharkov had been in radio contact with Lieutenant Radischev since the young pilot's departure. In spite of his concerns, he smiled in anticipation of the hunt. Somewhere out there, an enemy aircraft was headed his way.

It occurred to Kharkov that the Chinese might actually intend to bomb the airbase. He wondered if they knew what the Russians were guarding in Hangar Seven. It wasn't likely, but the Major determined then and there that he would defend the contents of that hangar at all costs.

* * * *

"I was afraid of this." Captain Desouza's attention was riveted to the radar console in the combat information center of the ship. He turned to Admiral LaSalle, who was beside him. "The storm is forcing LONE WOLF closer to the Russian coastline."

The Petty Officer at the console was not accustomed to having a Captain and an Admiral looking over his shoulder, but he was too intent on his duties to let that bother him. He shook his head and looked up at his Captain. "LONE WOLF has crossed into Russian airspace twice, sir," he announced. Just how far out to sea Russian territories extended had become a matter of dispute in recent years; of late, the Russians had claimed a much greater reach not recognized by NATO, the United States, or just about anybody else.

Desouza turned to the Admiral. "Sir, the Russians have an airbase near Vladivostok. If LONE WOLF keeps jumping in and out of their backyard, Commander Taublin and his crew are going to have company—real quick."

LaSalle let out a deep breath. "Get LONE WOLF on the horn and have them turn east. That'll put them back in the storm but it beats the alternative."

"It's no use, Captain. Storm's causing too much interference." The Petty Officer tried again, but got the same result.

Desouza stroked his chin and thought for a moment. LaSalle moved from the radar and walked to his side.

"Problems?"

"We're having trouble raising LONE WOLF, Admiral," Desouza's voice was low. "The front has moved in between us and them."

"We've got F-18s in the air now, don't we?" LaSalle asked.

"Yes, sir," Captain Desouza said.

"Okay." The Admiral had an idea. "Order them to go after LONE WOLF and make contact. Let's get that Viking back here before the Russians take an interest in it."

Captain Desouza took the mike from the radio operator and relayed the order to the pilots. A minute later the two Hornets were headed north.

* * * *

Lieutenant Radischev could see very little except the rain hitting his windshield. He had entered the same storm LONE WOLF was trying to avoid. The turbulence was getting worse but it wasn't anything he couldn't handle.

His radar was giving him conflicting images, but it appeared he had come in behind the unidentified aircraft. He strained to see ahead, but sighting his quarry visually was out of the question.

The fighter was equipped with an infrared device that could locate aircraft by detecting "hot spots," like engine exhaust. Radischev knew he would need that now, and flipped a switch to activate the system. Almost as an afterthought, his gloved hand moved across the console and keyed the weapons systems. Tucked under each wing, in the aircraft's bomb bays, below the port and starboard engine intakes, were a pair of ST-3 Malat air to air missiles—which he hoped he wouldn't have to use.

* * * *

"It's clearing up." Although he couldn't shake his anxiety completely, there was some relief in Taublin's voice. The rain had almost stopped. Between the breaks in the clouds the crew could see the sun more and more often.

Two miles behind them, Viktor Radischev also noticed the change in weather, but the clouds prevented him from seeing anything. He looked up, to the left and right, half-expecting to see some type of fighter escort for the plane he knew was ahead of him, but saw nothing. That was good, but it puzzled him. His quarry was moving too slow to be a fighter. It might be a Chinese bomber, but if that were the case wouldn't it need—

There it was.

Radischev saw it only for an instant before it disappeared into the clouds again, but he definitely saw it—a small aircraft, with two engines and what appeared to be a couple of external fuel tanks. His infrared imaging system locked on at almost the same instant, and Radischev accelerated the fighter into the clouds.

Major Kharkov was pacing the floor in the control tower when Lieutenant Radischev's voice, crackling with static, filled the room.

"It appears to be a small bomber, with … yes, there it is

again … I think—it's gone, Major. Back into the clouds." Even with the breaks in the weather Radischev was having a hard time maintaining visual contact. But the infrared image remained constant. He described what he had seen—and what his instruments saw—to Major Kharkov.

The Major frowned. The Chinese did have a new short-range bomber. It was a two engine aircraft that carried cruise missiles slung under the wings.

With that in mind, Kharkov made a fateful decision.

There was a long silence. When the Lieutenant heard Major Kharkov's voice again, it was firm, but very quiet.

"Are you within range to fire your weapons, Lieutenant Radischev?" He already knew the answer to that.

"I am within range, sir." *This is getting out of hand,* he thought.

Kharkov breathed deeply. "Target the aircraft and fire."

"Sir," Radischev said slowly, "We have not confirmed the identity of this aircraft. Allow me to—"

Major Kharkov cut him off. "Listen to me carefully, Lieutenant. You are closing on a Chinese bomber that has violated our airspace. We are now tracking two more aircraft moving at high speed toward your position. These are undoubtedly fighters." Kharkov knew this was a gamble, but if he was right there wasn't much time. "Target the aircraft and fire."

Radischev noted the approaching aircraft on his own instruments. Using the infrared imaging system to designate the target, he selected one of his missiles and activated the launch sequence.

* * * *

Coats was the first to get the message. "New orders from WOLF PACK, Commander. 'Turn east—'"

"Yeah, I've got it too," Taublin said over the intercom headset. It was comforting to see the radar images of the two F-18s thirty miles behind them, but what was that—

"Missile warning!" Coats shouted. The onboard threat receivers had suddenly activated. "Missile on our tail and locked on us!"

Taublin couldn't believe it at first but after a split second his training kicked in. Gripping the control column he turned the aircraft hard to the left.

"Where did that come from?"

Lieutenant Radischev watched as the infrared image of the aircraft banked to the west. He had to admire his adversary's piloting skills; the missile continued north, unable to maintain a lock on the target. Radischev checked his instruments and then turned to pursue.

"What have we got on radar?" Taublin asked. Coats checked the displays in front of him.

"Missile came from behind, but I show no aircraft except our Hornets," which, to his way of thinking, were not close enough. "You think it was a SAM?"

"Huh-uh, too small," Taublin said with a shake of his head. "Surface to air missile would've shown up sooner. That shot came from a fighter." He studied the electronic sensing instruments while banking the plane hard to the right. "Look there. Radar emissions on our six, about three thousand yards. Probably tracking us with infrared, too." He accelerated the plane. "Time to get out of Dodge, boys." *If we can*, he thought.

Radischev caught another glimpse of the target as both aircraft broke out into the open. Then it was gone again. He closed to within a thousand yards and selected the other missile. With only one left, he'd have to be careful.

Taublin didn't like being unarmed with an aggressor on his tail, but he still had a few tricks up his sleeve. He knew he could never outshoot or outfly an enemy fighter—the Viking had no offensive weapons—but with enough cloud cover he might be able to outmaneuver him long enough for the Hornets to get in range.

"Hang on, this could get rough!" Taublin gripped the control column and held his breath.

For almost five full seconds Lieutenant Radischev was un-aware that the infrared image on his screen was growing in size. When he realized what his adversary was doing he jerked the control column to the left. The fighter nearly flipped over as it banked to avoid the plane in front of it.

Taublin had opened the flaps completely but maintained his course, slowing the Viking to a fraction of its former speed and forcing the fighter to break off his attack or risk a mid-air collision.

Both Taublin and Coats strained to see as they broke out of the clouds, and for the first time they were rewarded with a quick glance at the fighter as it streaked past them on the port side of the aircraft.

"You see that?" Coats watched as their attacker flew into a cloud.

"I saw it." Taublin banked the plane to the right again. "Now where are those Hornets?" He was surprised too, but it wasn't over yet.

While Taublin and Coats had seen him, Radischev was too busy collecting his wits to get a good look at his quarry. He cursed his own stupidity for being tricked so easily then swung the fighter around for another run. For the first time he noticed he was sweating.

Taublin had twisted and turned the aircraft in an erratic pattern, then doubled back on his course. Even so, Radischev lost no time in re-acquiring his target. His radar was working much better now and he brought the fighter to within a thou-sand yards of the small 'bomber' ahead of him. He quickly checked to make sure the infrared tracking system was locked on, and then hit the launch switch. Nothing happened immedi-ately, then the second Malat slipped from the missile bay and began its run through the clouds.

"Missile warning—nine hundred yards and closing!"

Coats' words broke Taublin's concentration. He frowned, hoping it would take longer for the attacking aircraft to find them, then threw the plane into an abrupt right turn. LONE WOLF was out in the open again, and the missile broke through the clouds right behind them.

"Range?" Taublin's voice was calmer than he actually felt.

Coats bit his lip. He didn't like what his instruments were telling him. "Five hundred yards. Still locked on us."

Dante couldn't do anything but sit and wait. His body was thrown to the right as Taublin banked the plane into a left turn.

For a second or two, the missile lost its lock, but then re-acquired and adjusted its course. It passed them on the right side, but much closer this time. At a distance of fifty feet, a target detection device detonated the warhead.

Ten thousand metal fragments and large pieces of the missile casing itself shot through the air and impacted on the plane's starboard side, tearing through the skin of the aircraft and peppering the cockpit's interior with shrapnel. Taublin flinched as the deadly steel ricocheted off sensitive equipment, some of it piercing his clothing and tearing into his flesh. In the chaos of the moment he heard a muffled groan that was quickly silenced. At the same instant, the three hundred gallon auxiliary fuel tank on the wing was knocked off its mounts and fell into the sea.

Lieutenant Radischev emerged from the clouds in time to see the explosion and had to veer sharply away to avoid the blast. As the sunlight glinted off the mortally wounded aircraft he could tell this was no Chinese bomber.

* * * *

The two F-18s were now wingtip to wingtip as they closed on LONE WOLF's position. The radar intercept officer in the lead Hornet looked up from his scope. "LONE WOLF's all over the map."

"Course is pretty erratic," the pilot replied. He could tell the small plane was dodging something, and he instinctively knew it wasn't weather this time.

"LONE WOLF, this is HARDBALL Two-Four. We are

northbound and twenty miles from your position. What is your status?"

Taublin escaped serious injury and fought to regain control as the plane lost altitude. He could hear the F-18 pilot's voice in his earphones, but before he answered he looked to his right. Coats was doubled over in his seat, his flight suit covered with blood.

Looking behind him, he saw that Dante was shaken, but okay. Turning back to Coats, Taublin was nearly overcome with a sense of helplessness. As badly as he wanted to help his co-pilot, he knew that would have to wait. His most immediate concern was to keep the plane in the air.

What he didn't know was that it wouldn't have made any difference anyway.

Walter Coats was already dead.

The Russian pilot hesitated before heading back to the coastline. He checked his instruments, expecting the American to drop off his radar display and plunge into the sea, but the small plane remained aloft. As he watched, Radischev saw two more radar images approaching and decided it was time to head for home.

By the time Viktor returned to the airbase he was furious. He replayed the incident over and over again in his mind, and the image of the crippled plane only became more vivid. In his haste to obey orders—orders he knew were in violation of procedures—he'd created an international incident.

Radischev popped open the canopy as the fighter rolled to a halt, pulled off his helmet and slammed it to the tarmac below. The ground crew watched in amazement as the officer stormed off in the direction of the control tower. His confrontation with Major Kharkov minutes later was the talk of the base for days to come.

* * * *

LONE WOLF made it back to the carrier, but just barely. With all the structural damage caused by the missile's detonation it was touch and go. The two Hornets had formed up on either side of the stricken plane minutes after the attack, but the Russian fighter was long gone. Repeated efforts to locate it on radar turned up nothing.

Getting back to the ship was one thing. Landing was another. Commander Taublin had his hands full trying to bring the plane in safely. Touching down on the deck, the plane's tail hook caught the arresting wire, but one of LONE WOLF's landing wheels collapsed and the aircraft nearly flipped over. As it came to a stop the crash crews swarmed over the wrecked plane, pulled all three men out and carried them below decks to sickbay. The flight recorder and tailfin camera were also removed and taken to another part of the carrier.

The Admiral ordered the other ships in the group to a higher alert status. For the next six hours, a succession of warplanes took off from the carrier deck to practice air intercepts and also to protect against unfriendlies.

Word spread quickly aboard the *Bush*. By nightfall, Admiral LaSalle and Captain Desouza had another problem. Most of the crew on board were fighting mad and howling for blood. Both officers were worried that this incident might just give them the chance to spill some.

Chapter Four ✳ Strategies

I F THERE WAS A BRIGHT SPOT IN THE SQUALOR and poverty of the former Soviet empire, it was Ukraine. That was partially due to the fact that Ukraine had vast mineral and agricultural resources. Under communism, the country had been labeled the breadbasket of the Soviet Union, and with good reason; its pastures and farmlands were blessed with rich, black topsoil. A combination of fertile land and a warm climate made Ukraine the most productive of all the republics.

There were other reasons why Ukraine stood out, but those were mostly political. Since the 1990s the United States had looked at Ukraine and Russia with mixed emotions. Ukraine had great potential for destabilizing the pro-communist forces in Russia that were intent on restoring the old Soviet system. But while Ukraine looked promising, Russia made Western nations, like the United States, worry. The Russian people had suffered a great deal since the collapse of communism and began to yearn for the days when everyone had a job and knew where their next meal was coming from.

The free market system had simply not caught on, at least not very well. No former communist nation in the Commonwealth of Independent States had succeeded in making it work with any measurable success. There were a few exceptions, but this applied only to the very rich or those with powerful connections. For the most part, the common man was on his own. Without a model of capitalism at work to emulate, there was a real danger that these desperate people would restore the communists to power.

The United States recognized this. The solution Western leaders came up with was—on the surface—simple, if not costly. American financial aid began to pour in to Ukraine. The money was used to build up the farms and pay for the fuel to run the harvesting machinery. Advisors from the American business sectors were recruited by the U.S. government and sent to Ukraine. They counseled the people in everything from agriculture to corporate ethics, hoping that if America could export true democracy here, there might be a chance for the rest of the struggling republics that had broken away so many years before.

It was a noble experiment with a good chance of success. Soon, Ukraine began to operate more efficiently. Its people harvested their crops with the latest methods and technology. Natural resources were gathered with a mind toward environmental protection. Nuclear facilities were updated and managed with greater care. More and more goods were exported to other countries, and the Ukrainians began to enjoy a small measure of prosperity. All this while Russia watched with a wary eye.

In exchange for all its help, the United States had managed to get something in return. The Ukrainian government agreed to give up its inventory of Soviet era nuclear warheads, and by the mid-90s the majority of these had been returned to Russia—the ones that had been accounted for, at least. Occasionally, Ukraine would sheepishly admit that a 'forgotten' silo containing an ICBM had been found, and rarely, a small number of low-yield warheads would be located at an air base. The U.S. could almost excuse the Ukrainians for hedging their bets in case the Soviet Union surged back to life. However, discreet diplomatic efforts had persuaded Ukraine to be more transparent about these oversights in their nuclear arsenal. Western officials went so far as to negotiate a compromise. It was agreed that Ukraine would operate one dismantling station that would disarm the occasional warhead found in the surrounding republics. As long as the former Soviet nation played by the rules, NATO would share peaceful nuclear technology. The agreement was tacitly accepted by both sides, and the station was built just outside of Odessa, the port city on the Black Sea.

The choice of Odessa was made for practical reasons. Odessa was strategically located. Since American money had started coming in the port handled almost half of Ukraine's import and export business. As the home of the Black Sea fleet the port of Odessa was an important part of Ukraine's growing economic strength. The infrastructure for transportation was firmly in place, and getting the necessary equipment to the dismantling station was easily accomplished.

Trade was not the only factor that contributed to Odessa's growing role. Tourism had played a part, too. Each year thousands of visitors to Eastern Europe travelled down the Dnieper River, or cruised the Black Sea, stopping in Odessa to visit its historic sights. In the downtown district alone, it seemed that each building or street had a story to tell. Monuments and memorials were not uncommon.

Odessa's most famous landmark was located on the waterfront at the foot of the sprawling port complex. It was a monumental stairway known as the Potemkin Steps, the "grand staircase" of the city, and it offered a breathtaking view of the harbor and the surrounding coastline.

There were others who considered Odessa to be strategically located, but for far more sinister reasons. At the top of the Steps, two men scanned the waterfront and planned their next move.

Ivan Malyev and Sasha Kobrin mingled casually among the groups of tourists, dockworkers, and art students that came and went. They were both very common looking men in their mid-forties. Neither man was Ukrainian, although their passports and identification papers said otherwise. In reality they were Russian, each ex-Army veterans and each an expert in the field of explosives, demolition, and combat engineering.

Malyev took a long draw on his cigarette, a Western brand he had grown fond of and turned to his associate.

"Impressive," he said. "They've accomplished a great deal since I was here last."

Kobrin nodded, although he was preoccupied with other things. "How shall we proceed?"

The two men had spent the past hour looking over the waterfront, finalizing their plans. Malyev smiled as they turned to walk along Primorsky Boulevard. "Cautiously, Sasha." He cast a glance at the gray sky. It was late January and quite cold. "The truck is ready?"

"I have painted over the identification numbers and switched the plates. Only the loading remains."

"*Kharasho.*" *Very well.* Malyev crushed the cigarette on the sidewalk and picked up the pace. "We move out tonight."

Bethesda, Maryland
Near Washington, D.C.

In a restaurant halfway around the world, an old woman, bent by age and a hard life, opened her purse and counted the change inside. She was an immigrant from the old country, and had come to America with her husband many years before.

Michael Neill sat at the table next to hers, enjoying a few days leave and an early breakfast. He couldn't help but notice the pained look on her face as she counted her pennies. It didn't take a genius to figure out she was short on cash.

He finished his coffee, pulled out his wallet and left a tip. He held a larger, folded bill in his hand, then got up and walked toward the cashier, but stopped at the old woman's table first.

"*Dobre ootra,*" he said politely. *Good morning.* He'd heard her speak to the waitress earlier. Her thickly accented English told him she was Russian.

"*Dobre ootra*," she blinked, forgetting her problem for the moment. He wasn't wearing a uniform, but his closely-cropped hair told her this was a military man, probably a Marine. *Imagine that*, she thought, *a Marine who spoke Russian.*

She leaned forward as he pulled out the chair across from her and sat down. "How did you know—"

He smiled at her in a way that reminded her of her husband when he was a young man. Nicolai had been quite handsome at that age. "I heard you order breakfast," he said in flawless Russian. "How long have you been in America?"

The two talked for several more minutes—her name, he found out, was Natasha Lenkov, a teacher from Moscow—and they traded personal histories. Both were surprised to learn that the collapse of the Soviet Union years before had opened doors for both of their families. She had never gone back, and never really wanted to. Nicolai Lenkov had worked so hard to get them to America, and as difficult as it was to adjust to Western living, it was still better than the life they'd left behind. They'd never had much, but they were used to that. And as long as they had each other, that didn't matter. But now, Nicolai was gone, and—

Neill saw the faraway look in her eye and felt a little awkward. He got up to leave, but then looked down at the floor.

"What's this?" he asked, stooping low. When he stood again he held a ten dollar bill in his hand. "Here you go. Must've fallen out of your purse."

"But I didn't … " She started to protest. Then she looked up at him and smiled as he laid the ten next to her tea.

She was old, but certainly not stupid.

Neill felt her grab his hand and squeeze it in a way that reminded him of his grandmother.

Neill paid his bill and started to leave when something caught his eye. The cashier had a laptop next to the register, streaming a newscast with the volume turned down.

"I saw what you did for that old lady, Mike. That was real nice, man." Leo, the cashier, was also the manager. "She comes in a couple times a week for breakfast. Tough old bird. Gets a little bit from Social Security every month, but that's it." He shook his head. "She told the waitress she could use a job."

Neill sympathized. "Wish I could do more," he said. On the small screen he could see images of American warships and planes and then a reporter standing on the deck of an aircraft carrier.

"What's that all about, Leo?" Neill leaned in a little to try and catch what was being said. Naturally, anything dealing with the military was of interest to him.

"Ain't that somethin'? Russians shot at one of our jets, a fighter, I think. News guy said it was a Viking."

Neill frowned. "No, a Viking's not a fighter. When did this happen?"

"Late yesterday. Last night—I dunno, time zones and all that."

Neill hadn't seen anything about it in the newspapers, choosing to go for a morning run instead of catching the TV news. "Anybody hurt?"

"Yeah, co-pilot got killed." Leo shook his head. "No names yet; Navy has to do the next-of-kin thing first."

Lieutenant Neill headed for the door. Two minutes later he was on the freeway for the ten minute trip to his apartment.

* * * *

Anytime Russia did something out of the ordinary—which happened on a regular basis, these days—things got busy in the International Operations and Intelligence Office. Located in the Marine Barracks at Eighth and Eye in Washington, D.C., the IOI group advised the Commandant of the Marine Corps on political and military developments around the world. Lieutenant Neill manned the Eastern European desk, but was consulted on Russian matters as well.

With the morning briefing over, Sergeant Christina Arrens bolted from the conference room and headed for Neill's desk. The attack on the Navy plane off the Russian coastline was now common knowledge. The IOI staff had all the details, including the name of the dead co-pilot.

What bothered Arrens was the fact that the name sounded familiar. She knew that Lieutenant Neill had a classmate at the Academy named Coats, and that they had been good friends. Could this be the same guy? And what if it was—what then? One way or another, she had to be sure.

The pretty, hard-charging young woman quickly flipped through Lieutenant Neill's appointment book, looking for his list of indexed names and addresses, but came up with nothing. It occurred to her that Neill kept a rolodex on his desk—he could be a bit old-school when it came to stuff like that—and she began flipping through the cards looking for the name Walter Coats.

It didn't take long to find what she was looking for.

Neill had a bad feeling about this one. When he got home he changed into a fresh uniform, switched on the TV and tuned in to Fox News.

The news media had already dubbed the incident as "the Crisis in the Sea of Japan," and the networks were scrambling to get information from their far eastern bureaus. Details were scarce. Six hours earlier the Navy had released a statement that raised more questions than it answered.

TV crews and reporters converged on the White House, hoping for more information but getting none. Yes, it was true that an American reconnaissance plane had been fired upon by a Russian fighter, and yes, a naval aviator was dead. Beyond that, the whole situation was a big question mark. Finally, the White House press secretary appeared and assured the assembled journalists that the President himself would address the nation at eleven o'clock that morning.

Neill checked his watch. It was 8:30. Then he picked up the phone and punched in the number for the IOI office.

* * * *

Sergeant Arrens picked up on the first ring. The digital readout on the top of the phone told her where the call was coming from.

"Morning, Christina," Neill rarely called her by her first name—and as much as she liked hearing him say it, she knew this would not be a pleasant conversation.

For the next few minutes she told him everything she knew, but giving Neill the answer to the question he feared the most was the hardest part. One sad fact seemed to keep pushing to the surface: Walter Coats, Neill's friend, was dead, and Arrens could almost feel the pain in the voice at the other end of the line.

Neill pushed aside his own feelings for the moment. "He had a wife, Christina."

The sympathy she felt for Coats' widow—although she'd never met her—was quite real. Christina pictured Neill's face in her mind for a moment and then tried to imagine how she'd feel if—

"I know. A Navy chaplain is on his way down to Virginia right now." She paused. "The C.O. wants you in here right away, Mike." A cringe. *"Lieutenant."*

Neill drew in his breath and whispered a silent prayer for Brenda Coats. "I'm on my way," he said at last.

The White House

Step One was easy.

Gathering the available information was the first part of his job. This morning there was plenty of that. The most reliable sources came in from various intelligence agencies, including the CIA. News from the television and cable networks was useful, as well as the internet, but the newspapers were not:

the story had broken too late to make the morning editions.

Willis Avery sat in his plushly carpeted, mahogany-lined office down the hall from the President of the United States and concentrated on Step Two: fitting all the information together to form an overall picture. While that was a little trickier, it was the third step that was the toughest: advising the President and the Joint Chiefs of Staff on an appropriate course of action.

The small, wall-mounted sign outside the door identified Avery as the National Security Advisor to the President. Like most other offices in the White House, his was very busy this morning. Avery had gotten the call at 3 a.m. advising him of the incident in the Sea of Japan. By 4:30 he was at his desk. Now, at 8:45, he was gulping a second cup of coffee and fighting a losing battle with fatigue.

Richard Aultman, Special Assistant to the National Security Advisor, entered the room holding a thin file folder that contained additional information. He stopped in his tracks long enough to take in the scene before him.

Avery was a big man with a larger than life presence and a no-nonsense, squared-away reputation, but today's events had already taken their toll on his appearance. It amused Aultman to see his boss this way until he remembered that Avery had been up half the night and seen the sunrise from his office.

Avery looked up from his reports and saw the file in Aultman's hand. "Naval intelligence?" he asked.

"Naval intelligence," Aultman nodded. "Just came in. Photos from the plane's tailfin camera are right on top."

Avery took the file. "Did you look at them?"

"Mr. Avery, that's a top secret file," Aultman frowned, pretending to be offended.

"You looked at them," Avery said. "No matter. You're cleared for it." He opened the folder and pulled out three black and white photos, spread them out on his desk and whistled softly.

"The pilot was right," he said. "This is definitely in the

'Red Sky' category. Who do we have in the field that can check on this further?"

Aultman sat down in a chair across from Avery. "That's the problem. There aren't any field personnel in that area. For some time now we've suspected the Russians were up to something near Vladivostok, but security's tighter than a drum. Nobody can get close."

Avery winced. "Tell that to you-know-who." He stood and straightened his tie, then picked up the photos. "All right. I'll give these to the President. He's meeting with the Russian ambassador at 9:30 so I'd better get over there. Anything else?"

Aultman shrugged. "Not really. We got a message from Wesley Cobb yesterday, but it can wait."

"Cobb? Our ambassador to Ukraine? What's up?"

"Seems there's been a shake-up at the weapons dismantling station in Odessa."

"Oh? What kind of a shake-up?" Avery walked into the small bathroom adjoining his office and looked at himself in the mirror. The tussled mass of gray hair on top of his head was a mess. Stroking his chin, he realized he could use a shave, too.

"Command level type." Aultman's voice rose so he could be heard. "The station commander was replaced, a Major named Mayakovsky."

Avery pulled a cordless razor out of a drawer. "Any idea why?"

"No. Cobb didn't say, so I'm assuming he doesn't know either." He heard a buzzing sound as Avery began to shave. "Kind of odd, don't you think?"

"Very odd. Did Cobb say when all this happened?"

"Two weeks ago."

Avery switched off the razor and re-entered the room. "Two weeks?"

Aultman nodded. "Mayakovsky was replaced by a Colonel in the Ukrainian Air Defense Forces, a man named Andrei Ulyanov."

"I know that name." Avery was fully intrigued now. "We've got someone going over there in a week or so to verify their disarmament procedures, don't we?"

Aultman got up and pulled another folder from a cabinet in the corner. "Got the file right here." He handed it across the desk to Avery.

The National Security Advisor scanned the pages inside. "Here it is. Marine Lieutenant Michael Neill. Leaves in twelve days." He sat down and read a little more, then smiled for the first time all morning. "Well, well, well ..."

Now Aultman was curious. "What is it?"

"Did you say it was the dismantling station in Odessa?"

"Yes," Aultman said.

"Do you know where Lieutenant Neill is headed?"

"I'll take a wild guess and say Odessa."

Avery chuckled. "You've got a bright future in intelligence, my boy. Want to know something else?"

"Humor me."

"It was Colonel Ulyanov who recommended Neill for the job."

"Wait a minute, I'm a little confused. What job?"

Avery's voice took on the tone of a patient scholar instructing a student. "Several years ago we negotiated with Ukraine to return its stockpile of nuclear weapons."

"What a can of worms that turned out to be," Aultman snorted.

"Can't argue with that," Avery replied. "Every year or so a few more turn up. Which was the primary reason we agreed to the Odessa facility—we wanted to ensure disarmament was really happening. On-site verification was always a sticking point, though. Their military bristled at the idea of having American personnel on their turf."

"I remember that," Aultman said. "Didn't our foreign aid money soften them up a bit?"

Avery shook his head. "Not completely. We only reached an agreement after a high-ranking member of their negotiating team—Colonel Andrei Ulyanov—recommended Neill to do the job."

"Why did he do that?"

"Because Ulyanov and Neill know each other."

Aultman was really confused now. "I don't get it. How does a Ukrainian Colonel get to be buddies with an American Marine? And why put Ulyanov in charge of that station? He has no background in weapons disarmament."

"That's where things get a little murky," Avery answered. "But to answer your first question, it seems that Neill grew up in Ukraine. His parents were missionaries there or something. As for your second question, I don't know."

"I still don't see how this Neill got the thumbs up from Ulyanov."

Avery shrugged. "That part I'm not sure about either. But the bottom line was that the Ukrainian government was satisfied and so were we. And it gets better." He slipped on his jacket and looked almost presentable. "Dismantling nukes isn't in his resume, but Ulyanov is—or was—the commanding officer at Ukraine's tactical air base in Nikolayev, which puts him in a position to help us."

Aultman had learned that turning any situation into an advantage was a crucial step in achieving political goals. Avery was a master of that.

"How so?"

"Colonel Ulyanov was in their military even in the days before the Soviet Union broke up. I'm sure he still has contacts in the Russian Republic. If that's the case, maybe he can tell us more about this—" he held up one of the photographs— "and what the Russians are up to near Vladivostok."

Aultman could see where Avery was going with this. "Do you think our Lieutenant Neill could persuade him to do that?"

Avery shrugged again. "That's something we'll have to ask Neill." With that, he gathered up the photos and headed down the hall for his meeting with the President.

Chapter Five ✷ An Old Threat

Moscow, Russian Federation

SINCE THE TWELFTH CENTURY, THE HISTORY of the Kremlin was one of siege, fire and sword. The citadel was situated on the bank of the Moskva River, and it began as a small stockade while the city grew up around it. Over the years it was destroyed and rebuilt several times.

Even its name spoke of conflict. The word Kremlin meant fortress and conquering armies from the Poles to the Tartars laid siege to the city. In those days, there seemed to be no shortage of foreign invaders, and each would-be conqueror reached deep into Russia to strike at her heart.

But Moscow survived them all to become an important trading center and a symbol of the Russian empire's might. By the time Napoleon invaded in the 1800s the city had taken on much of its present appearance. By the middle of the 20th century Russia and her satellite countries were regarded as one of the greatest superpowers on Earth.

Those humble beginnings mirrored the career of Russia's current leader. President Arkadi Murovanka stood at the window of his office in the Kremlin and watched as the snow fell outside, absorbed in his thoughts.

Murovanka had served the Soviet Union from his youth, entering the army at seventeen and rising quickly in the ranks of the officer corps. It was there that he fully embraced communism. His superiors were pleased and impressed with the young officer's sense of duty and commitment and urged him to join the communist party. He did, but ambition drove him further.

After establishing a name for himself as an effective soldier, Murovanka surprised everyone by leaving military life for politics. Those who knew him well regarded him as a cold and calculating man, and they were right.

Only two events in recent memory had truly appalled Arkadi's deep sense of nationalistic pride. The first had been the demise of the Soviet Union. He had been in Moscow that fateful day in December of 1991, working as an aide to a high-ranking member of the Politburo. He watched as the crimson flag of the Union of Soviet Socialist Republics faded from the sky in the shadow of *Krasnaya Ploschad*—Red Square. The end was oddly anti-climactic. While many of his comrades shrugged it off, the events of that day would fester in Murovanka's soul for years.

The second blow came only eight years later, when Arkadi's political career began surging. The West—and by extension the United States—had reached across Eastern Europe and brazenly challenged Russia by offering NATO memberships to Poland and Ukraine. Murovanka saw their actions as openly hostile and their march across the steppes of the formerly Soviet states had led him down a path of desperation …

The career of General Leonid Karpenko paralleled that of the President, but where Murovanka had chosen to leave the military for the cause of the party, Karpenko decided to remain in the army. Now he served Murovanka as his most trusted advisor. Between them, they shared power unrivaled anywhere in the Russian Federation, and while they were not exactly friends, they did share a common vision; both men wanted to rebuild the Soviet Union, and restore the glory of the fallen communist empire.

Murovanka turned from the window and back to his desk. It was early evening; Moscow was eight hours ahead of the eastern seaboard of the United States. While Washington D.C. was waking up to the news of the attack on the Navy plane, reports of the incident had consumed the better part of the Russian President's workday.

Murovanka picked up his phone and instructed his secretary to ask General Karpenko to join him. Moments later, the General entered the room, careful to close the door behind him and took a seat across from the President.

"Any word from Anatoly?" Murovanka asked.

"Ambassador Bazhenov should be meeting with the American President—" Karpenko checked his watch, "—even as we speak."

"Good." Murovanka turned to the credenza behind him and poured two glasses of mineral water. Unlike his predecessor, he had never acquired a taste for vodka. "You instructed him as to what he should say?"

"Of course, Mr. President." The General stood and took the glass Murovanka offered him. " *'The position of the Russian government is one of deep regret. We share the sorrow of the American people in their time of loss. Our people are looking into this tragic accident'*, et cetera, et cetera." Karpenko sipped from his glass and thought how much better mineral water tasted with ice. "Bazhenov is good with words. He will say all the right things."

Murovanka leaned back in his chair. "We should remove the aircraft from Vladivostok."

"Agreed," Karpenko said. "Closer to Moscow. Or the Baltics."

The President looked thoughtful. "No; I think not."

"You have someplace else in mind?"

Murovanka took his time answering. "We still have an agreement with Ukraine to exchange technological information, yes?"

Karpenko was puzzled. "Yes," he replied slowly. "But why Ukraine? They move closer to NATO with each passing day. Putting the aircraft there will only expose them to the Americans."

"And you think that hasn't already happened?" Murovanka asked. "Secrecy was lost when Kharkov ordered the attack on their plane." He shook his head. "All eyes will be on Vladivostok for the short term. Tensions will be high."

Karpenko's frustration became evident. "That may be true, but I still don't see the logic of this."

"Take the long view, Leonid," Murovanka said with a smile. "Ukraine just discovered more than two dozen of our warheads. I want them back."

He was right about that, Karpenko knew. The communique had come directly from Pavlovsk's office. "And how does giving the plane to them accomplish that?"

"Providing them with access to the aircraft—for a brief time—will give us some leverage. In return, we will negotiate with them for the return of the weapons."

The idea had some value, but Karpenko wasn't sold. "Ukraine has already agreed to turn them over to us." *After they've dismantled them*, he didn't add.

Murovanka shrugged. "I'm sure they will. Perhaps we can expedite the process by sweetening the pot."

"So where do we send the aircraft?"

"I'll leave that detail to you," Murovanka answered. It was a military matter that the President was more than happy to push down. This whole business had become tiring. "Which brings us to the pilot. What shall we do with him?"

"You must remember, he acted under orders, orders which he questioned. It was Major Kharkov who gave the authorization to fire the missile."

"You agree with Kharkov's decision?"

Karpenko shook his head. While he was willing to defend the actions of the pilot, the Major was another story. "No. Kharkov acted carelessly. As a result, he will also be re-assigned." At this the General smiled wryly. "In a few days he will be in charge of maintenance … or food services. Somewhere in … I'm not sure yet. It's a pity, really."

Murovanka felt no sympathy for Kharkov or anyone else.

"In what way?"

Karpenko went on. "Kharkov only acted to protect our new aircraft at Vladivostok. I cannot fault his judgment in that respect. Still, we have to blame someone." His eyes met those of the President. "Perhaps none of this would have happened if ..."

Murovanka returned his gaze. "If what?"

General Karpenko took a sip of his water before going on. "Mr. President, if I may speak frankly—"

"You always have, Leonid," Murovanka said softly. "Do continue."

Karpenko stood to his feet and walked to the window. "Right now our troops are massed at the Chinese border. We have flexed our muscles, but we did not achieve the desired effect. Instead of proving to the world that we are still a force to be reckoned with, we now have a dragon by the tail." He turned to face Murovanka. "This dragon has muscles, too, Mr. President."

"And teeth," Murovanka agreed.

"Exactly my point."

"What do you suggest?"

Karpenko breathed a little easier. He was getting through to his leader. "A phased withdrawal of our troops. These 'military exercises' began abruptly; we shall end them in the same manner."

Murovanka leaned forward. "We would lose face in front of the whole world."

"This operation has been conducted solely on Russian soil," Karpenko pointed out. "Only its close proximity to our Chinese neighbors makes it unique. We simply declare the exercise a success and order our commanders in the field to stand down."

Murovanka considered it for a moment, then frowned. "I am not entirely comfortable with that idea."

"Perhaps you would be more comfortable with all-out war," Karpenko moved to the front of the desk and rested his fingertips on its smooth surface. It was a rare occasion when he spoke to the President so bluntly. "Let me put it another way, Mr. President. We stand on thin ice." He lowered his voice. "We have thousands of troops who are at this moment standing eye to eye with the Chinese, and we have attacked an American reconnaissance plane without provocation. If we do not withdraw our forces and find some way to appease the Americans, we will be condemned as an aggressor nation."

The room grew very quiet.

Murovanka took a long sip of his mineral water and pursed his lips. "You are right, Leonid," he said at last. "Begin the withdrawal and congratulate our Generals in the field on a job well done. I will personally telephone President Breese and convey my condolences for their dead airman."

Karpenko breathed a sigh of relief and placed his empty glass on a table. But he wasn't finished yet.

"There is another matter."

"Concerning?"

"Concerning our 'agents of persuasion.' "

" *'Agents of persuasion?'* " Murovanka said with a snort. "You mean our terrorists, don't you?"

Karpenko winced. He would have preferred that word to remain unspoken in this office. 'Terrorists' was not a term he was fond of. But it was chillingly accurate.

For several months Murovanka and Karpenko had secretly been sending teams of patriots to the smaller republics. Their job was to persuade them that life under the old communist rule was better than democracy. The teams were to infiltrate military weapons arsenals, power plants—even hospitals—in order to steal small amounts of nuclear material. So far these teams had been successful in planting radioactive canisters in parks and railway stations in several large cities.

Two of the canisters were found in Lithuania, sending the local government officials scrambling to assure the public there was nothing to fear, but the damage had been done. Many began to long for the old days, when the Soviet Union was strong, and public sentiment for a return to rule under communism grew.

Which was exactly what Murovanka wanted.

"Your tone suggests there is a problem," the President noted.

"Yes, Mr. President." Karpenko replied. "One of our contacts has been arrested."

Murovanka blinked. It was rare that he was visibly disturbed. "Arrested? Who?"

"Major Mayakovsky, at the weapons dismantling facility in Odessa."

"On what charge?"

"Conspiracy. Treason. There are other charges, but they are somewhat inconsequential." Karpenko could see the concerned look on the President's face. "Fortunately, it appears our agents there have managed to slip away, although it has been almost two weeks since we have heard from them."

"They are undoubtedly laying low." Murovanka said.

Karpenko nodded. "That is my feeling as well. An abandoned farmhouse had been selected for just such a contingency."

"Too bad. As I recall we paid Mayakovsky a great deal of money to cooperate with us." Murovanka stood and began slowly pacing the room. "What are the names of our agents in Odessa?"

"Ivan Malyev and Sasha Kobrin."

The President considered this new development. It was a setback, but not a disaster—at least not for him. Murovanka and Karpenko had covered their tracks well. Even if Malyev and Kobrin had been captured, it would be difficult to prove that the President of the Russian Federation was behind their criminal acts. He had gone to great lengths to distance himself from their activities.

" 'Agents of persuasion,' " Murovanka said quietly to himself. It surprised him sometimes to think that he was now resorting to scare tactics to bring the republics back under his control. But for him the ends justified the means. He shook his head and sat down in a chair next to the General.

"Leonid, the time may come when we have to disassociate ourselves from those who serve us ..."

Karpenko knew exactly what he meant. Knowing Murovanka the way he did, the General was not the least bit surprised ...

The White House

Anatoly Bazhenov did not enjoy taking the blame for his country's mistakes, but as Russia's ambassador it was sometimes unavoidable.

It had been a busy day for Bazhenov. After his meeting with President Breese early that morning, Bazhenov's limousine whisked him back to the Russian Embassy. From there he telephoned Moscow, making his report and receiving further instructions. Next came the President's televised address to the nation, which Bazhenov watched with great interest. Bazhenov noted that the President never disclosed the type of aircraft that had fired on the Navy plane. That was good, he thought. *Perhaps we can keep the secret a little longer*. But that was naïve. He had to assume that Breese knew more than he let on.

No sooner had the address ended when Bazhenov received a phone call from the White House; the caller, Richard Aultman, strongly urged him to return at once for a meeting with the National Security Advisor. An hour later he found himself sitting in Avery's office, somewhat nervous and very much on the defensive.

"Sorry to keep you waiting, Mr. Ambassador," Avery said wearily as he entered the room. It had been a long day, and actually he wasn't the least bit sorry. He dropped a folder on the desk in front of Bazhenov as he made his way behind his desk. "These just came in. Take a look."

The ambassador opened the folder and pulled out several

photographs, close up stills of a badly damaged Viking aircraft.

"Your Malat missiles are quite effective," Avery said as he leaned back in his chair. "What does Malat mean, by the way?"

Bazhenov closed the folder and handed it across to Avery. "It is the Russian word for hammer."

Avery raised an eyebrow. "Hammer? Very appropriate, wouldn't you say, Mr. Ambassador?"

Bazhenov ignored the thinly veiled sarcasm in his voice long enough to try and change the subject.

"Your pilot must be very skilled to bring in an aircraft as badly damaged as this one," he said in a thickly accented voice. He decided to push his luck a little. "A pilot with his skill should have had no problem respecting our airspace."

Avery blinked. "Come again?"

Bazhenov shrugged. "Of course, you cannot blame our pilot for wanting to protect his Motherland in the face of Western aggression." His voice had taken a decidedly nasty edge.

"Are you saying this incident is our fault?" Avery was leaning forward now. "You can't be serious."

"I have never been more serious, Mr. Avery. Western expansion into former Eastern Bloc countries serves only to damage relations between Russia and the United States."

"Go on." Avery had underestimated the Ambassador, but in spite of that he was also mildly amused, although he didn't show it. This Russian had spunk, that was for sure.

"In the past, neutral nations acted as a buffer between East and West," Bazhenov continued. "Now NATO is expanding, reaching deeper into Eastern Europe." He stared across the desk at the National Security Advisor. "Such actions have produced a feeling of vulnerability among my people. You can see with your own eyes the results." Bazhenov jabbed a finger at the folder of photos on Avery's desk. "Germany has re-united. The Warsaw Pact is dissolved. Yet the West has made no effort to consider how this affects my country."

Avery was able to glean quite a bit from the Russian's tirade. Both of the events he mentioned had happened years before, but he could still hear the anger in Bazhenov's words. "Do you really regard NATO as such a threat?" Avery asked, taking a more conciliatory tone. He hoped to pull more information out of him, but he couldn't do it as long as the ambassador was so agitated.

"You would do the same if our positions were reversed, Mr. Avery." The ambassador had calmed down considerably. "Your current experiment in Ukraine is one more reason why we worry in Moscow."

Avery silently conceded that point. The West had dangled a NATO membership in front of Ukraine, but President Pavlovsk had publicly stated that the decision to join should be decided by a public, national referendum. And while everything Bazhenov said up to that point might have been just so much hot air, Avery knew that Russia's concerns for its former satellite country were very real indeed.

Murovanka had pledged to spend trillions of rubles—billions in U.S. dollars—to strengthen the Russian military over the period of a decade. It was a two-fold effort. The first phase was in response to NATO's plan to deploy a network of missile defenses, protecting Europe from potential attacks. The second step was designed to upgrade Russia's capability to defend against threats in the modern age.

Bazhenov was right; if their roles were reversed, the West might react in the same way. The Russian republic could just be making preparations to defend itself, but Avery feared there might be more to it than that. He hoped they would see the folly of challenging their Chinese neighbors and stand down, but since the fall of communism, the Russian bear was a very unpredictable animal.

Chapter Six ✶ Danger on the Waterfront

Odessa, Ukraine

❝ THIS IS NOT A GOOD OMEN, COMRADE.”

Sasha Kobrin struggled with the gears of the truck and cast a worried glance at Ivan Malyev, who sat next to him in the passenger's seat.

"What is wrong now?" Malyev asked.

Kobrin shook his head as the vehicle lurched along Suvorova Street between the port complex to their left and the towering Potemkin Steps on the right.

"I don't know. It could be the transmission." Kobrin stood on the clutch pedal and tried to downshift. This time the gears seemed to catch.

It was well past midnight and there was not another vehicle in sight. Kobrin parked the ailing truck about fifty meters beyond the foot of the Steps and turned off the ignition. Then he took a deep breath and forced himself to relax.

"Tell me about the shed," Malyev said as he lit a cigarette. Kobrin watched with some concern in the rearview mirror as a car rounded the corner.

"It was built about ten years ago as a storage area for road-work equipment." The car passed them by without stopping, and Kobrin continued. "Shovels, tools, that type of thing." He smiled. "Of course, there was no money to fund road repairs at that time, so it has been all but forgotten."

Malyev grunted, then opened his door and jumped down from the cab of the truck. It was a two and a half ton military vehicle with a tarpaulin covering stretched over the back. As were most military vehicles in the former Soviet Union, it was painted green.

Kobrin got out and both men walked to the back, swung open the tailgate and climbed inside.

It was an especially black night, but even in the darkness Malyev could see it; a steel container, five feet long, two feet deep and another two feet high, a metal box that both men simply called 'the device.'

Mounted on top, in the center, was a flat keypad control panel, about one inch thick, with a digital display. On either end of the container were handles that folded into recessed depressions. The outside surfaces were very smooth. While it looked very heavy, it was not. It was constructed of titanium, an alloy much stronger—and lighter—than ordinary steel.

The two men grabbed the handles and pulled the container to the open rear. Malyev jumped to the ground and looked in every direction. He was just as anxious to get this over with as Kobrin; he just didn't let it show. Peering into the darkness, he was pleased by what he saw. So far, so good, he thought. Kobrin picked up a tool bag and laid it carefully on top of their cargo. They might need it soon. A minute later they had unloaded the container and manhandled it into the dense tree line that covered the hillside. Only then did they stop to catch their breaths. The device wasn't so heavy that two men couldn't carry it, but after some distance it became burdensome.

Malyev could see the maintenance shed just ahead, a small featureless structure built into the hill where the incline began. It was overgrown with weeds and shrubbery, perfectly camouflaged and hidden from the road, which was only thirty meters away. If it was everything Sasha had said it was, it would do nicely.

They picked up their cargo and continued toward the door

of the shed. It was padlocked, but Kobrin produced a pair of bolt cutters from the tool bag and with a little effort they were inside. Kobrin closed the door quietly behind them, then pulled out a flashlight and switched it on. In the cold light of the beam, Malyev surveyed the room and smiled. A heavy, musty smell filled their nostrils.

"Perfect," Ivan said. "You were right. No one has been here for years."

They wasted no time moving tools and equipment out of one of the corners, clearing an area large enough to accommodate the steel container. Their work didn't take long. Soon the device was in position. Malyev covered one end of it, including the control pad on top, with an old canvas tarp he found among the tools. Then both men stood back and surveyed their efforts.

"There." Malyev said. "It looks almost natural here, wouldn't you say?"

Kobrin said nothing, instead bending down to uncover the control pad. He flipped on a start-up switch and the small hard drive built into the console hummed to life. He worked quietly as Malyev peered over his shoulder.

"The system is active?" Ivan asked.

Kobrin keyed in a command on the control pad. "Starting the diagnostic program now." He had barely finished speaking when the digital readout began to glow red. Malyev read the display out loud:

INITIALIZATION COMPLETE
SYSTEM READY — ENTER PASSWORD

His mouth suddenly felt very dry.

"All right," he finally said. This really wasn't necessary. "We know that it works. Now it is time to go."

Instead of standing, Kobrin remained where he was. His eyes never left the control pad before him.

"Do you realize how easy it would be, Ivan?" he said softly.

Malyev eyed his associate warily. "How easy what would be?"

"To activate the sequence—to detonate the warhead right here and now."

Malyev placed his hand gently yet firmly on Kobrin's shoulder. "That is not our purpose here, Sasha. It may come to that, but we will not proceed in that direction without orders." His voice became just as firm. "Do you understand, *tavarisch*?"

"Yes, but what good is a bomb if you don't intend to use it?" Kobrin was trembling now. "We have poured weeks of our lives into this, and now you are ready to just walk away?"

Stealing a nuclear weapon had been Kobrin's idea and by doing so the two men—three, actually, including Major Mayakovsky—had gone far beyond their original orders of simply taking radioactive materials. In fact, not even their superiors knew about the bomb. He doubted they would appreciate their initiative. The two had only briefly discussed how to inform them.

Malyev crouched down and looked his friend in the eye. "Sasha, listen to me. We have been through this before. This device can serve many purposes, even if it remains intact." He ran his hand along the smooth surface of the container. "And we are not just walking away."

Kobrin was insistent. "Then why leave it here? Why not take it with us?"

Malyev shook his head. That just wasn't going to happen. "No. We cannot possibly get across the border with this—they will be looking for us."

"But what if someone finds it here?"

"That is the beauty of it." Malyev smiled. "Think of the effect it will have on those traitors who conspire with the West—a nuclear warhead sitting right next to their precious port." The thought was clearly amusing to him now and for that reason Malyev had no intention of using the bomb. "They will beg Moscow to take them back and protect them from such acts of terrorism."

"You oversimplify the situation, Ivan. The people of Ukraine have begun to feel the hand of prosperity—thanks to the Americans. I think they prefer democracy."

Malyev nodded grimly. "They have tasted success, that is true. But only a taste. The wealth of this land once belonged to Mother Russia. And it will again." He wanted to leave the discussion there, and hoped he'd said enough to convince his friend.

Ivan rose to his feet and moved toward the door. "Now let's get out of here."

Kobrin bent over the control console once more and sighed. He knew it was pointless to argue with the man. He pulled the tarp over the end of the container, his fingers moving quickly over the keypad, but before he finished he entered a command that Ivan Malyev was completely unaware of.

Once outside again, Malyev secured the door with a new lock he had brought with him. Then they moved away from the wooded slope and back toward the truck.

Crouching under the cover of some overhanging branches, Malyev's eyes searched the street for any signs of activity. There was no one in sight. Then they walked out into the open and headed back to the street.

Kobrin slid into the driver's seat as Malyev got in next to him, quietly closing the door. They were almost home free.

* * * *

Sergei Goncharov was a five year veteran of the Odessa police force known as the militia. The waterfront was his beat, and at that particular moment he was completing his shift with a quiet stroll down the Potemkin Steps. He was almost at the foot of the Steps when a truck parked along the curb caught his attention. He sighed. Tonight's shift had been uneventful and he was looking forward to shift change. That might have to wait now.

* * * *

Kobrin slipped the key into the ignition. He couldn't believe how smoothly it had gone, and still no one had seen them. It was even easier than he had expected.

But his rising confidence faded when he turned the key. Instead of roaring to life, the engine was still.

* * * *

"Try it again," Malyev said in a steady voice.

Kobrin nodded and turned the key a second time, but the engine refused to turn over. By now raw fear had replaced his self-assurance.

Malyev remained calm. "All right," he said quietly. "We will get out and check under the hood. Probably just an electrical short—"

Before he could finish, a bright light shone into the cab, blinding both men for an instant.

"Forgive my intrusion." Sergeant Goncharov immediately sensed that something was out of place as he shone his flashlight into the faces of the two men in the truck. He was now standing at Kobrin's door. "But we don't get many visitors to the waterfront at two o'clock in the morning."

Malyev's eyes were just beginning to adjust when Sergeant Goncharov lowered the beam. He could see Goncharov's uniform and realized they had been surprised by a police officer.

"Sergeant," Malyev said in a friendly voice. "We seem to be having some mechanical problems. Do you know anything about engines?"

Goncharov ignored the question. "What are you men doing here?"

A pause. "We were delivering some machinery to one of the ships docked below," Kobrin spoke up, a little too nervously.

Goncharov stole a quick glance at the harbor. "Machinery? What kind of machinery?"

"Heavy equipment. Shaft assemblies for automobiles, that type of thing." Malyev said.

"And you've just come from the port complex?"

It was the way he phrased the question that made Kobrin edgy. "That's right." Sergeant Goncharov's hand was now resting lightly on his holster.

"Then let me see your shipping manifest." It didn't sound like a request and it wasn't.

Kobrin was sweating now. His mind raced for an answer of some kind, but he just couldn't think of one. Finally Malyev spoke up again.

"I'm sorry, officer," he smiled broadly. At the same time his hand moved slowly into his jacket. "The manifest was delivered with the cargo."

Goncharov was not amused. "Then show me a copy of the harbormaster's receipt."

Malyev shrugged. "His office was closed. We were unable to obtain a receipt."

"Really?" Goncharov was more than suspicious now. "The harbormaster's office never closes."

There was an awkward silence. Malyev was no longer smiling.

"Let me see your papers. And step out of the truck," Goncharov ordered. The hand that had been resting on his holster now unfastened it.

Kobrin's trembling hands reached into his pocket and pulled out his I.D. He held it out as Sergeant Goncharov reached up toward the cab. That was a mistake. Before he could take it, Kobrin dropped the papers and grabbed him by the wrist.

Pulling up as hard as he could, Kobrin slammed the Sergeant against the door frame. It was an awkward attack, but momentarily effective. He released his grip and pushed the door open with his shoulder, knocking the stunned officer to the street.

Goncharov was disoriented from the impact against the door, but still managed to pull his sidearm. Kobrin jumped to the street and swung at him, but this time Goncharov managed to avoid the blow.

Malyev leaped to the ground, his own gun in hand. He

rounded the front of the truck just as Sergeant Goncharov staggered back and raised his weapon, pointing it at Kobrin's chest.

Kobrin froze, but the shot that rang out came from Malyev's weapon, a Russian-made Makarov 9 millimeter. Goncharov whirled, clutched his chest and then slumped to the pavement.

As quickly as it had started, the scuffle was over.

Malyev quickly put away his gun and looked all around. Even at this late hour he knew the sound of a gunshot would not go unnoticed for long. A frown passed over Kobrin's face as he bent over the fallen policeman.

"Is he dead?" Malyev was now at Kobrin's side.

For the moment, there was still no one in sight. Kobrin took Sergeant Goncharov's wrist. He felt nothing. Then he placed three fingers on the officer's neck. Here he found a slight pulse. He unzipped the officer's jacket and checked the wound. "No," he said. "His pulse is weak and he is bleeding badly. But he is alive." Kobrin looked up into Malyev's face. "What now?"

Malyev had acted without really thinking and was at a loss for words. Everything had gone so well—and now this. His instinct for survival told him to run away, to get as far from the waterfront as he could. And it was in these kinds of desperate situations that Malyev let his instincts take over ...

He gripped Kobrin by his coat and pulled him to his feet. Looking down at the man he'd shot, Malyev felt something, an emotion he couldn't quite identify. It wasn't pity or remorse, but it grated against what little conscience he still had.

He forced himself to put aside these strange feelings. With Kobrin in tow, both men began to run, looking back briefly at the still figure of the policeman lying in the road. In a moment's time they had disappeared into the night.

The relief officer who found Sergeant Goncharov two minutes later saved his life. Fresh from military service, the young Corporal applied some basic first aid and stopped the bleeding, then radioed militia headquarters for backup and an ambulance.

The first responders arrived shortly after that. The hospital was not far, and an hour later a surgeon removed the bullet from Goncharov's lung and sewed him up. After receiving several units of blood his condition improved and the doctor began to think he just might pull through.

Nothing else happened until dawn, when the militia commander ordered a complete investigation into the shooting. He knew the assailants would be long gone, but the truck they'd left behind might give them some clues. The vehicle was towed to police headquarters, but a thorough search turned up nothing. The commander was not surprised; whoever had used this truck had carefully removed any registration papers that might have been used to trace it.

In the greater scheme of things, the incident was hardly noteworthy from the local news media's perspective. The Odessa newspaper buried the story far from the front page. By mid-morning the investigating team concluded their work at the scene of the crime and headed back to headquarters to compare notes. The investigation had centered on the truck, so no one paid any attention to the maintenance shed hidden in the tree line.

In fact, none of them knew it was even there.

Chapter Seven ✶ Additional Duties

L IEUTENANT WALTER COATS WAS BURIED AT
Arlington National Cemetery with full military hon-
ors. About a hundred people attended the services,
including the Vice President, the National Security Advisor,
and several other key administration officials. The Russian
ambassador had expressed his desire to attend the funeral, but
his request was graciously denied.

Brenda Coats had asked Neill to say a few words before her
husband's casket was lowered into the ground. As the pallbear-
ers silently placed it into position, the Marine Lieutenant took
his place.

Wearing his dress blue uniform, Michael looked as if he'd
stepped out of a Marine Corps recruiting poster. He cleared his
throat and looked out at the sea of faces before him. Christina
Arrens sat in the front row of folding chairs, next to Brenda
Coats. The Commandant of the Marine Corps, General Bradley
Cole, was also present. Cole caught Neill's eye and gave the
young officer an encouraging nod. Neill nodded back and then
began to speak.

"If we could see things from Walter's perspective, none of
us would feel the need to grieve—but grieving is only natural,"
he said. "Right now he stands whole in the presence of the King
of Kings, without pain, without worry, and completely at peace.

"Every time an American puts on the uniform of his country,

he—or she—assumes some risks. We've come here today to honor the memory of a man who knew the risks, but felt they were worth taking."

Neill turned slightly and ran his hand along the closed lid of the casket. It was not theater, but an effort to fight the emotions of the moment. "Walter Coats took an oath to defend his country and its people. He gave his all in pursuit of that oath, but long before his devotion to duty placed him in harm's way, his faith in Christ put him in God's hands.

"If you'll look around you, you'll see a hillside dotted with white stones. Each one tells a story of honor, service, and sacrifice. The marker that will be placed here will be no different." The cold January wind that blew at his back seemed to carry his words even farther.

Sitting next to the Vice President, Willis Avery was deep in thought. His grandfather had been a country preacher in the hills of Kentucky, and Avery had grown up listening to the old man telling him stories from the Bible. As an adult he'd walked away from the faith, but he'd never forgotten the quiet integrity that defined Grandpa Avery's life.

Neill began reading from the Old Testament. His words caught Avery's attention.

" '... *Acknowledge and take to heart this day that the Lord is God in heaven above and on the earth below. There is no other* ... '

"The Scriptures tell us that wisdom is found in trusting God's promises. It goes on to say that a life sacrificed in service to Christ is really no sacrifice at all." Michael closed the Bible.

"Walter Coats understood that. He knew that God truly is in control." His voice cracked slightly as he spoke the words, and the emotion in his voice was clear to everyone present.

"Now's your chance," Richard Aultman whispered to his boss.

The honor guard had folded the flag draped over the casket, and then Lieutenant Neill knelt before Brenda Coats and presented it to the young widow. The two shared a heartfelt look. No words were necessary to express the pain of losing a friend and a husband. Brenda clutched Michael's hand and nodded, her body trembling slightly as she fought to maintain control of her emotions. Michael's gloved hand squeezed hers in return. It might not have been protocol, but Neill was beyond caring about that. He leaned forward and embraced her just as Brenda's sobbing began.

A small group of musicians played the Navy Hymn. When they finished, the chaplain concluded with prayer and quietly announced that the service was over.

With the ceremony at an end, Neill watched as Brenda was enveloped by her family. They shared a forced smile before her parents—along with Walter's—escorted her slowly away from the crowd and back to the road. Michael rejoined General Cole for the short walk back to the Commandant's staff car. The two officers had nearly reached the vehicle when they heard a voice behind them.

"General Cole?"

Neill turned to see Willis Avery approaching, with two other men following slightly behind. One was Richard Aultman. The other was a Secret Service agent.

"Willis," General Cole stopped and let Avery catch up. The two men shook hands. "I thought I saw you up on the hill. You riding back with the Vice President?"

Avery smiled and shook his head. As usual, his hair was a mess. "No, I've got my own ride." He gestured to a car across the street. Neill saw that Avery had a driver and another Secret Service agent waiting for him.

Avery turned his attention to the Lieutenant and stuck out his hand. "Sorry about your friend, Marine. That's a tough shot to take." As brusque as he could be at times, even Avery found the moment awkward.

"Thank you, sir."

"Do you mind if we take a few minutes to speak privately?"

"Not at all, sir," Neill took a step back and looked at the

Commandant. "General, if you'll excuse me, I'll just wait over here—"

"No, no, Lieutenant," Avery chuckled and gripped the General's arm. "I don't want to talk to this old warhorse. It's you I'm here to see."

Neill was confused. "Me, sir?"

"That's right, you. General?"

General Cole raised an eyebrow. "Fine with me, Willis." He turned to Neill. "I'll send a car back for you, Lieutenant."

"No need for that, General. My driver can take him when we're finished."

The General had a driver too, a Marine Gunnery Sergeant. The Gunny opened the car door and Cole slid into the backseat. A moment later the vehicle pulled out onto the drive and Neill found himself alone with the President's right hand man.

"Lieutenant," Avery began slowly. "What we're going to talk about is classified information …"

* * * *

"Nearly three weeks ago there was a command shake-up at the weapons facility in Odessa." Avery carried a manila envelope under his arm as they talked. "Colonel Andrei Ulyanov is in, Major Vadim Mayakovsky is out. The trouble is nobody knows why."

Neill nodded. He'd been briefed about the situation the day before and was just as puzzled.

"I've read your file, Lieutenant," Avery continued. "You've got quite an impressive resume. Born and raised in Ukraine— your family spent a long time there, didn't they?"

"That's correct, sir." Neill replied.

"Must have been a real culture shock when you got back to the U.S.," Avery observed. "You did your senior year of high school stateside. Then a Congressional appointment to the Naval Academy—where you took the Marine Corps option. At graduation, your class standing and fluency in Russian made you a shoe-in for a job at the IOI office."

"That just about covers it," Neill conceded, not knowing exactly what else to say.

"Why the Corps?" Avery asked. "Was that your uncle's doing?"

Michael took a deep breath. "The Master Gunny was a big influence, yes. But that's a long story."

The National Security Advisor decided to leave that for another time. He wore a shrewd look on his face as he sized up the man before him. "And it doesn't end there, does it?"

"I'm not sure what you mean, sir."

"Two years ago Ukraine and the United States formally agreed to on-site disarmament verification—that was after one too many warheads showed up unexpectedly in their country. We needed some assurances that they weren't getting sloppy. The President himself pressed for American representation on their soil. The Ukrainians didn't like it at first, but they finally came around—especially after Colonel Ulyanov recommended you for the job. That part's not in your file. So I'm curious about why he would do that."

Neill was somewhat surprised by Avery's subtle probing. "The Colonel is an old family friend, sir. You're aware that my parents were missionaries."

"I got that part," Avery nodded his head slowly. "Go on."

"My dad's vision when he first arrived in Eastern Europe was to distribute Bibles to the troops in the Ukrainian military. Colonel Ulyanov—actually he was a Major back then—was the C.O. at one of the air bases. Dad approached him with the idea—"

"And the Colonel went for it?"

Neill shook his head. "No, not at first. But shortly after that he became a believer—have you ever heard his testimony, sir?"

Believer. Testimony. Grandpa Avery had used words like that. "Can't say that I have."

"Well, to make a long story short, the Colonel asked my dad to start a Bible study—right on the base." Neill was clearly fond of the memory.

Avery was thoughtful for a moment as the wind did further damage to his hair. "Tell me about Ulyanov," he said at last.

"Fighter pilot from the old school. Highly decorated, very dependable. And he has some pretty good political connections, as well." That was an understatement, but Neill wasn't prepared to disclose everything he knew about his old friend. "An excellent officer in every respect. But I had no idea he knew enough about nukes to take charge of a dismantling station."

"As far as we know, he doesn't. But you don't have to be a subject matter expert to be in charge," Avery pointed out. His eyes brightened a little. "Which brings us to you, Lieutenant."

The conversation had gone far enough for Neill to make an educated guess about what Avery was leading up to. "Me, sir?"

"Don't play dumb with me, Marine," Avery chuckled. "Your flight leaves in a few days from Andrews. When you get to Odessa I want you to do a little detective work for me."

"Am I being re-tasked?"

"Think of it as an additional duty." Avery said. "Kind of like a favor; but more than that."

"Yes, sir," Neill answered.

"Find out what's going on, why Ulyanov is in charge. My guess is that it has something to do with his friendship with Ukraine's president. Check on Mayakovsky, too. He seems to have dropped off the face of the earth. That's not supposed to happen over there anymore, so there must be a good reason for it."

Neill seemed to find that humorous. "The Cold War may be over, but not much has changed since then," he smiled. "Is that all, sir?"

"No," Avery said, shaking his head. "There's one more thing." His eyes narrowed. "Have you ever heard the phrase 'Red Sky at Morning'?"

Neill turned that over in his mind and then nodded. "CIA

buzzwords. 'Red Sky' denotes technologies used by the Russian air force. 'Morning', 'Afternoon', or 'Night' pinpoint geographic locations in the eastern, central, or western parts of Russia." Neill wondered what all of this had to do with his mission in Ukraine.

He didn't have to wait long. Avery opened the envelope he'd been carrying and pulled out some photographs.

"I want to show you something. These were taken four days ago." Avery handed him the photos. "What does that look like to you?"

Neill studied the pictures for a moment. "I'm no expert on aircraft; but it appears to be a fifth generation fighter. Cockpit configuration would suggest this might be a two-seater."

Avery shook his head. "More like a *sixth* generation fighter. Take a closer look—vertical and horizontal wing surfaces blend with the air frame. Definitely a step beyond current design. In one of those photos, the plane's skin is almost indistinguishable from the background."

"Low-observable technology," Neill nodded. He'd heard of this. "Stealth in all aspects."

"For a ground-pounder, you're well informed," Avery smiled. "And yes—for all practical purposes, this aircraft would be invisible to the human eye under certain conditions. On top of that, its aerodynamics would ensure LPIR—Low Probability of Intercept Radar. We suspect it has other features that make it a game-changer."

"Such as?" Neill's security clearance didn't extend beyond 'top secret', but he decided to press for more details anyway.

"Cyber warfare capabilities; directed energy weapons." Avery was being very forthcoming. "Probably some advanced situational awareness technology that would make it next to impossible to sneak up on." He shook his head. "I remember the day the last F-22 rolled off the assembly line—ending production on that aircraft was a big mistake."

"This all sounds like science fiction." Neill continued thumbing through the images. "That kind of stuff is pretty expensive; I'm guessing it would be hard for a government to justify technology like this in a post-Cold War world."

"Only if you're interested in the well-being of the people you serve," Avery grunted. "Otherwise, you skim from the top of the GDP and roll it all into your military. There are more than a few nations with those kinds of priorities. China, Russia, for starters. North Korea. Definitely Iran. A few other third-world countries practice it on a smaller scale." The mention of Russia brought to mind a briefing Avery had received that morning. The latest intel suggested that Russian forces were posturing to take a step back from the border they shared with China. The National Reconnaissance Office, or NRO, had picked up radio chatter to that effect.

"Mr. Avery, if you've been to Russia, you've *been* to a third-world country." Neill's assessment reflected years of first-hand observation. "There's something to be said for having an overwhelming military advantage. In the right hands, it ensures peace. But the countries you've mentioned don't see it that way. They've practiced that policy while their people starve. There's only so much common grace in the natural world. Decency persuades the conscience, but real faith is what morality's built on. Without it, the goodness of man doesn't go too far."

Avery gave the younger man a quizzical look. Neill's eulogy at the grave side brought back memories of Grandpa Avery. His words now did the same. But despite their ringing indictment of humanity, Neill spoke them without sounding judgmental.

"Well, I wasn't expecting a Sunday School lesson," Avery said slowly. "But I think I see your point. And you're right— these photos are evidence of just that."

"Where were these taken?" Neill slid the photos back into the envelope.

"Sea of Japan, off the Russian coast."

Neill looked up the hill where his friend's grave was, then back to Avery. "This is the fighter that attacked Walter's plane?"

Avery nodded. "Those pictures were taken by the tailfin camera of Lieutenant Coats' Viking," Avery said. "We think the Russians have more—possibly a squadron at an air base near Vladivostok."

Michael was surprised. "An entire squadron?"

Avery shrugged. "Well, at least another prototype. Like you said, this type of weapons program would be very expensive. You'd need more than one for comparative testing."

" 'Red Sky at Morning'." Neill said, handing the envelope back to Avery. "I think I see where you're going with this."

Avery tucked the photos under his arm. "I need your help, Lieutenant. You have something of an investment in this incident. We don't have enough eyes on that part of the world. And the Russians seem to have the lid on pretty tight."

"That should tell you something right there."

"It does," Avery agreed. "It tells me that they don't want us nosing around. But you have the background that could tell us more. I want you to find out anything you can about this plane and report back to me."

"Odessa's a long way from Eastern Russia, sir," Neill pointed out.

"Colonel Ulyanov spent a great deal of time in the Soviet Air Defense Forces. He may still have friends there." He turned and began walking slowly back to his car. "I know it's a slim chance, but it's the best one we've got. I'm authorizing you to bring back anything that might tell us what the Russians are up to."

The afternoon sun was casting long shadows on the sprawling grounds around them. As the two men approached Avery's car his driver got out and opened the door. "Bear in mind that this is all a bit delicate. Do the best you can, but use discretion. Oh, there is one thing—" Avery pulled a sealed white envelope from his coat pocket and handed it to Neill. Avery's name and the White House logo were printed on the front. "It's a letter—giving you authority to act on behalf of the U.S.

government. If anybody on our side gives you a hard time, show them this and tell them you're working for me."

Neill was thoughtful as he slipped into the back seat of the car with Avery. The National Security Advisor had just given him wide latitude to accomplish his mission, one that would dead-end in a hurry if Colonel Ulyanov couldn't—or wouldn't—cooperate. As the car pulled out onto the drive and back towards Washington, D.C., Neill pushed the day's events out of his mind and concentrated on what lay ahead.

It occurred to him that once in the field, he might have to roll with the punches and maybe even improvise a little. As a Marine officer, he was used to that.

* * * *

Moscow, Russia
The Kremlin

"I have some disturbing news."

President Murovanka looked up from the paperwork on his desk as General Karpenko entered the room. The look on the General's face caused him to fear the worst.

"What now, General?" Murovanka was not at all pleased with the interruption. He'd spent the past few days trying to undo the crisis caused by the attack on the American aircraft and he was bone tired. NATO had condemned the action and demanded a full investigation. Murovanka had appeased the international community somewhat by appearing on television and announcing a full withdrawal of all Russian troops located at border 'hotspots', including China. For the moment, the world seemed satisfied, but the republics that once belonged to the Soviet empire looked with suspicious eyes toward Moscow.

Karpenko pulled a chair close to the President's desk and sat down. "I have just received two reports from Ukraine. The first concerns our agents in Odessa."

"Malyev and—" Murovanka frowned, trying to remember their names.

"Kobrin, yes," Karpenko said, then paused. "It seems Malyev shot a police officer as they were preparing to leave the country."

Murovanka began to quietly fume. "Where are they now?"

Karpenko held up a folded piece of paper. "The report comes from Major Pirogov."

Murovanka had never met the Major, but he knew that Pirogov acted as the contact for Karpenko's agents in the field. It was Pirogov who had recommended and recruited Malyev and Kobrin nearly two years before.

"Pirogov received an encrypted radio message yesterday. Kobrin and Malyev intend to fly out of the country in two days and rendezvous with the Major at our training camp in Bryansk."

"Did you say fly out?" Murovanka asked.

Karpenko nodded his head. "They have a small plane at their disposal, hidden at the farmhouse."

The President was deep in thought. "I see. And the other message?"

"We have received word that the Ukrainian militia has stepped up its patrols. Their border guards have also been ordered to search and question anyone leaving the country."

"Casting their nets," the President mused. "What is the condition of the man who was shot?"

Karpenko shrugged his shoulders and frowned. "Details are hard to come by, but we think he is alive."

"That is unfortunate. If he survives, he might be able to identify his assailants." There was nothing they could do about that now. Murovanka pushed himself away from his desk and walked to the window. He drew the curtains back and allowed the morning sun to spill into the room. Outside, ice glistened as it clung to the ancient walls of the Kremlin.

"There is a very real danger that Kobrin and Malyev might still be captured, General," the President said slowly. "But perhaps we can turn this situation to our advantage."

"How so?"

"The republics are worried," Murovanka continued. "Worse than that, they are afraid; our agents have done their jobs well." He turned to face General Karpenko with an evil smile. "Suppose Major Pirogov and his troops captured the training camp in Bryansk and apprehended the terrorists at the same time? Even better, suppose those terrorists met an untimely end?"

General Karpenko's eyes fixed on the President as he considered the idea. There seemed to be no end to Murovanka's diabolical thinking.

"The plan has merit," Karpenko said. Now he was smiling too. "The republics might actually begin to believe we are on their side after all. And with Kobrin and Malyev out of the way we reduce the risk of being associated with their criminal activities." Then something occurred to the General. "But what about our teams in the Baltic states and elsewhere? We can't simply eliminate them, too."

Murovanka returned his gaze to the city of Moscow. No matter how chilling the weather was outside, his heart was colder still.

"The Major's actions must be ... *dramatic*, shall we say? We need to send an unmistakable message. Contact Pirogov. Tell him to recall the rest of our agents and quietly disband them. The fate of Kobrin and Malyev will serve to force their silence." He turned again to face the General. "Any questions, Leonid?"

"No, Mr. President," Karpenko said, standing to his feet. "I will make the arrangements myself." Karpenko excused himself and left the room.

* * * *

Once back in his own office, General Karpenko lifted the receiver of a secure telephone and punched in a rarely used number. He was thankful to give the order that would end their collaboration with terrorists. The President's plan had worked—up to a point. The republics had reacted as they had hoped to the presence of radioactive materials within their borders. But Karpenko was never entirely comfortable with the scheme. He was always concerned that it might come back to haunt them. So far, none of the breakaway governments had taken the next step; embracing Moscow's offer of protection.

There was a delay as the connection was made, then the General heard a familiar voice on the other end of the line. The conversation was brief, sprinkled with pre-arranged, coded phrases in case some unwanted listener overheard what was being said. It was important that Karpenko make himself understood, so he repeated his orders and within minutes, Major Pirogov had received—and confirmed—his new instructions.

Chapter Eight ✷ The Master Gunny

I T WAS A NIGHTLY ROUTINE. AT SIX P.M. EACH evening, Daniel Gavin Neill, USMC (medically retired), stared at the television with a frown on his face and a growl in his throat as he watched his favorite cable news show. Tonight the partisan politics that played out in front of him seemed particularly infuriating. And it wasn't just the *other* side—sometimes his own party—or what he'd always *believed* to be his party—was the one that gave him fits. Neill sighed heavily. Maybe this was just a consequence of growing older, but that ran counter to what he'd always believed— that maturity brought with it a more mellowed disposition. The past few years had disproved that old axiom. More and more often, as he absorbed the day's events, he found himself shaking his head and on several occasions the not quite prime-time broadcast caused him to consider hurling the remote at the screen.

Tonight the elder Neill had company, which was the norm whenever his nephew was in town. Seated in a recliner next to him, in the den of a quiet bungalow in suburban Anacostia, Michael Neill opened a container of Thai food—carry-out from a local restaurant—and started eating, while on the screen a congressman answered questions posed to him by the broadcast's anchor.

"Politics as usual," Daniel Neill muttered. He reached into

a paper sack on the coffee table in front of them and retrieved his own meal. "Just more of the same. Guys like that are more interested in getting re-elected than they are in making a real difference. It's all tit for tat; this party scores today; then tomorrow, the other side retaliates. And the American people suffer."

It was a familiar rant. Michael swallowed his fried rice before making an observation. "I thought you stopped watching the news."

Daniel's bowl of Pad Thai was almost cool enough to eat. "No," he replied. "I stopped reading the *newspapers*." He bit the end off that word with particular vigor. "Cancelled my subscription. Still get it on Sunday, though." Michael gave him a curious look. "Coupons," he winked in explanation. He peered into the bottom of the sack. "You brought spring rolls. Awesome."

"Roger that, Master Guns."

The two consumed their meals in silence as they sat in the den—or the 'Marine Room', as it had come to be known. All manner of Marine Corps kitsch decorated the walls, for the most part tastefully, but in some cases not. Michael eyed a bumper sticker adorning a framed poster that read 'Opinionated Marine on board.' The sentiment was an appropriate description of his uncle and brought a smile to Neill's face.

The broadcast was over and the rice was gone. Daniel Neill got up and steadied himself—one of his legs being a prosthetic limb below the knee, the result of an IED blast in Iraq—and took the empty food containers to the kitchen for disposal. Michael followed behind him and found the coffee pot, then poured two mugs of coffee. It was strong, just the way both men liked it.

"Saw some footage of the funeral the other day," Daniel offered, leaning against the counter. Michael added cream and sugar to his mug and took a sip. "The camera lingered on you, Mike. But then, the media always loves a Marine in his dress blues. Except for the haircut and the uniform, you looked a whole lot like your dad."

Michael nodded but didn't say anything in reply. The memory of Walter Coats' death was still too fresh. He handed his uncle one of the mugs.

The elder Neill could tell he'd struck a nerve and changed the subject. "So you're headed back over there?"

'Over there' was Ukraine, of course. Michael's face brightened now, and he seemed thankful to discuss a topic that wasn't so raw.

"I leave in four days."

Daniel nodded and then headed back to the den. He turned down the volume as the two reclaimed their chairs. "What's it been, six years now?"

"Going on eight," Michael corrected. "I hear a lot has changed." He glanced outside the window. Night had fallen, the temperature had dropped and a light rain began to fall.

"Never been there myself," Daniel said. "Your dad always wanted me to come over, but I was always on orders somewhere …" The memory of that was a happy one. "I wish I'd taken him up on it now." Neill turned to face his nephew, feeling the need to segue into a deeper discussion. "How do you feel about going back?"

"That's hard to answer." Michael wore a thoughtful look. "Overall, I'm looking forward to it. The mission is a bit unusual for a Marine, but I know what to look for." His answer sounded a little awkward even to himself, and even more so to Master Gunnery Sergeant Daniel Neill.

"What *is* the mission, Mike?" The Master Gunny was aware of the broad strokes, but his nephew seemed preoccupied and unusually quiet about the whole thing.

"Disarmament. Proper techniques. Specific safety measures, compliance with the fine points of the treaty," Michael answered. That was the *official* line. It was the additional tasking that bothered him. He wondered if he should broach the subject with his uncle.

"But there's more to it than that, isn't there?" Daniel could tell the younger Marine had something on his mind. "Want to talk about it?"

"They've asked me to look into the aircraft that attacked Walter's plane." Michael settled into the recliner and cradled the mug of hot coffee. "Willis Avery suspects it might be a sixth generation fighter."

Daniel Neill whistled softly. "They've actually got one?"

"It looks that way." He recalled the photos Avery had shown him, but didn't elaborate.

The Master Gunny considered that for a moment. "Russia's a big country. And Ukraine's nowhere near where that plane was shot at."

Michael nodded his head. "I told him the same thing. But he knows Colonel Ulyanov's a big part of the picture."

Daniel's brow furrowed. "And he thinks he can fill in the gaps. Good idea. Who knows, he might be right."

"Well, it makes a lot of sense. I doubt there's much that goes on in the skies over Russia that the Colonel *doesn't* know about."

The elder Neill adjusted the recliner, pulling his prosthetic limb up in a more horizontal position. Sometimes when the weather changed, or he sat for too long, the scar tissue at the point of amputation became painful. He fought the discomfort by constantly shifting his body weight. "So let me get this straight," he said slowly. "On top of verifying their disarmament procedures, they want you to investigate a new Russian fighter? That's a pretty tall order, Mike."

Michael drew in a deep breath and let it out slow. "It's not every day they get to send in someone who speaks the language—*and* knows somebody who can provide answers," he observed. "Avery's just making the most of the opportunity, I guess. And I don't doubt his motives. I think his heart's in the right place."

"But you're not so sure."

The younger Neill smiled thinly. His uncle was certainly intuitive. "About my abilities, no. Granted, I've been trained to ask all the right questions. And I know the obvious things to look for. But this is a brave new world and sometimes I wonder if they've picked the right guy for the job. Everybody sees me as some kind of invincible knight or something. But sometimes when I look in the mirror I just see ... *uncertainty*."

Daniel Neill had that look on his face. Usually it preceded some pithy thought or statement. "Michael, not many people want to be leaders. Most of the time it's because they don't think they can. But sometimes we don't have a choice. You're a Marine—and an officer at that—so leadership is your default setting." A pause. "Everything you learned at the Academy boils down to a few simple things; first, you find out what the job is. Then you embrace it. You do that by putting your best foot forward; make yourself proficient at it, without shrinking back. Define the mission and follow through on it."

There was silence for a moment. The Master Gunny sipped his coffee and a wistful look spread across his features. "I'm not sure how this figures into it, but I'm gonna say it anyway. There'll be times when life hands you an extraordinary opportunity. When that happens, press your advantage; and do good when you can.

"You're not alone, Mike. I've experienced times of uncertainty myself and had the same feelings you're having." He ran a hand over his artificial leg. "Misery and fatigue are a staple of life. You have to fight through it. The years can fly by so fast, but sometimes the pain seems to crawl." He paused to remember his brother—Michael's dad. "And there's something your father taught me. Took a while to sink in, it's true, but just remember—when we cry out to God, don't think for a minute that He doesn't hear us. Sometimes we just have to wait for the answer."

The Master Gunny decided that was a good place to end the discussion. If he kept going, he knew the whole thing would end in some maudlin, overly emotional mess. There was no point in letting things degenerate to that point. And emotionalism just wasn't his thing. Still, something else needed saying and he couldn't stop without throwing it in.

"Don't ever forget that your dad would be very proud of you, Mike." *Pivot*, he told himself; *don't make the lad uncomfortable*. Then he grumbled, "I guess I am too—even though you went rogue on me and became an officer."

Michael met his uncle's gaze with a smile and seemed to be his old self again. "You're not gonna start with the waterworks, are you?"

"Don't forget that I'm Old Corps, my young Lieutenant," Daniel replied. He cranked the recliner back. "That's not how we do things.

"Besides, it's almost time for Jeopardy."

Chapter Nine ✴ Disturbing Questions

NEILL USED A TOWEL TO WIPE THE SWEAT from his face, then drained the contents of his water bottle. The gym at Joint Base Anacostia-Bolling, in Washington D.C., wasn't far from the IOI office and he had decided to get in one more workout before his flight to Ukraine. The events of the past week had built up considerable stress, and Neill needed to bleed some of it off.

Today's session was a little longer than most—an extra thirty minutes on the elliptical—but Michael felt much better for it. Far from being a gym rat, Neill visited the fitness center only three times a week, varying his routine between cardio, calisthenics and free weights. Today's session was no different—in the wake of Walter Coats' death, he still felt the need to maintain his schedule.

Michael grabbed his sweats from the locker room and made his way toward the exit. On the way out, he passed the cardio machines. A young woman on one of the treadmills caught his eye and smiled. A bit winded, it took Neill a split second to recognize her, then he returned her smile.

"You come here often, Lieutenant?" Christina Arrens said playfully. Her stride continued without interruption.

"When I can," Neill answered, stopping by her machine. He was momentarily distracted, but in a pleasant way. Arrens wore a sweat-soaked, form-fitting tank top—and a pair of athletic shorts that revealed her long, muscular legs. Michael allowed himself to notice her sinewy beauty for the briefest of moments, then looked back up at her face. Her auburn hair was pulled up in a bun. "I don't think I've seen you here before."

She drew in a lungful of air before replying. "Couple of times a week," she said. Which was true—since she found out Neill was a regular there. "A girl's gotta do what she can to stay in shape."

And it's working, Michael didn't say. "You still doing kettle bells?"

"Yeah, that's next." Arrens nodded enthusiastically. "Great for the core. This your cardio day?"

"Cardio, arms and chest." Neill stood a little more erect, his chest expanding slightly to fill his t-shirt. It wasn't intentional, but—

"I can tell." *Snap*. She probably shouldn't have said it and knew her actions might be interpreted as just a little flirtatious. The Marines frowned upon fraternization between the enlisted and officer ranks—and particularly between genders; but after all, she was a young, single woman—and catching the Lieutenant's admiring glance, she doubted Neill would be offended by her remark. Besides, as a professional and an NCO, she knew the difference between appropriate and inappropriate behavior. She wasn't about to cross *that* line.

Neill felt his ears glow just a little. He decided to change the subject.

"My flight leaves tomorrow. I appreciate your help with the arrangements."

Wow, she thought. *Is that it?* "No problem, Lieutenant. That's my job." Her reply had an edge to it and she regretted it. *Give the guy a break. One of his best friends just died.* She decided to try one more time.

"Hey, you did good the other day. Up at Arlington, I mean. Your words were … special. Very touching." She hoped he caught the sincerity in her voice.

Neill nodded, wiping sweat from his brow. This time it had

nothing to do with his workout. "Thanks." He would have liked to carry this a little further, but thought it might be best to move on. "I'm gonna head out. Need to pack." That much was true. "See you when I get back, Sergeant."

Really? *Did he have to address her by her rank?* Arrens looked down at the treadmill's digital display as Neill turned to go. She punched a button and increased the machine's resistance, feeling somewhat disappointed as she picked up the pace.

The room was filled with mirrors. Christina found one with a clear view of Neill as he headed for the exit. She fixed her gaze on his frame and watched as he tossed his towel into a bin by the door.

Come on, Neill, turn around, she urged him silently. *You know you want to.*

Michael stopped in mid-stride; there weren't any mirrors by the exit, but he could clearly see her reflection behind him in the glass doors. As their eyes locked, he decided to do something completely spontaneous.

Arrens turned her attention to the display as soon as she saw Neill walking back toward her. Suddenly she was intensely focused on the calories she'd burned, the distance travelled and anything else the machine could tell her. She acted surprised when she heard his voice again.

"Hey, I'll be gone for a while, Christina," Neill's tone was more subdued, almost awkward. "Maybe I could buy you lunch after you're done here."

Michael wasn't good at this. Arrens looked down at him and smiled, her heart racing a little faster. Sweat trickled down her neck and beads of perspiration dotted her face and shoulders.

"I think my time's about up." She pulled a towel from the hand rails and dried her face. "Let me grab my stuff and I'll be ready to go."

Neill frowned slightly. "You said kettle bells were next, didn't you?"

Christina smiled in an inviting way. "They can wait."

* * * *

Three days after his meeting with the National Security Advisor, Lieutenant Neill's flight lifted swiftly off the runway at Andrews Air Force Base and climbed north. The plane was a Gulfstream VC-20, a sleek blue and white trimmed military version of an executive jet that carried various diplomats and couriers with assignments in Eastern Europe and Germany.

Presently the aircraft reached cruising altitude and Neill settled back in his seat by the window to enjoy the view. The New England coastline rushed by below and soon the little jet was over Canada, then the Labrador Sea.

It was an uneventful flight. Neill tried to strike up a conversation with a few of the other passengers, but the low-level bureaucrats around him thought themselves too important to pay him much attention. Despite that, the plane made good time and before long began to descend for a refueling stop in Iceland.

The ground crew performed their tasks quickly. Neill didn't envy them their duties in the frigid weather. Once again the jet was climbing into the sky, headed for Ramstein Air Force Base in Germany; and as Neill watched the cold waters of the North Atlantic pass beneath him his thoughts raced ahead.

He'd felt good about his assignment a week earlier, but now things were different. Now his mission bothered him, but he couldn't quite put his finger on what it was. Walter's death had shaken him up, to be sure. Losing a comrade in arms was never easy. He'd allowed himself to be vulnerable after hearing the news, knowing that burying his grief was not a healthy way of dealing with it. The tears had flowed; the pain was real, and it lingered. But he knew that someday he would see his friend again, in a place where uniforms and reconnaissance planes and nuclear weapons were no longer needed ...

Neill finally decided that it was the unanswered questions that bothered him the most. Why had Colonel Ulyanov assumed command in Odessa? What had become of Major Mayakovsky? Had something gone wrong? Terribly wrong? He wasn't sure he wanted an answer to that last question.

He closed his eyes and recalled something his dad used to say. "I don't know what tomorrow holds, but I know who holds tomorrow." It was a comforting thought and it seemed to push aside his other concerns, at least for the moment. Soon he was fast asleep.

Neill awoke just as the plane began its descent. He straightened his tie and squared away his uniform as the landing gear brushed the runway at Ramstein; a Marine on an Air Force base was not a rare sight, but he wanted to make a good impression anyway.

He grabbed his bags and disembarked with the rest of the passengers, then made his way through the passenger terminal. It was one of the larger ones used by the armed forces and Department of Defense personnel. At the Air Mobility Command counter, an Air Force Staff Sergeant was on duty. She pretended not to notice him too much.

Neill dropped his bags and opened his wallet, then produced his I.D. The Sergeant looked at his card then scanned a sheet attached to a clipboard. "Lieutenant Neill, USMC." She handed back his identification. "Welcome to Germany, sir."

"Thanks, Staff Sergeant. It's been awhile since I was here." Normally Ramstein would have been one of his stops on the way back from Manas, but the rotator had landed at Leipzig instead. "Sandwich shop still open upstairs?"

She smiled back. "Closes at twenty-hundred hours." That was eight p.m. in military parlance. "The USO's still open, but if you want a hot meal I'd try the chow hall."

"Sounds like a plan." Neill picked up his bags. "What time does my flight leave in the morning?" He already knew, but wanted to double-check.

She looked at the flight manifest for the next day and then noted the destination. Behind Neill was a flat screen TV monitor that displayed incoming and outgoing flights over the next few days. "Your non-stop to Odessa leaves at ten a.m.—same aircraft you came in on."

Neill turned to read the mission number on the screen and matched it up with the aircraft type. The point of debarkation was listed as ODS—Odessa, Ukraine.

Looking at the manifest she noticed something else. "This is interesting—looks like you're the only passenger." She was duly impressed and just a little curious, then checked the show time. "Be here at 0800 tomorrow morning and they'll fix you right up."

Neill nodded and headed for the door. "Thanks, Sergeant," he flashed her another grin. "You've been a big help."

She smiled back again. "Not at all, sir. You know where lodging is?"

"Yep. Across the street." She watched him as he left, and her eyes followed him through the window as he made his way toward his quarters.

Neill stowed his gear in the room. Billeting was impressive and almost made him wish he'd joined the Air Force. Then he headed over to one of the base dining facilities for a late supper. He wasn't disappointed; he was hungry and the food was good. Half an hour later he finished off a cup of coffee and some apple pie—an after dinner habit he'd acquired in Manas—and headed back to his room.

The flight had taken its toll on him physically, but after a hot shower he felt a lot better. Next he powered up his laptop and answered a few email messages sent from the IOI office, then composed a few of his own. The dispatches he sent were all routine and twenty minutes later Neill shut off the computer. He spent a few minutes pressing his uniform and then got ready for bed. The past few days were catching up with him and he was spent.

He was asleep almost as soon as his head hit the pillow, but before he drifted off it occurred to him that the next time he bedded down it would be in the Ukraine; and maybe by then he'd have the answers to some of those disturbing questions.

* * * *

Odessa Countryside,
Ukraine

From the road half a mile away, the old farmhouse looked completely abandoned. Its windows were broken, or cracked at best, and the ancient roof sagged in several places. Overall the structure appeared to be sinking into the earth; the vines and shrubbery that clung to the walls only added to the impression. Mold and mildew added a speckled appearance and gave the illusion of camouflage.

A combination of bad weather and even worse economic conditions made the surrounding fields useless as farmland. In recent years a nearby lake had regularly overflowed its banks during the rainy season, reducing the soil to a marsh-like bog. And before that, there was simply not enough money to buy the fuel oil needed to keep the harvesters running.

For all practical purposes, the property was worthless. Passersby rarely gave it a second glance, but if they had looked a little closer they would have found that the farmhouse was not quite as empty as it seemed.

Ivan Malyev stepped out of the ramshackle building and looked up into the night sky. The air was cold and crisp, and a million stars twinkled overhead. A light snow had fallen earlier in the day, but now there was not a cloud in sight.

As Malyev studied the horizon, Sasha Kobrin emerged from the shadows, wiping his hands on a greasy rag. Snow crunched underfoot as he approached his associate.

"The plane is ready?" Malyev asked.

Kobrin nodded. "The engine is in good condition and we have plenty of fuel." The two had a small, propeller driven airplane carefully hidden in a tractor shed behind the house and hoped to use it as a means of escaping the country. An open field—untouched by the marsh—sat nearby and was used as a landing strip. They had visited this site often. It had become their base of operations when they were in Ukraine. "In any event," Kobrin went on, "it should take us farther than the truck."

Malyev grunted in agreement, recalling their narrow escape a few days earlier at the waterfront.

Getting out of the city after the shooting hadn't been easy. They'd caught a bus to the outskirts of town, then took another one into the countryside. After that, they walked the last few kilometers under cover of darkness, arriving back at their hideout at dawn. They'd expected their every step to be dogged by the militia, but that hadn't happened.

That was now in the past. Malyev turned toward the road and drew in a deep breath, the cold air refreshing as it filled his lungs. In the distance, he could see the lights of Odessa glowing on the horizon. There was danger there, but tomorrow they would put that far behind them.

At least that was the plan.

Chapter Ten * Shot from the Sky

THE STAFF SERGEANT AT RAMSTEIN HAD been right; as the Gulfstream lifted into the skies over Germany Neill found himself alone in the passenger cabin. He knew the flight would be a relatively short one, so he decided to pass the time by reviewing some technical manuals for the mission at the weapons facility.

The content was pretty dry stuff. Neill loosened his tie and stretched his legs. He'd waded through about twenty pages when the pilot's voice filled the cabin, announcing that they had entered Ukrainian airspace. Neill put aside his notes and looked out the window. Lying on the seat next to him was a historical novel by a famous Polish author—there was only so much he could take of the manuals.

Far below lay the rich farm land of Ukraine, lying fallow for the winter and looking a lot like a patchwork quilt in places. Here and there the ground was covered by snow and occasionally sunlight would reflect off a lake or river.

As he enjoyed the view the co-pilot made his way from the cockpit to the rear of the plane.

"You must be pretty important, Lieutenant," the officer said.

Neill looked up and saw the co-pilot grinning from ear to ear. "How's that?"

"Not too often we make a run into Ukraine with only one passenger," he gestured to all the empty seats. "But an armed escort—you must rate pretty high." He leaned over and pointed out Neill's window.

A Sukhoi SU-27 fighter jet had taken up position about three hundred yards off the port side. Neill could see the blue and yellow of the Ukrainian flag painted on one of the jet's vertical stabilizers, as well as a pair of Malat air to air missiles mounted on the end of each wing.

"There's another one off the right wing," the co-pilot said. "Showed up almost as soon as we crossed the border. Spooked us real good till one of the pilots radioed this message." He handed Neill a folded slip of paper.

Michael unfolded the paper and read the message.

TO MICHAEL NEILL, U.S. MARINE
SENDING TWO GUARDIAN ANGELS TO TAKE
GOOD CARE OF YOU. WELCOME HOME.

REGARDS,
COLONEL ANDREI ALEXANDREYEVICH
ULYANOV
P.S. HOPE YOU BROUGHT TOILET PAPER

Neill laughed out loud and pocketed the message; this one was definitely a keeper.

An hour later the Gulfstream touched down on the runway at the international airport in Odessa. The aircraft taxied to a stop and Neill was allowed to disembark. Overhead, the fighter escorts made one pass over the airfield, then headed for home.

It was Neill's first trip back to Ukraine in eight years. Stepping off the plane and onto the tarmac, he was immediately struck by the improvements that had been made in the air terminal—Western foreign aid had certainly made a difference. He took a deep breath and let it out slowly, the flood of emotions he'd half expected never materializing. Then he let his eyes sweep the landscape. The ancient, Soviet-era planes and helicopters that had once littered the field had been removed. Every hangar and building had received a facelift. One thing hadn't changed, though; a bas-relief sculpture of Lenin still clung to the wall near the top of the terminal. Neill made a mental note to ask someone about that later.

A small delegation of military personnel waited on the tarmac as Neill stepped off the plane. He lowered his bags to the deck and saluted the group.

Colonel Andrei Ulyanov, the stern-looking, robust officer with classic Slavic features, stood at the front. Up until his conversation with Willis Avery, Neill hadn't expected to be greeted by the Colonel, but with the news about Mayakovsky, things had changed. Ulyanov's uniform shimmered with medals and badges, and the light blue shoulder boards and band around his visored cap identified him as a member of the Air Defense Forces. Standing a head taller than the others, there was no doubt that he was the man in charge. He stepped forward and returned Neill's salute.

"Lieutenant Neill," he boomed. "On behalf of the President and the people of the Democratic Republic of Ukraine, I welcome you." Then his chiseled face broke into a grin and the legendary fighter pilot threw his huge arms around the young Lieutenant in an embrace.

Michael was sure he'd heard his ribs cracking.

Grigory Valentin, the field's chief of security, noted Neill's arrival with mild interest. Westerners came and went with increasing frequency these days, but to his recollection, none had warranted an official welcome from the Ukrainian military. This particular visitor appeared to be a U.S. Army or Marine Corps officer. He found that odd, but not enough to question it. Grigory was naturally curious, but reasoned that while the American had an escort from the armed forces, his presence didn't warrant further suspicion. It was his job to protect the facility, but in this case, the visitor seemed harmless. Besides, this appeared to be a military matter, and Valentin was content to let it remain that way.

Another of Grigory's duties was to screen who got access to the field's controlled movement areas, particularly when it came to the taxiways and runways. Just an hour and a half earlier, he'd met with a representative of the military—a Captain, whose name he'd written down, but promptly forgotten—checking their I.D. cards and papers, giving permission for the group to drive their vehicles through the gate to a ramp near the runway. Grigory had insisted on documenting the identity of the ranking officer. Although the Captain had seemed a bit reluctant at first, the name Valentin was given belonged to Colonel Ulyanov.

Grigory wrote that down too, then watched as his staff opened the gate and ushered the entourage of state vehicles onto the tarmac. He was aware that the Ukrainian Air Force shared the field and knew many of their officers and enlisted men personally, but the men riding in these cars were unfamiliar to him. He decided that they might be from the weapons station, seven kilometers west of the city.

Grigory walked back to the terminal and watched as the group parked their cars and prepared their reception. All things considered, it was the most interesting thing that happened all day.

* * * *

"We will speak in your language, yes?" Ulyanov asked in his best English, which wasn't very good.

"We will speak in my language, *no,*" Neill replied in Ukrainian. "Unless your English has gotten better in the past few years. *Sir.*"

The Colonel was smiling as Neill opened a large envelope he'd pulled from his briefcase, relieved to know he would be conversing in his native tongue. Despite his best efforts to learn English, his progress had been slow.

Neill pulled some documents from the satchel he carried. "Colonel, I have letters of greeting from the Chairman of the Joint Chiefs of Staff and—"

Ulyanov snapped his fingers. "I have letters, too, Michael. Dmitri?"

A Captain stepped forward and handed the Colonel several sheets of parchment. He was a young man, a little older than Neill, his uniform accented with the red markings used by the rocket forces.

"Captain Dmitri Yaroslav, my aide de camp." Ulyanov said, smiling broader than ever. Neill shook the Captain's hand, then noticed that Yaroslav's left arm hung in a sling. He thought that to be a bit curious, but protocol and common courtesy prevented him from asking any questions.

By now it was quite plain that Colonel Ulyanov was one happy man. The officers behind him glanced at each other and smiled—it was good to see their new commanding officer in such a jovial mood. In the three weeks since Ulyanov had taken charge of the weapons facility, none of the troops had seen him quite so relaxed.

Both men put away their official documents for the moment. The Colonel took Neill by the arm and steered him over to his awaiting staff, and soon formal introductions had been made.

Neill saw several cars parked in a neat row near the terminal gate. At a nod from the Colonel, two enlisted men came forward and took his luggage. Neill's bags were quickly stowed in the trunk of one of the vehicles. The assembled group then climbed in; the limos made their way toward the exit, and within minutes the fleet of cars was headed downtown to take the American visitor to his hotel.

* * * *

Malyev and Kobrin had been airborne for over two hours

and were rapidly approaching the border between Russia and Ukraine. With each passing mile their confidence grew; it looked as if their escape plan just might succeed.

Kobrin piloted the small aircraft while Malyev studied a map. Below them the treetops rushed by at a dizzying pace.

"We are close, yes?" Kobrin asked. Malyev noted a trace of anxiety in Sasha's voice, but decided not to comment on it. Kobrin had been a little edgy lately, more so than usual. Malyev wondered if he was beginning to lose his nerve, then dismissed the thought. He knew that this type of work—if you could call it that—wore down even the best of men. Even Ivan felt a certain level of fatigue.

"Yes, we are close," Malyev said after a moment. "The border is just ahead." He folded the map and smiled at Kobrin. "Soon we will be safe in Bryansk."

Kobrin breathed a sigh of relief and began to think his friend was right. He was anxious to be finished with this whole business. They knew the militia would be watching the roads and railway stations for them, but a small plane was another matter. Flying low to avoid radar contact, they hoped to make good on their escape. And so far everything had gone smoothly.

As they left the border behind them, Kobrin increased the aircraft's altitude. They were in Russian airspace now, with their own country's soil beneath them, and that put both men more at ease.

Neither man knew that the greatest danger lay ahead.

* * * *

Squinting into the southern sky, Major Pirogov saw something just above the treetops that caught his attention. He raised his binoculars to get a better look. Pirogov stood at one end of a makeshift runway a few miles west of Bryansk. A squad of heavily armed Russian soldiers waited anxiously in the tree line behind him.

The Major watched intently as the object drew closer. It

was definitely an aircraft, most likely the one he and his men had been waiting for. He watched for a moment longer, then lowered the binoculars and ordered his troops to stand by.

Kobrin decided to make a low pass over the runway before setting the aircraft down. A thin blanket of snow covered the field, and he didn't want to risk hitting a partially hidden branch or tree stump.

Malyev surveyed the area as the plane began to descend. He could make out several figures at the far end of the runway. Beyond that he could see the huge *dacha* that had once been used by party members as a type of country club. Those days were gone. More recently it had been utilized to train men like Malyev and Kobrin in the ways of terrorism.

At Pirogov's command a two-man fire team bolted from the trees and crouched down in the snow. Each carried a hand-held surface-to-air missile launcher.

Lifting the weapon to his shoulder, the first soldier looked through the telescopic sight attached to the side of the tube. He centered the crosshairs on the small plane and waited for the electronic seeker system to do its job. Almost immediately the device began to beep, confirming the weapon's lock on the target and an instant later the missile streaked into the sky.

From a kilometer away, Malyev's trained eye saw the flash and the puff of smoke and instantly realized that they were under attack. Kobrin saw it too, and instinctively banked the plane to the left in a desperate attempt to get away from the clearing.

It was too late. The missile accelerated, snaking through the air until it was clearly visible to both men. It exploded on impact, completely severing the tail section. As the cockpit and wings plummeted toward the trees, the ruptured fuel tank exploded, turning the twisted, falling wreckage into a huge fireball.

Kobrin was killed instantly, but Malyev was thrown clear. He remained conscious long enough to see the trees rushing up beneath him, then blacked out.

Sasha's last act had saved Malyev's life. Ivan's tumbling body bounced from branch to branch as he fell into the forest. The tree limbs seemed to reach out for him, bending and snapping, unable to hold his weight for long, but nonetheless slowing his twisting descent.

He landed flat on his back in a pile of snow. The sudden impact briefly drove the air from his lungs, and he lay quite still for several minutes.

Major Pirogov was looking through his binoculars again. The forest blocked his view of the wreckage, but he could see a thick column of black smoke rising into the sky above the treetops.

"Sergeant!" He barked.

"Sir!"

"Take a detail into the forest," Pirogov ordered. "Put out that fire and bury the debris."

The Sergeant saluted smartly then turned to gather his men.

Malyev came to his senses and struggled to his feet. Every joint and muscle seemed alive with pain, but as he checked his injuries he was surprised to find only minor cuts and abrasions.

The blast and his fall through the trees had left him dazed, but when the smell of smoke filled his nostrils everything came back to him. He forced his aching body to move and headed toward the clearing.

He trudged through the snow, crouching as he went, picking his way around fallen branches and an occasional piece of smoldering wreckage. When he reached the edge of the tree line he dropped to the ground.

Malyev suspected treachery. Looking out across the snow-covered clearing, his worst fears were confirmed. Several men stood at the far end of the runway. Ivan could tell they were soldiers, but their camouflaged uniforms made it difficult to see them against the backdrop of the forest. As he watched their movements, one of the troops stood out, and Malyev recognized the unmistakable figure of Major Pirogov.

Ivan saw four of the men moving in his direction. He quickly considered his options. They had already tried to kill him once—but why?—and must have thought they'd succeeded, since none of them appeared to be in any hurry. Staying anywhere near the plane's wreckage was dangerous—clearly the troops had been waiting for them. When Pirogov's men discovered only one body, they would most certainly search the woods.

Malyev still had his pistol, but the odds were against him; one man with a small pistol against four combat-ready infantrymen wouldn't last long. And he didn't want to do anything to make their job easier. Besides, even though he was an avowed atheist, he was thankful to be alive, and he didn't want to do anything to jeopardize his new-found lease on life.

In the final analysis only one option was really practical. If he wanted to survive, he'd have to run. Adrenaline coursed through his veins and his body was wracked with pain. But he was alive.

Crouching as low as he could, Malyev retraced his steps and headed back into the woods. Escape was his first priority; finding food and shelter would be next.

The Sergeant poked through the wreckage while his men shoveled snow and earth on the smoking debris. He'd found the charred remains of one body—there wasn't much left—but where was the second?

He thought it over for a moment. The other man might have been incinerated when the plane exploded; after all, the fire had consumed almost everything else, hadn't it? He was convinced that if he dug deep enough, he'd find another body at the bottom of the debris.

If he dug deep enough ...

The image of the raging fireball falling to earth was still fresh in the Sergeant's mind; no one could have lived through that. Still, a motivated soldier would have made a more thorough search of the wreckage, but fortunately for Ivan Malyev the Sergeant didn't fit that particular description.

Exhuming bodies was the work of gravediggers, not soldiers. The Sergeant picked up a shovel and helped his men finish burying the wreckage. An hour later his official report to the Major listed two bodies, not one.

Chapter Eleven ✷ Design Flaws

Central Ukraine

IT WAS THE MAINTENANCE CHIEF'S DAY OFF, but he was far too excited to take advantage of it. He arrived at the hangar at six a.m.—an hour before his shift normally began—and had spent most of the morning scrutinizing the object of his fascination. It wasn't every day that he got an opportunity like this one. In fact, over the course of his fifteen years of service to the Strategic Air Forces, no other piece of hardware had captured his attention in quite the same way.

He was a *Starshina*, or Master Sergeant, actually—the term Chief was an acknowledgement of the position he held as the senior enlisted man of a group charged with maintaining jet aircraft. Today he was positively giddy, but had managed to moderate his enthusiasm to the point where few of the other technicians assisting him noticed. Earlier he'd directed them to wheel out a maintenance cart with a host of various instruments. He juggled a tape measure and calculator to determine dimensions and lift ratios. He consulted a clipboard from time to time, jotting down notes and figures, walking back and forth from one corner of the hangar to the other, his eyes fixed on the sleek airframe carefully parked before him. Ordinarily, access to such an advanced piece of technology would have been restricted, but the conditions surrounding this plane had changed of late.

The fighter and its pilot had flown in the day before, and to the Chief everything about this plane seemed different. From the ground up—where the wheels of the landing gear were chocked—to the bubble canopy above and the wing surfaces that swept back toward the twin engines, the design was unique. The Chief wasn't an artist, but he couldn't resist sketching some of the machine's more impressive features. For the rest of the aircraft's characteristics, he simply took photographs.

Occasionally, he found himself nodding his head in appreciation as he discovered new aspects of the plane's detail, or innovations designed to solve old aerodynamic problems. Those were inspiring to behold. But as he considered the angles of the control surfaces, one thing stood out—and it bothered him.

He picked up a rag from the cart and wiped grease from his hands. From the eastern end of the hangar, a door opened and the morning light spilled in. The Chief turned to see the silhouette of a lanky young man in a flight suit. His gait was less of a walk and more of a march. As he got closer, the Chief recognized him as the pilot of the fighter jet he'd been examining.

"*Dobre ootra.*" *Good morning.* Lieutenant Viktor Radischev extended his hand and introduced himself. No smile, no emotion, but polite and respectful nonetheless. He'd just come from the air operations office, submitting his transfer paperwork and receiving in return his flight line authorization and access badge to the controlled movement areas of the base.

The Chief responded in kind. "Yevgeniy Rada," the Sergeant said. "We met yesterday." The two men eyed each other's uniforms; similar, but different in subtle ways. That was to be expected; their respective countries were both part of the Commonwealth, after all.

"I remember," Radischev replied. Honestly, he didn't, but he felt it would be rude to admit that. The leadership at the air base had gone to great lengths to give him a proper welcome, and there were many people to whom he'd been introduced. The day's events had become a blur.

Rada could tell. "You've traveled a long way, Lieutenant," the Chief observed. "I'm just sorry it had to be under these circumstances."

The look on the Lieutenant's face told Rada that he appreciated the sentiment, but he felt awkward nonetheless. By now everyone at the airfield knew about Radischev's brush with fame and the reason he was here. He and his aircraft had been shuffled thousands of kilometers to the west in an effort to keep them out of the spotlight. Most of that had been a concession to the politics between nations, in addition to the concerns of the Russian military—and those were *very* real.

The Lieutenant had been caught in the middle; he hadn't been reprimanded for attacking the American plane—or the death of the U.S. Navy airman—but he certainly wasn't being commended for it either. For the time being, he was in limbo.

The Chief didn't want to belabor the point. He turned his attention back to the fighter. "A remarkable aircraft, Lieutenant. She and I have bonded together this morning." Radischev noticed a frown on the Sergeant's face. "But I have a few questions for you."

"Ask anything you'd like, Sergeant," Viktor replied. There was no reason why he couldn't be cooperative while he was here. Being helpful would only make his stay—however long that might be—more enjoyable. And the man standing before him would be his new crew chief. Having a good rapport with him was as important as anything else the young pilot would need on this base.

"She's a thing of beauty," Rada went on. As a rule he didn't care much for officers, but this one seemed different. "Very sleek. Her designers have minimized the occurrence of right angles in the airframe. How does she handle in flight?"

"Like a dream," Radischev answered. "She's the fastest plane I've ever flown."

"Speed is a consideration. I don't doubt that it's agile," the

Chief agreed. "But what about buffeting? Have you encountered any unusual turbulence?"

The Lieutenant didn't know where the Chief was going with that. He considered his question carefully before answering. "There was one incident I recall," he said slowly. The recollection was clearly an unpleasant one. Before he could explain himself, the Chief continued.

"Did you experience any instability ..." he paused, drawing in a breath. "... during combat operations?"

Radischev frowned. "Yes," he answered. "Briefly, over the Sea of Japan." He eyed the Chief curiously. "And how do you know this?"

"I've been taking some measurements," Rada explained. "As I said, this is a remarkable aircraft. But it appears that some trade-offs have been made; a few shortcuts were taken." He shrugged slightly. "Performance cannot trump physics; there's always a price to be paid when you try to bend the rules." The two were standing in front of the fighter, the nose of the plane just a few feet away. "Let me show you."

The chief got the attention of one of the technicians working in the back. "Yuri—turn on the power cart and stand by the cockpit." The young journeyman nodded at Rada and moved quickly to a small, mobile generator positioned next to the jet. He flipped a few switches and the device hummed to life. For the first time, Radischev noticed several cables running from the cart to the plane's side.

Rada took the Lieutenant by the arm and pointed directly ahead. "Look straight down the central axis of the fuselage. Do you see anything unusual?"

Viktor squinted. Nothing stood out to him about the plane. "Forgive me, Sergeant, but I don't."

Rada nodded. "And that's understandable. Perhaps we're too close." He turned and trotted toward the center of the hangar. Radischev watched him, mildly amused. Clearly, this Sergeant was passionate about his craft.

The Chief stopped and motioned for Viktor to join him.

The younger man walked to where Rada was and they turned to survey the plane from a little further away.

"Now look again; pay close attention to the leading edges of the wing and the position of the missile bay doors."

Radischev did as he was instructed, but all he saw were the smooth surfaces of what he considered to be an impeccably designed airplane. The wings were symmetrical, and the missile bays equivalently positioned on both sides. "I'm afraid you've lost me."

"No matter. Follow me and I'll explain." Again, Rada took off briskly. Radischev brought up the rear dutifully.

They stopped this time at the point where one of the wings joined the airframe. Rada pulled a tape measure from his belt and extended it a few feet, then tapped the leading edge. "Do you see this?" He raised his voice to be heard above the drone of the cart on the opposite side.

Viktor's eyes narrowed. It was difficult to distinguish, but a four or five inch section of the wing surface appeared to be slightly buckled. It was very subtle, and only a discerning eye would have seen it. Now that it had been drawn to his attention, it was very apparent to Radischev.

The Lieutenant whistled softly. "Does this—*anomaly*—exist on the other wing?"

Rada nodded. "It does—in the same location, as you would expect if this were a condition endemic of her design characteristics." The Chief ducked under the aircraft with Radischev behind him, then pointed to the same position on the other wing. Sure enough, the condition was mirrored in exactly the same place.

"Would this be the cause of turbulence the plane might encounter in flight?"

This time the Chief shook his head. "No, Lieutenant." He gestured again to the affected area. "Not the *cause*. This is merely a *symptom* of the turbulence. A flaw in the design." He looked up toward the cockpit and gave Yuri a nod. The technician returned the gesture and reached into the cockpit, activating a series of switches. The bay door swung inward, revealing the missile compartment—which was empty.

Viktor considered what the Chief had said. This was alarming news. "What would cause this?"

Rada moved closer to the missile bay and gestured to the interior. "With the aircraft configured for combat, I can demonstrate this more fully. Imagine the plane in flight, with the weapons system activated."

Just as it had been when I fired on the American, Radischev thought to himself.

"The airframe is designed to move through the air with the least amount of resistance possible," the Chief explained. It was a fundamental tenet of flight, one the Lieutenant was very familiar with. "This is accomplished by creating surfaces that minimize drag and conform to basic aerodynamic principles. And for the most part, this aircraft does that."

"For the most part?"

"Yes," Rada nodded. "However, once the bay doors are open, drag is increased."

Radischev was aware of that also. "But as I understand it, the blended fuselage concept mitigates the effects of drag."

"Quite right; that was obviously the intention of the designers. And I can see where they tried to maximize the effect. But they must have miscalculated."

"In what way?" Radischev now wore a frown on his face.

Rada held out his hand in front of him, fingers outstretched and parallel to the hangar floor. "In flight, air moves across the wing surfaces and around the body of the aircraft. But not always in a strictly linear fashion." He brought up his other hand and positioned it in a similar way. "When the bay doors are open, the air continues to flow along the curvature of the plane, like this." He ran one hand over the other. "But when it reaches the weapons bay—and the doors are *open*—the compartment acts as a scoop."

"Increasing the drag."

Again he nodded. This officer *was* different. "In such a

way that it stresses the aircraft." Rada pointed to the buckled skin. "And this was the result."

"But our ground crews examined the plane before I left Vladivostok," he protested. "Surely they would have noticed this."

The Chief shook his head. "Not necessarily. The effects might not have been visible then. And as I said, you've travelled a long way. Your flight here only compounded the problem."

"Creating further fatigue in the airframe," Viktor observed. "How serious is this?" By that he wondered how dangerous it might be to continue taking the plane aloft.

"That's difficult to say." Rada replied. He wanted to break it to the Lieutenant gently. "It's certainly a problem the designers need to address. I haven't determined the tensile strength of the composite materials, but until I can run further tests, caution should guide us." That was a tactful way of saying the plane was grounded.

The Chief took a long look at the fighter. With all the admiration he had for the machine there was also disappointment. "I'm surprised this problem didn't come up in some kind of computer modeling. Can you tell me who the design bureau was?"

"It was a collaborative effort," Viktor answered vaguely. "There were rumors that some of the technology was borrowed from the Chinese."

Rada nodded. He suspected as much.

Chapter Twelve ✶ Full Disclosure

❝ You speak Ukrainian." Oksana Marpova was impressed.

Neill stood across from her at the front desk of the Londonskaya Hotel and signed the guest registry. "Yes, ma'am," he answered. "My Russian's not bad either. I studied in school," he added casually with a slight shrug. He didn't mention that it was in a *Ukrainian* school. Operational security was something Neill was always mindful of in foreign countries; there were some things the locals just didn't need to know.

"But you are an American, yes?" The squat, older woman studied Neill's military ID and passport before handing them back across the counter.

Michael nodded, growing a little impatient, but not allowing it to show. "That's right." He returned the ID to his wallet and pocketed the passport. Some of the hotel's guests wandered through the lobby on their way to lunch, slowing their pace as they gave Neill a second look. Ulyanov's driver had just dropped him off ten minutes before. "Am I too late for check-in?" It was almost noon.

Oksana squinted at the clock on the wall. It was next to the spot where Lenin's portrait had once hung. "The maid cleaned your room this morning," she said, producing a card key. "You're on the second floor, room 210. How long will you be staying with us, Mr. Neill?"

Michael smiled to himself. *She's sly, this one,* he thought. The duration of his stay—including the date he planned to check out—was right in front of her, on the antiquated computer she used to check him in. He knew she was just trying to draw out more information. Like many Ukrainians, she was wary of Americans—even if they did speak the language.

"A week. Possibly two, if I decide to extend my visit," he replied. He leaned forward and adopted a very serious tone. "It all depends on how long this job takes."

Oksana knew he was toying with her, but she was taken by the sound of his voice. She had noticed that this young American officer was quite handsome. "And what job is that?"

Neill put a finger to his lips, suggesting secrecy. He then smiled and turned to take the stairs up to his room.

Neill's arrangements for a room at the Londonskaya Hotel weren't without a little controversy. Colonel Ulyanov objected at first. He and his wife, Irina, had insisted that as long as Neill's mission kept him in Ukraine he would stay with them. The couple had taken an apartment in Odessa only three weeks earlier. Michael wasn't exactly comfortable with the idea, reminding the Colonel that such an arrangement might be seen to color his judgment during the inspection. Ulyanov relented, but made it clear he wasn't happy about it.

Neill's first full day in Odessa started early. A hearty breakfast in the hotel dining room followed morning devotions, and it was still dark when he walked the two blocks to the Ulyanov's apartment. The Colonel answered the door and ushered Michael inside. The apartment was sparsely furnished, but did contain a few items the Ukrainian couple had brought from Nikolayev. Irina squealed at the sight of Neill, hugged him, fussed over him and then poured another cup of tea from a large *samovar*. When Neill politely declined her offer of breakfast, she spent ten minutes scolding him for being too skinny.

"How do you expect to get a nice Ukrainian girl looking

so thin?" She shook her head, returning to her stove. "Talk to him, Andrei."

Ulyanov sat down at the breakfast table, finishing a plate of sausage and eggs. He winked at Michael over the rim of his own cup, smacking his lips as he swallowed his food. "Of course, *mati*. We'll discuss it over a large lunch."

Irina made her presence known from the kitchen. "Be home early for dinner, both of you. I'll be cooking all day."

"I'll wear my stretchy pants," Neill promised with a grin. It had been years since he'd had a home cooked Ukrainian meal.

Irina Ulyanov gave him a look, then frowned. *"Pah!"* Another shake of her head.

The Colonel finished his tea and his eyes widened. "I almost forgot. I have tickets for the Opera—Puccini's *Turandot*, next Wednesday night. Wear your dress uniform."

"Well, since you put it *that* way—" Neill said with a grin.

Ulyanov wiped the corner of his mouth with a napkin. "What, you have plans? Don't force me to make it an order. Besides, you're a guest in this country. Allow us to treat you to a night of culture."

After tea, he and the Colonel prepared for the drive to the weapons facility. Neill had suited up in his digital, camouflaged uniform—it had the virtue of being both warm and comfortable—and Ulyanov was similarly dressed in camouflage utilities of his own.

The Colonel's car arrived a little before seven o'clock, driven by a member of Ulyanov's staff, a punctual and efficient Corporal named Sevnik. Neill kissed Irina on the cheek as she shooed him out the door, then double-checked his briefcase, making sure he had everything he needed.

Neill had no sooner stepped outside when two figures at the end of the hall caught his attention. Both were burly young men dressed in dark suits. Michael's eyes narrowed. He put out a hand to stop Ulyanov as he brought up the rear.

"Colonel—"

Ulyanov chuckled as he clasped Neill's shoulder. "It's all

right, Michael," he reassured him. "It's just Oleg and Pavel. My security detail." The Colonel nodded and the two men returned the gesture, their faces betraying no emotion. "There are two more in a car downstairs."

"I didn't see them earlier," Neill said.

"You weren't supposed to. They divide their time between Irina and I," Ulyanov explained. "The SSD seems to feel my job here is very important."

* * * *

The road leading to the dismantling station snaked out of town and into a heavily forested region. There were few structures in this part of the province, only a vast sea of trees, their branches left barren by the long winter. Along the way, Michael spied several small ponds through the tree line, a fine mist rising from their surfaces like a patchy fog as the early morning sun rose over the horizon.

After a journey of about six kilometers, they arrived at their destination.

"Looks like a prison," Neill observed. The staff car turned off the highway onto the road leading to the weapons complex. He glanced behind him. The other two members of Ulyanov's protective detail followed in a sedan closely behind.

Nuclear Dismantling Facility Odessa was a series of large, almost featureless buildings. During the Soviet era, it had served as a small armory and had been the home of a Russian tank battalion. All of that was gone now and the facility had undergone a complete renovation. In its new role, storage bunkers dotted the grounds and were used to temporarily house the weapons once they arrived. Located next to the bunkers were two high-tech X-ray labs. The actual work of dismantling the warheads was done in heavily guarded underground bays. A tall electrified fence surrounded the perimeter. Guard towers were discreetly located at each corner, obscured somewhat by the trees. Neill could see armed soldiers patrolling the grounds inside the gate.

"Very impressive," Neill said. "Security looks tight."

"It is now," the Colonel said slowly.

" '*Now*'?"

Ulyanov looked Neill in the eye and forced himself to smile. "We'll discuss that later, little Michael."

"There's no time like the present," he gently prodded.

The Colonel sighed. "You have a job to do—what I have to say might distract you from your duties."

"Does this have anything to do with Major Mayakovsky?" Neill asked quietly.

Ulyanov's face darkened at the mention of Mayakovsky's name, but he nodded nonetheless.

Corporal Sevnik stopped the car at the gate. Two security personnel emerged from the guardhouse, one holding an automatic rifle, the other with a sidearm strapped to his waist. One of the men approached the car and checked everyone's I.D.s—including the Colonel's—before waving them inside.

"My job is easy." Ulyanov said, smiling again as Corporal Sevnik parked the car. "I can show you where everything is, but if you have any technical questions, I'm afraid you'll have to ask Captain Yaroslav."

A few minutes later Ulyanov and Neill were inside the facility's administrative office where further security checks were made. Neill was issued a visitor's badge and instructed to wear it in plain sight at all times. After the formalities of checking in were observed, the two officers were joined by Captain Yaroslav.

"Good morning, gentlemen," Yaroslav smiled warmly and shook Neill's hand. Morning pleasantries were exchanged between the men. Neill noticed that the Captain still wore the sling on his arm. "We'll start slowly with a tour of the entire station. Did you bring a camera today, Lieutenant?"

"It's back at the hotel." Michael hadn't expected a question like that. He carried his cell phone, which had excellent digital capabilities, but nothing more elaborate. "I didn't think flash photography would be allowed here."

Yaroslav nodded. "I appreciate your sensitivity. But in your case, we will permit it. It will be necessary to fulfill your mission, and we want to cooperate in every way possible. Are you ready to begin?"

Michael nodded his head. They were already off to a good start.

"Lead on, Captain."

* * * *

The three men exited the administrative office and made their way toward one of the compound's large concrete bunkers. Michael was immediately struck by the overall appearance of the facility. The place was spotless, even by Western standards.

That was curious. Two vehicles caught Neill's eye. Parked in front of one of the storage bunkers were a pair of Russian GAZ Tigers—essentially the Russian counterpart to the Western Humvee. The military vehicles were a recent addition to the Russian Ground Forces and boasted a powerful, turbo-charged diesel power plant capable of propelling the Tiger at high speeds. Michael had seen footage of the impressive Tigers when they were rolled out in Moscow a few years back, but had no idea they were in use in Ukraine. He filed it away in the back of his mind and planned on asking Ulyanov about it later.

"The treaty between our two countries is three-fold, Lieutenant." Yaroslav began in a friendly tone. His deep baritone voice and easy manner made him a natural-born public speaker. "The first step, of course, is dismantling the weapons. The next calls for the destruction of our delivery systems— conventional rockets, submarine-launched ballistic missiles, whatever the case may be. All of that is easily accomplished." Yaroslav paused. "But the third step—"

Neill nodded. "My guess is you're running up against the same problem our people have: storage."

"Exactly." The Captain's eyes lit up, impressed by Neill's educated response. "Already we have more enriched uranium and plutonium than we know what to do with. Of course, the nuclear material is eventually turned over to Moscow. But in the meantime, we must find a place for it somewhere."

"Wouldn't the Russians prefer to have the weapons intact?"

Yaroslav nodded. "*Da.* In the beginning, we simply returned the warheads. But dismantling the warheads here serves two purposes; it gives us experience with the weapons; knowledge is good, don't you agree?"

Neill nodded. "Depends on what you intend to do with that knowledge. What's the second reason?"

Yaroslav smiled wistfully. "Giving back a dismantled warhead makes it harder to use."

"What type of policy do you have in place for storing the materials?" Neill began jotting down notes on a small pad.

"A small amount is kept here. The rest is taken to specially-constructed silos, where it is transferred by train to Russia." Here the Captain paused, laughing softly. "But forgive me, Lieutenant. I'm getting ahead of myself."

The trio stopped in front of the bunker and Yaroslav continued. "Once the weapons arrive they are stored here in Bunker #1. As you can see, this building is heavily fortified."

"Looks pretty sturdy to me," Neill agreed. "How do you get inside?" There weren't any visible doors.

"Two four-thousand pound concrete blocks guard the entrance. Each requires a forklift to move them out of the way—and the keys are kept in my office."

"So no one gets in or out—"

"—without my permission," Yaroslav finished. "Let's visit the radiography bay, shall we?"

The Captain led them into a nearby building that looked more like a surgical operating room than anything else. Two large turntables were situated in the center of the room, with heavy diagnostic equipment hung on gantries fixed to the ceiling. A computer system linked to several television monitors lined one wall.

"Before the warheads are disassembled it is necessary to

x-ray them." Yaroslav continued. "It is important to know the condition of the weapon's inner workings before they are taken apart. The entire process is controlled by a computer and monitored by our technicians.

"Once the evaluation is complete, the dismantling process can begin. Follow me, please."

They left the x-ray lab through double doors at the far end of the room and walked down a long hall to another door. Yaroslav punched in an access code on a keypad mounted on the wall and the door swung open. Two more security personnel—each armed with automatic weapons—waited for them in a small room on the other side.

"Before entering the disassembly bays, we must be cleared by security," Yaroslav explained. "No one—including the Colonel or myself—can go beyond this point without proper authorization."

Neill surveyed the room carefully. Two chairs and a computer console occupied the space along one wall. There was an elevator immediately to his right. A small surveillance camera had been installed near the ceiling.

Once again, each man was thoroughly scrutinized by the security team, then one of the guards produced a key and opened the elevator doors. Neill and his hosts stepped inside and descended to the underground disassembly area.

Michael was impressed with the security measures and said so, but Captain Yaroslav assured him that other improvements had yet to be made. "Soon we will be installing voice-recognition equipment and retina scans," Yaroslav said. "But I cannot take credit for those implementations. They were Colonel Ulyanov's idea."

Ulyanov only smiled, shrugging in an embarrassed sort of way that belied his keen sense of thoroughness.

After the elevator ride the three men passed through a series of more doors and then into the disassembly bay itself. Technicians wearing lab coats, face shields and heavy gloves worked behind a large Plexiglas window that separated them from observers.

"The fissionable cores of each warhead are dismantled here," the Captain said quietly, as if not to disturb the technicians. "Each weapons' outer casing is removed and the process begins."

"How long does that take, generally speaking?" Neill asked.

"Our pace is unhurried. The procedure may last a day, or as long as a week. It depends on the complexity of the weapon." The Captain turned to face Neill. "Tomorrow is Friday, but on Monday morning our technicians will begin work on one of our large-yield, two-stage warheads. We have recently received a consignment of several weapons." At this, Yaroslav seemed embarrassed. Michael had been briefed about the warheads found in the warehouse, but didn't press for details. "You may inspect our disassembly procedures then."

Neill examined the ceiling from one end of the room to the other. "What type of shielding do you have for the bays?"

"We are twenty-five meters below the surface," Yaroslav said. "The walls are three meters thick and enclosed by heavy layers of concrete."

"Is that enough? I mean, suppose a technician makes a mistake—"

"—and detonates the warhead?" Yaroslav smiled. "An accidental chemical explosion might occur during the disassembly process, but a nuclear blast is very unlikely." Almost as an afterthought, he added, "Come with me; I want to show you something. I think you will find this interesting."

The Captain led them to the end of the room to a case resting on a workbench. He opened the case and turned to face Neill and Ulyanov.

"We have recently adopted a method of disabling the weapons, one developed by your lab in Los Alamos." He pulled out a handful of thin wire from the case; to Neill, it looked just like so much uncooked, metallic spaghetti. "We call it coring, or core-stuffing. This procedure is ingeniously efficient; and prevents the plutonium from being used again in a weapons system."

Neill was intrigued. "How does it work?"

"It's a bit complicated, as you might imagine," Yaroslav continued. "At the heart of each weapon is a core of nuclear material."

"Plutonium or highly-enriched uranium."

"Correct. And at the center of *that* is a hollow tube used to introduce another element—causing a chain reaction and detonating the warhead."

"Where do these wires come in?"

Yaroslav separated a wire from the bundle. "One of these is inserted into the tube, stuffing the core as it tangles. When a sufficient amount is inside—"

"—it stops the tube from being compressed?"

"Preventing a nuclear reaction *and* detonation," the Captain smiled. "You have done your homework."

"And it's verifiable?" That was the other side of the coin.

Yaroslav nodded. "The effect is permanent and inexpensive. And it can be done quickly."

Michael nodded slowly. Even for someone with little knowledge of disarmament, the technique was simple enough and made a lot of sense. It offered a level of transparency to the process that would go a long way in satisfying the West.

They watched the technicians at work for several more minutes then returned to the surface level. Once there, Captain Yaroslav directed the group to a row of dirt-covered bunkers at the rear of the facility.

Security was even tighter here. Neill watched as armed soldiers with guard dogs paced back and forth in front of the heavy bunker doors. It didn't take him long to figure out why.

"Let me guess—plutonium?" Neill asked.

Yaroslav nodded grimly. "Correct. Once the warheads are dismantled, the plutonium is stored here temporarily." He gestured toward the guards. "Our security forces have orders to shoot first and ask questions later."

"What happens to the plutonium when it reaches Russia?"

"Storage is a problem," Yaroslav frowned. "Some have suggested that we blast it into space. Another possibility is to combine the plutonium with conventional nuclear fuel—I believe your own Nuclear Energy Institute favors that solution."

Neill nodded. A great deal of the material had ended up in the States, used for just those purposes. It was ironic, in a way. "Congress supports that idea as well. What's your opinion?"

Yaroslav shrugged. "Perhaps there is more than one answer. But for now, guarded storage is the least expensive and most effective way to prevent—"

The Captain stopped suddenly and shot a glance at Colonel Ulyanov, but the unflappable senior officer only smiled.

"Perhaps now is a good time to break for lunch," the Colonel said casually.

The officers interrupted their tour with an early meal in the facility's dining hall. Neill wasn't too surprised to see a fully functioning kitchen, complete with a small staff of food services personnel. The station was far from the city limits, and it made sense to provide easy access to meals right on the base. It also helped ensure accountability and minimized the possibility of a breach in security; once inside the gate, no one left until their shift ended.

By mid-afternoon the three men concluded their exploration of the main buildings and returned to Colonel Ulyanov's office in the administrative wing. Ulyanov waved the younger men towards a long sofa along the wall, then settled into his own chair behind the desk.

Michael looked around the room. The office had that 'just-moved-into' look, with boxes stacked in corners and noticeably bare walls. This was a brand new command for Ulyanov and it occurred to Neill that the Colonel probably hadn't had too much time to decorate.

"What do you think, Michael?" Ulyanov couldn't quite bring himself to address him as *Lieutenant Neill*. He'd watched the young man before him grow up, and still thought of him as the son he'd never had. "Are you pleased with our little facility?"

"Much more than I expected to be," Neill admitted. "The layout here is very close to our own station in Amarillo."

"Ah, yes, your Texas facility." The Colonel locked his fingers together behind his head and leaned back. "I visited there three years ago—right after you graduated from that little school in—" Ulyanov frowned. "—what was the name of that place?"

Neill grinned. "You mean the Academy?"

A mischievous light danced in the Colonel's eyes. 'Yes, that's the place. In Minneapolis, correct?"

"Annapolis, sir."

Ulyanov's good-natured ribbing helped to ease the tension Neill had felt earlier in the day. Even Captain Yaroslav seemed more relaxed now.

But in spite of the good feelings they shared, Neill was inwardly restless. He'd seen nearly every inch of the facility, but was still no closer to getting answers to those troubling questions. In fact, the mystery only seemed to grow.

As they continued their friendly discussion, Neill began to pray silently. Soon he had the opening he'd been looking for.

"And what of our security measures, Lieutenant?" Yaroslav asked. "How do they compare with Western standards?" The room grew quiet as both Ulyanov and the Captain fixed their eyes on Neill.

"You've done an admirable job here, Captain," Neill began. "I'm impressed—but at the same time I'm concerned ..."

Yaroslav frowned. "Concerned? In what way?"

"Let me explain," Neill said slowly. "Security doesn't seem to be your problem here. But it is something you've emphasized ever since I arrived—in a reactionary kind of way."

" '*Reactionary*'?" The Captain asked.

Michael nodded. "The guard dogs, armed sentries, security checkpoints, retina scans—all necessary, to be sure. But it's almost as if you've done all this in *response* to something." He looked directly at Ulyanov. "I can't help but get the feeling that there's more here than meets the eye. Am I right?"

Colonel Ulyanov sighed heavily and a look of resignation spread across his face. He'd hoped to enlighten his young friend much later, after he had completed his mission, but Neill was far more intuitive than Ulyanov remembered. Michael's own father had once told the Colonel that there was no book easier read than Ulyanov's face. He'd taken the jibe as a compliment then, but there were many times since then that he wished it wasn't true.

"Very well, Michael," Ulyanov said after a long, awkward pause. "You are right. There are some details that the Captain and I have kept from you. In time, we would have given you more information."

"Colonel, are you sure you want to pursue this further?" Yaroslav asked.

"Forgive the Captain, Michael." Ulyanov said calmly. "He is ... how do you say it ... 'between a rock and a hard place.' On one hand he wants to comply with the terms of our treaty; but on the other he is concerned for the security and well-being of our homeland."

"I can appreciate those concerns, sir," Neill replied. "But to honor the spirit of the treaty we have to cooperate—and that means no secrets."

Ulyanov considered his words carefully and nodded in agreement. State secrets were sometimes the hardest to keep, and with Neill's suspicions aroused, there was no turning back now.

"Very well," the Colonel began. There was a hint of relief in his voice. "Four weeks ago, this facility suffered a serious security breach—and I'm afraid Major Mayakovsky was deeply involved."

Michael leaned forward. "Involved in what?"

"Our intelligence agencies have determined that the Major collaborated with terrorists," Ulyanov continued. "And with his assistance, they successfully penetrated our defenses and stole a low-yield warhead."

"A nuclear warhead?" Neill's voice was steady. Both Yaroslav and the Colonel expected some kind of reaction, but the young Lieutenant remained calm; Neill already suspected far too much to be surprised by Ulyanov's frank admission.

Michael began to assess the importance of everything he'd been told—and what he'd seen so far—and it all began to fall into place. Mayakovsky's sudden disappearance was no longer a mystery, but this new revelation only complicated matters and brought other questions to mind. What he had regarded as a straightforward mission only weeks before had now been transformed into something quite different.

"All right," he breathed at last, settling back into his seat. He was somewhat relieved himself—at least the Colonel seemed willing to cooperate. Willis Avery had been right; Ulyanov was in a position to answer a host of questions. Neill was encouraged by his openness so far. As a dozen thoughts flooded his mind, Michael looked Ulyanov in the eye and silently wondered just how far his cooperation might extend.

"Suppose you start at the very beginning."

Chapter Thirteen ✭ Betrayal

OKSANA MARPOVA LEFT THE LONDONSKAYA Hotel and lit a cigarette, then walked past the Opera House on her way toward the waterfront. It was time for her break. The morning was crisp, but the sun had been up for some time, and as long as she stayed out of the shadows the bitter cold was almost bearable.

She reached into her purse and found her cell phone. She turned on the device and waited till she got a signal, then selected a number in the directory. Oksana pushed a button on the display and was thankful she didn't actually have to punch all the digits; while the sealskin gloves she wore were quite warm, they didn't make it easy to use the phone's keypad.

Oksana waited as the call went through. The party on the other end picked up after two rings.

"*Odessa Today*. Viktoriya Gavrilenko speaking."

"Viktoriya, this is Oksana." A stiff breeze had begun to blow.

"You're going to have to get out of the wind, Oksana. I can barely hear your voice."

The older woman positioned herself in a doorway and cupped the phone with her hand.

"Is this better?" she asked.

"*Neem mnoggah,*" came the answer. *A little bit.* "What do you have for me?"

"An American checked in to the hotel last night."

There was a heavy sigh. "A lot of Americans check into hotels these days, Oksana."

"An American *military* officer," Marpova continued. "And he speaks Ukrainian. Like a native."

A pause. "Go on."

Oksana told the woman on the other end of the line almost everything she knew about Neill. She spoke quickly; the cold seemed to be reaching all the way to her bones. She wanted to end the call and go back to the hotel where it was warm. "Is that useful to you?"

"It has certain value."

"How much value?" Oksana pressed.

"Two cartons of cigarettes?"

"Make it three," Oksana replied. "And I'll tell you his name."

"All right. Three it is—but I want to know why he's here."

Oksana shivered and started walking back toward the center of town. "You're the *reporter*, Viktoriya. Why don't you ask him yourself?"

On Ukraine's black market, nearly anything could be bought or sold. The collapse of the Soviet federal government years before had left a gaping hole in the system. People had need of basic necessities, but they had become dependent on something that no longer existed. When they couldn't get them through legal means or the approved sources, they could be forced to go far beyond the limitations of the law. And human nature being what it was, sometimes it was hard to distinguish between need and want.

Viktoriya Gavrilenko knew that all too well. As a journalist, she'd built her career delving into the darker side of the black market. Her bylines included dozens of stories uncovering the illicit world of drugs, sex for sale, counterfeit goods and pirated software. And all were tied to trade on the underground.

The most sensational example was that of a city adminis-
trator in Kharkov who profited from human trafficking—or
more specifically, prostitution. Viktoriya spent months on that
one, and found so much evidence that it couldn't be swept
under the rug. The public couldn't get enough of her stories.
Circulation and readership actually increased while the newspaper ran her series. And her blog had ignited righteous indig-
nation in the hearts of people across Ukraine.

At twenty-five, Viktoriya's investigative skills had served
her well, earning accolades from her peers and a promotion
from her bosses. But in Kiev—recently a hotbed of illegal
commerce and the next target of her journalistic acumen—
those talents had earned her a few death threats, too. She had
poked a stick in one too many hornets' nests. The seriousness of those threats was enough to persuade her to ply her
trade someplace safer. Her superiors were also convinced and
transferred her to a sister publication in Odessa—to the *Odesa
Sivodnya*, or Odessa Today.

Viktoriya didn't see it as running; always the pragma-
tist, she knew she couldn't continue to write, couldn't effect
change, if she were dead. And she knew she was slinging
stones at a Goliath that would like nothing more than to see
her end up that way. The people she implicated didn't play
games, and her position in the fourth estate—or her popularity
with her readers—wouldn't protect her forever.

She needed a new angle, but it had to be something worthy
of her skills as a journalist. She had already proven herself.
Right now she was the flavor of the month, but that wouldn't
last. Her editors had short memories, so she had to act while
her successes were still fresh in their minds.

Viktoriya was noodling on that very thought when her
phone had rung hours earlier. She sat at her desk and read over
the notes she'd taken from Oksana's call. *Maybe opportunity
has just knocked*, she thought to herself.

Michael Neill. She stared at the name she'd written on her
notepad. An American military officer in Odessa was more

than a little unusual. But the fact that he spoke the language added a level of mystery that intrigued her. What was he doing here? Who was he? His identity only added to her questions—he may have spoken Ukrainian, but his name was clearly Western. Did his presence signal the beginning of some joint exercise being conducted by the United States and Ukraine?

There was a story here; Viktoriya just knew it. This was just the thing she needed to sink her teeth into. She smiled to herself in anticipation, then pulled out her cell phone and considered a number from her directory. Oksana was only one of the sources she'd cultivated since arriving in Odessa.

She had questions, but she knew where to get more answers.

* * * *

The voice seemed to come from nowhere.

If you seek, you will find ...

Malyev jerked awake and sat up, abruptly ending his troubled sleep. Several seconds passed before he was alert enough to remember where he was and how he got there.

The first thing he did was to check his surroundings. His hotel room in downtown Bryansk faced west. The late afternoon sun glowed behind the curtains as his eyes adjusted to the light. It was a small room and sparsely furnished. Ivan scanned its contents quickly, and once satisfied that he was alone—and safe for the moment, at least—he looked at his watch. It was nearly five p.m.

He pushed aside the blankets and sheets and became painfully aware of the dull ache he felt all over his body. As a cold-hearted mercenary, Malyev regarded his discomforts merely as a passing inconvenience; his crashing descent into the forest may have bruised and battered him, but at least he was still alive.

And that was more than he could say for Sasha.

The memory of his fallen comrade caused a frown to pass over his face. Malyev staggered to his feet, then bent over the bed and retrieved his pistol from beneath the pillow.

He stuffed the weapon in his belt—Ivan had slept fully clothed—and was reminded of how vulnerable he really was. Malyev had managed to evade Pirogov's troops for the present, but he knew that if the Major's soldiers ever caught him in the open, his small handgun would be practically useless. He needed a heavier weapon, something that would give him the edge, but until then the pistol was all he had ...

As his mind slowly stirred to alertness, Malyev mused on how drastically things had changed in the past forty-eight hours. After the ambush in the clearing, he'd trudged through the forest for more than a kilometer before reaching the highway that led into town. A farmer on his way to market in Bryansk had given him a lift in his truck. By nightfall Malyev had checked into this hotel—under an assumed name, of course, paying with cash—and for two days he left his room only to take meals in the restaurant on the first floor, or to buy a fresh set of clothes in the small clothier's shop situated next to the hotel.

He feared pursuit, but curiously, none came.

Ivan flipped on the television as he made his way to the bathroom and the old set hummed to life. He'd pre-selected a channel that broadcasted its signal from Moscow. As a news commentator's voice filled the room he turned his attention to getting cleaned up.

Entering the small bathroom, Malyev turned on the hot water, closed his eyes and hung his head. The steam felt good on his face as it rose from the basin, but Ivan's mind could find no rest. Each passing moment held the possibility that Major Pirogov and his men would find him. As he soberly considered his options, Malyev decided that might be best; death in battle against a superior force was far more heroic than running in fear for the rest of his life.

After all, where could he go? Staying in Russia meant that sooner or later he'd be found. If Pirogov had orders to kill him, then someone at a much higher level of authority wanted him dead. Ivan had no doubt about who that might be. And what if the Major was simply acting on his own? Malyev shook his head—Pirogov's obsession with finishing a job gave him little hope.

Ukraine, or any other republic for that matter, was also out of the question. By now every police officer and intelligence agent from Kiev to the Crimea would know about his criminal activities in Odessa. No matter how he looked at it, Ivan Malyev was a marked man.

* * * *

"Who else knows about this?"

Colonel Ulyanov adjusted his collar to keep warm as he and Neill walked the streets of Odessa, an evening snowfall swirling around their feet. The two men had taken Friday to get away from their official duties and were dressed in layers of civilian clothing. Oleg and Pavel followed discreetly behind them.

"Our State Security Directorate—the SSD—has been involved from the very beginning," Ulyanov explained. "They were quick to identify one of Mayakovsky's conspirators as a man named Sasha Kobrin. SSD believes the other man to be Ivan Malyev."

"Russians?" Michael noticed that Ulyanov didn't address Mayakovsky by his former rank.

"Russians," the Colonel replied. "Both men have military backgrounds, with experience in demolitions. One has rudimentary training with low-yield nuclear warheads—Kobrin, I believe." Ulyanov trembled, but not because of the cold. The incredible breach of security at the weapons facility, compounded with Mayakovsky's treasonous assistance, still affected the Colonel emotionally.

"Rudimentary?" Neill asked. "Does that mean he's capable of detonating it, or are we talking about a dirty bomb here?" The thought of a nuclear bomb, even one with a low yield, in the hands of trained terrorists didn't encourage much optimism.

Ulyanov shook his head. "We aren't entirely sure. Kobrin's training would enable him to devise either one. Our facility would provide all the tools required."

"How did they get access to the weapons station?" Neill could see that his questions were having a painful effect on his old friend, but he had to ask them anyway.

"Mayakovsky had command, Michael," the Colonel grated out. "In addition to those duties, he assumed responsibility over security as well. He bypassed standard security procedures and brought in Malyev and Kobrin as 'x-ray technicians'—under assumed names, and with counterfeit identification papers, of course."

"Why?" Neill asked, each answer begging a new question. "Didn't anyone get suspicious?"

The Colonel smiled wryly. "Captain Yaroslav was—uncomfortable—with Mayakovsky's rule-bending, but couldn't act immediately." They could see the harbor and the sea beyond, the setting sun obscured by the clouds on the horizon. "His first step was to document the Major's actions. Then, after several weeks, he quietly contacted the Directorate and shared his suspicions."

"Risking his military career on a hunch," Neill added thoughtfully. "The Captain's a good man."

Ulyanov grunted in agreement as they entered the business district, lights burning brightly in the shops and kiosks that lined the street. Michael wanted a copy of the evening paper, and as they made their way toward a newsstand the Colonel continued his story.

"Yaroslav found Kobrin and Malyev—with Mayakovsky— late one night in the receiving bay, loading something onto the back of a truck."

"The bomb?"

Ulyanov nodded grimly. "The Captain tried to stop them— he subdued Mayakovsky, injuring his arm in the process, but ..."

"—Kobrin and Malyev escaped," Neill finished for him. He picked up a newspaper as they stopped at the little kiosk and scanned the headlines. "What about security? How did they get the truck past the gate?"

The Colonel fairly seethed. "Mayakovsky had dismissed the guards earlier. Kobrin and Malyev drove out of the facility without a shot being fired." Neill didn't answer. Ulyanov looked at the younger man to see if he'd heard him. "SSD has determined that they used the facility's labs at night—after hours—modifying the weapon to suit their—are you listening to me, Michael?"

Neill still didn't answer. Instead, he shoved the front page under the Colonel's nose. The lead story caught him by surprise.

* * * *

Nearly eight hundred kilometers to the north, Ivan Malyev was getting his own dose of headline news. Emerging from the bathroom he was confronted with a televised image of the man who had tried to kill him.

Ivan quickly crossed the room and adjusted the set's volume. The display at the bottom of the screen told him that the program was being broadcast from Russia's news station in Moscow. Swallowing hard, Malyev focused his attention on the figure center-stage.

Major Pirogov stood behind a podium, imposing in his full dress uniform. He was obviously the center of attention for what appeared to be an official press conference. Off-camera, Malyev could hear a host of reporters as they shouted questions. In the wings Ivan recognized the face of none other than General Leonid Karpenko.

* * * *

" 'Russian Forces seize terrorist training camp' ..." Colonel Ulyanov's eyes widened as he read the headline aloud, then a frown passed over his wide face and he handed the paper back to Neill. "Read it, Michael," he ordered impatiently. "I left my glasses back at the apartment."

Neill scanned the page and picked up where the Colonel left off. " 'Russian commandos have captured what they describe as a terrorist training camp in Bryansk, 380 kilometers from Moscow. Two armed men were killed as they tried to escape.'

" 'The camp, hidden deep in the forests near the city, contained an extensive armory that included automatic weapons, explosives, rocket launchers and a large cache of ammunition.' "

Ulyanov leaned over Neill's shoulder, trying to read the grainy newsprint. "The men who were killed ... does it identify them?"

"I'm getting to that," Neill said. " 'Initial reports indicate the camp was used as a base to launch terrorist acts against civilian targets in Ukraine, Lithuania, Estonia and other republics ... '

" 'Major Alexei Pirogov, commander of the ground force that secured the camp Friday, confirmed the deaths of two terrorists, killed in an attempt to escape—' " Michael paused, then lowered the paper and looked the Colonel in the eye. "Pirogov," he breathed. "I know that name."

"This hidden outpost was clearly a threat to the outlying republics," Pirogov was saying. "We believe the terrorists used this location as a base from which they mounted terrorist activities in Ukraine and in Lithuania." The Major's voice had a decidedly sinister edge to it, even now. "Some of their criminal acts included the use of radioactive materials, I'm afraid."

Malyev watched breathlessly as Pirogov conveyed a sense of disgust at the terrorists' actions, tasting the bile as it rose in his throat.

"Look at this—even Karpenko is quoted here," Neill said. "Karpenko?" Ulyanov asked. "General Karpenko? The

Russian President's military advisor?"

Neill nodded, then continued. " '… the two men killed were misguided Russian nationals identified as Sasha Kobrin and Ivan Malyev—' " He opened the paper and found the rest of the story continued inside, complete with Kobrin and Malyev's passport photos. " 'General Leonid Karpenko was quick to point out that these men acted independently, condemning the use of terrorism against the republics and praising Pirogov and his men for their capture of the terrorist stronghold … ' "

* * * *

"The danger is over." General Karpenko stood at the podium now, hands raised in an open, friendly gesture, a broad smile on his face. "Once again, Russian forces have demonstrated our commitment to the safety and well-being of all members of the Commonwealth. Major Pirogov will continue to work diligently, ferreting out—"

Malyev had heard enough. He snarled disgustedly at the image on the screen, then reached over and switched off the set, trying to silence Karpenko and Pirogov just as coldly as they had silenced Sasha. He knew it wasn't the same thing, of course, but right now nothing was exactly as it seemed.

Only three things were real for Ivan at that moment.

Duty and betrayal were two of them.

Malyev had been paid well for his work in Ukraine, but in spite of his mercenary tendencies he believed in the cause, had wanted to see Russia strong again.

Pirogov had violated the code, even if he was under orders from a higher authority. He and Sasha had acted in good faith and Sasha had paid for it with his life. Malyev would've been dead too, had it not been for—what? Fate?

To Ivan's way of thinking, duty defined his—and Sasha's— actions, while betrayal distinguished him from General Karpenko and the Major.

Vengeance, the third reality, was something else altogether.

Chapter Fourteen ✳ The Journalist

❝ 'Broken arrow'?" Richard Aultman asked. He'd just read Neill's latest classified message for the second time.

Willis Avery sat at his desk in the White House and shook his head.

"'*Empty Quiver,*'" he grumped. "The warhead was stolen. And in this case, the intent would appear to be terrorism. *'Broken Arrow'* refers to an *accidental* event."

"This changes things," Aultman observed. *Dramatically*.

"It certainly does," Avery agreed. Sitting back in his chair, he folded his hands behind his head and stared at the ceiling. Normally he'd be more vocal, but Aultman could tell his boss was thinking.

It wasn't clear what they were dealing with. The device might have been converted to an RDD, or it might have retained the functions of a conventional nuclear warhead. An RDD, or radiological dispersion device—a dirty bomb, as it was known—would have more of a psychological effect. While it was the lesser of two evils, it could still be very lethal. Aultman wasn't sure what the current code phrase was for that. As a traditional weapon, detonating the nuke would cause far more devastation and loss of life. But neither option was acceptable.

Avery was feeling a rather heavy dose of disappointment.

First, the sudden and unexpected appearance of the warheads in Donetsk. Now this. He couldn't lay the blame solely at the Ukrainians' feet—Russia had been sloppy in maintaining a firm grip on their weapons as well. Now, their inattention to detail and recklessness threatened innocent lives.

"What's our next step?" Aultman asked, breaking the silence.

"I'll advise the President," Avery answered. "We'll quietly inform a few of our commanders in the field—we've got people in a few countries near their border. Prep them in case we need to offer some type of assistance." He wasn't sure what that might be. Aultman watched as Avery pulled out a lined pad and began jotting down a few names. "Ukraine's a sovereign nation," he observed finally. "In the end, we just have to trust people to do their jobs."

"Are you talking about our friends in Kiev?" Aultman asked. "—Or Neill?"

Avery looked up and stared into the distance. "Both," he replied.

Neill had always found it difficult to run in cold weather, and for more than a few reasons. Layering up kept his joints and limbs warm, so that wasn't really a problem. Today he wore a micro-fiber long sleeve tee under his sweatshirt, with a hoodie over that. To keep his legs warm, he wore long underwear beneath his thick, cotton sweatpants, rounding out his PT gear with two layers of socks and his athletic shoes.

It was Michael's lungs that always seemed to suffer. Drawing in cold air during the course of a run caused pain. It was a discomfort that he didn't experience at any other time of the year. In fact, he seemed to thrive under humid conditions. But not in winter. To combat that, he wore a breathable scarf to minimize the flow of frigid air into his chest. Unfortunately, all the extra clothing caused other problems.

After thirty minutes of hoofing it in the cold, Neill would

start to perspire. Sweat-soaked clothes just did not make for a good running experience. Michael's solution was to run into the wind. That helped, but only postponed the inevitable. Besides, with the wind in his face, his eyes began to water …

Neill mulled all that over as he pounded the cobble-stone roads of downtown Odessa and decided he was being a wimp. *Pick up your feet, Marine,* he told himself. *And quit your belly-achin'* … He could almost hear the voice of his uncle in his head.

The streets were mainly empty as he made his way up from the park near the city's business district. That was fine by Neill. He needed a break to clear his mind and the morning run had done the trick. The past few days had been a rush of early mornings, late evenings, and detailed briefings at the station. At times those bordered on overload. The news of the stolen warhead hadn't helped his frame of mind, either.

Being back in Ukraine had also brought a flood of boyhood memories. Neill smiled to himself, and he could see his breath; while Odessa was unique in many respects, it had a certain look and feel common to other Eastern European cities. When it came to the old—particularly with regard to culture and architecture—that could be a good thing. But like other municipalities spread across the former Soviet Union, Odessa shared a more recent history, one colored by revolution, fire and blood.

Neill pushed all that from his mind and decided it was time to get indoors. He rounded a corner and began walking the rest of the distance to the hotel. After a block or so, he jogged up the steps of the Londonskaya's landing—taking them two at a time—then stood just outside the building's ornate glass doors to catch his breath. His appearance did not go unnoticed from inside the main lobby.

"Is that him?" Viktoriya Gavrilenko kept her eyes on Neill as she pretended to read the morning paper. Her chair near the front desk had a good view of the hotel entrance.

Oksana Marpova glanced up from her duties behind the counter. "How did you know?"

Viktoriya shrugged. "A journalist's instincts. Besides, only an American would go out in this weather," she answered.

From her vantage point, she could tell the young man on the landing was very athletic, even under the layers of warm clothing he wore. She caught a glimpse of his profile and raised an eyebrow. "You were right, Oksana—he is *very* handsome."

Oksana smiled ruefully. "That should make your job even easier."

"I'm sure I don't know what you mean," the younger woman huffed. She folded the newspaper and laid it down on the arm of the chair. Either subconsciously or quite deliberately, she glanced at her reflection in the mirror on the far wall and stood to her feet, then gauged her steps as she moved to the center of the room.

Showtime, she thought silently to herself.

Michael wiped the sweat from his face and turned to enter the building. The warmth of the lobby was a welcome change as he stepped through the door. He managed to get only a few feet when his peripheral vision warned him that his personal space was about to be invaded.

Neill tried to put on the brakes, but it was too late. The young woman had turned on her heel and moved directly in his path. The collision was inevitable.

Neill heard a loud *ooomphh* as Viktoriya plowed directly into him. She had seriously miscalculated his body mass. Completely unbalanced, his momentum was enough to knock her off her feet. She landed unceremoniously before him on the floor before Neill could even attempt to save her from falling.

Michael was horrified. Steadying himself, he looked down to see who it was he'd just met head-on. He focused his attention on the woman beneath him. In spite of the circumstances, he had to admit it was a pleasant sight.

Viktoriya was now returning his gaze, her dark eyes flashing as her auburn hair framed the contours of her face. She leaned back on the floor and caught her breath. Neill noticed everything about her. She wore a bright red leather jacket over a black turtle-neck sweatshirt. Her blue jeans looked brand new and she wore a pair of tan boots, with fringed, suede outers that went up nearly to her knees. He was immediately struck by her beauty and tried to ignore the fact that she seemed to have been poured into every stitch of her clothing.

She recovered quickly and didn't appear to be any worse for wear from the impact. Viktoriya shook her head and laughed softly, then placed her hands over her face. Neill knelt down and reached out awkwardly.

"I am so sorry," Viktoriya began. "*Prastityeh minya.*" *Please forgive me.*

Michael shook his head, his cheeks reddening. "Not at all," he replied in Ukrainian. "I should have been watching where I was going. Are you all right?"

Viktoriya laughed again, then looked directly at Michael and batted her eyes. "I'm fine. Just clumsy," she cooed. "Would you mind helping me up?"

From behind the front desk, Oksana shook her head as a thin smile spread across her face. *A performance worthy of the Opera*, she concluded. A bit heavy-handed, but the young American *was* a man, after all. And all men were naïve in the presence of a woman like Viktoriya.

"You sure you're okay?" Neill asked.

Viktoriya sipped her tea as the two sat in the hotel restaurant. She smiled back at Michael before answering.

"I'm sure," she said. She put down her cup and looked at him reassuringly. "Please, think nothing of it. I'm quite all right." She reached out and touched Michael's arm, then frowned slightly. "I didn't hurt you, did I?"

"Nah, I'm good." Neill drank from a bottle of water the

waitress had brought him. He was quite comfortable now, pulling off his hoodie and laying it beside him in the booth the two now shared.

"Thank you for the tea."

Neill smiled now. "The least I could do after running you over."

"It wasn't that bad," she laughed, then extended her hand. "My name is Viktoriya. Viktoriya Gavrilenko."

Michael noted the warmth of her touch. "Michael Neill."

Viktoriya looked briefly puzzled. "You're an American?" She shook her head. "But you speak the language like a native. Where are you from?"

"Here in Ukraine, just outside of Kiev. But yes, I am an American. My parents lived here when I was born."

Her eyes crinkled as she laughed. "Well, of course. If you were born here, it stands to reason they were also living in Ukraine."

Michael nodded, slightly embarrassed. "I guess that didn't come out quite right."

The restaurant manager eyed the young couple with a frown. Proper attire was expected in fine dining establishments. Neill's sweats certainly didn't meet those standards, but the manager decided to let it go. The dining room was nearly empty anyway. Besides, it would have been too much trouble to ask the American to leave now.

"So, Mr. Neill—what brings you to Odessa?"

"Business. And please, call me Michael."

"All right, Michael," she laughed softly. "What *kind* of business?"

He took another drink of water as he thought about how to answer that question. He knew that sooner or later it might come up. "I'm here as part of a comprehensive security initiative for our respective governments."

She wore a frown now. "That sounds serious. What type

of security?"

"Issues that could surface when the United States and Ukraine interact." *There*, Neill thought. *Broadly accurate, but vague enough not to compromise operational security.*

"Is that like a status for forces agreement?" Viktoriya asked.

That was curious. Most people didn't ordinarily use that phrase in everyday conversation. "Something like that," Michael answered. "My job is to act as a liaison, more than anything else."

"So you are a government official?"

"In a manner of speaking," Neill replied slowly. In the back of his mind, a small flag just went up. "I'm in the U.S. military. The Marines."

Viktoriya's face brightened. "Oh, I see. That's very impressive. The United States Marines have quite the reputation." She leaned forward, her eyes expressing a newfound interest. It was the kind of look almost any man would have welcomed from a woman as beautiful as she was.

Her statement was an attempt at flattery, but for the first time in the conversation, Viktoriya hadn't ended her sentence with a question. It was a tactical error on her part. Neill wasn't completely taken in by Viktoriya's wiles and took advantage of the opportunity to steer the discussion in a different direction.

"What about you, Miss Gavrilenko? Are you a guest of the hotel, or is Odessa your home?"

"My friends call me Viktoriya." She looked down at the table for a moment and glanced at Michael's hand, her smile softening. *No ring,* she thought. And no evidence of one. *So he's single.* "I moved here from Kiev six months ago."

Neill smiled to himself. *And here we go.* Her line of questioning had raised his suspicions. *She talks a lot, but doesn't really say much,* he thought. "What do you do here in Odessa, Viktoriya?"

She realized her mistake; she'd been in control of the conversation, then lost it when she failed in her follow-up. Now she was cornered, forced to give up a little information about herself. "I'm a journalist, Michael. You've read the Odessa Today?" Viktoriya held her breath; would this American be gullible enough to keep talking once he knew who she was?

Neill smiled broadly. "I have. Just this morning," he said. He folded his arms and settled back in the booth. The game was over. "Is this an interview, Viktoriya?"

The young woman looked embarrassed—Neill decided that was probably part of the act, too. After a pause, she let out a sigh, squared her shoulders and looked Michael right in the eye.

"It's who I am, Michael. I'm sure you're just as passionate about what you do." She reached out and touched his hand, gave him her most alluring smile and hoped for the best. "I meant no harm."

"You're very good at what you do, aren't you?"

No such luck, she thought to herself.

"I realize you're just doing your job, but were the theatrics really necessary?" Neill picked up his hoodie and sat on the edge of the seat. "If you wanted an introduction, all you had to do was walk up and say hello." He stood to his feet and stuck out his hand. "It was a pleasure to meet you, Viktoriya—even if you were just fishing for a story." Any other man might have been angry, but Michael's voice carried a compassionate tone that surprised her. "Maybe we'll see each other again before I leave."

She took his hand and shook it, not sure exactly what to say, then watched without saying a word as Neill left the room, leaving her sitting all alone. She felt somewhat ashamed of herself. It was not an emotion she experienced often.

Chapter Fifteen ✳ A New Plan

IVAN WOKE EARLY AND PACKED THE FEW PER-
sonal belongings he had in his possession. He showered
and dressed, but did not shave; although he was convinced now that no one would be looking for him, his three-
day growth of beard would be helpful in disguising his features—just in case.

He left his hotel room for the last time and took the elevator
to the first floor. Once there, he made his way to the restaurant
and ordered a large breakfast. His food arrived shortly and he
spent his meal deep in thought, contemplating his plans for the
day.

He'd had plenty of time to think. Ivan recalled the telecast
from the night before and considered Pirogov's words, trying
to separate fact from fiction. Culling together all the truthful
information he had and distinguishing it from speculation and
probabilities was crucial if his plan was to succeed ...

Major Pirogov—and the General—had betrayed him, that
much was certain. He'd trusted them and nearly paid for it with
his life. Malyev couldn't explain the treachery, but it was there.
Maybe his superiors had simply grown tired of their terrorist
tactics and decided to sever the ties in the most expedient method available: by eliminating all witnesses.

That type of speculation could go on forever, so Malyev put
those thoughts aside. He might never know the real reason and

it didn't matter anyway. The waitress refilled his empty tea cup and Ivan moved on to his next consideration.

Fact two: Sasha Kobrin was a dead man; but so was Ivan Malyev. Pirogov had said so, and the morning papers had confirmed it. As far as Malyev knew, Pirogov really believed it—or did he? What if the Major had only said that, knowing Ivan to be alive and waiting for him to surface again so he could finish the job?

Malyev shook his head; that didn't make sense, especially when Pirogov had ample resources to eliminate him right after the ambush. He was a lone man against well-armed and well-trained troops. He concluded that the only reason they hadn't found him was that they hadn't looked for him. Dead men don't run, Ivan thought, and Pirogov must have complacently assumed that the plane's explosion was something no human being could survive.

The fact that everyone thought he was dead gave Ivan a new freedom, but not for long. Dead or alive, the news media had labeled him a terrorist. If he was ever found in Russia—or the republics—he would face assassination at worst or a public trial and execution at best.

Those thoughts—and his desire for vengeance—fueled a new plan.

He paid for his breakfast, settled his hotel account and then headed out the door into the city. For his plans to succeed, he'd need a disguise of sorts, and he knew just where to get one.

* * * *

"Your procedures are strictly by the book," Neill said as he entered the Colonel's office in the administrative building. In one hand he carried a clipboard, his laptop clutched in the other. It was Monday afternoon and both men were back in their camouflage utilities.

Ulyanov's head came up from his paperwork and he motioned for Neill to sit down. "Everything is to your satisfaction?" the Colonel asked casually.

"Yes, sir," Michael said, depositing the clipboard and computer on a small table. He pulled off his cover—the Marine Corps' term for headgear—and sank into the sofa across from Ulyanov's desk. "Security, storage, safety precautions—your staff's performance exceeds the recommended standards by a wide margin," he said. "Dismantling seems to be moving at a glacial pace, but—"

"Michael," the Colonel grinned, sitting back in his chair. "If you were taking apart a nuclear bomb, would you do it quickly?"

Neill considered that and began to smile to himself. "I think I see your point." Then, frowning, he added; "Unfortunately, your inventory is still short one weapon. Any word from SSD regarding our two friends killed in Bryansk?"

"Malyev and Kobrin?" Ulyanov shook his head. "Not a word. The news reports—on TV or in print—make no mention of a bomb being found, which doesn't surprise me."

"Oh?"

"Our own security directorate is understandably hesitant about contacting the Russian government," Ulyanov sighed heavily. "SSD can't exactly call them and say 'by the way, one of our bombs is missing; you didn't happen to find one at the terrorists' camp, did you?' " He frowned. "It would be a political embarrassment."

"Not to mention the panic it might produce if it became common knowledge." Neill clasped his hands behind his head, a thoughtful look on his face. "So you don't think they took it with them?"

"Not at all." The Colonel filled two small cups from a *samovar* he kept behind his desk, then turned and handed one to Neill. "They would have no need for it in Russia. No, Michael, the bomb is still here."

"What makes you say that?"

"Major Pirogov said that Kobrin and Malyev were misguided patriots." Ulyanov took a sip of his tea. "I believe him on that point. They were using terrorist tactics—"

"—and nuclear weapons," Neill threw in.

"Yes, that's right," Ulyanov agreed, "—to scare the republics, frighten them into accepting protection from Mother Russia. With that in mind, it makes no sense to bring the bomb with them back to their own country."

"But leaving it here in Ukraine, at a strategic location to frighten the local government would make sense, is that what you're saying?"

The Colonel nodded, a twinkle in his eye. "Let's review what we do know, Michael. For nearly a year, subversive groups—men like Malyev and Kobrin—have threatened the republics by planting radioactive materials in key republic cities." He liked to voice the facts; it always helped in assessing the next course of action.

"Like the canisters found recently in Lithuania," Neill nodded, leaning forward. "Something we've been monitoring in the States, too. What's your read on that?"

"Blackmail, plain and simple," Ulyanov said flatly. "These … anarchists … are trying to push us into a closer dependence on Moscow. Of course, the Kremlin has promised that if we accept their offer of protection, these criminals could be crushed."

"A tempting offer, I'm sure," Neill said. "But that would mean losing some of your independence—and I doubt Moscow would stop there." Neill shook his head. "A restored Soviet Union is a pretty high price to pay for security."

The Colonel nodded his head in agreement and took another sip of his tea. "The Russians are desperate, Michael. Lately they've become quite ruthless—" Ulyanov looked at Neill in a curious sort of way, "—as you are quite aware of, I think."

Neill returned his gaze but didn't quite understand.

"The American pilot who died recently," the Colonel began slowly, his voice very quiet. "Do you know what type of aircraft was used in the attack?"

Michael blinked. "I'm supposed to ask you that question," he admitted. This was certainly an odd turn of events. "Our information on that is a bit thin, to say the least." He got the feeling that the Colonel's intel was a little more elaborate.

The Colonel nodded his head, just the hint of a smile on his face. Neill was about to question him further when Captain Yaroslav entered the room, his arm no longer hindered by the use of the sling, and the subject of Russia's newest fighter faded as abruptly as it had come up.

Ulyanov waved the Captain to a seat and turned his attention back to Neill. "You said you knew Pirogov's name—how?"

Neill drained the last of the tea from his cup before speaking again. "I did a paper on Russian counter-terrorism tactics during my last year at the Academy," he explained. "Pirogov's name kept coming up in my research. Seems the Kremlin put him in charge of protecting the state against troublemakers, but he'd practically disappeared by the time I went to work in the IOI office three years ago."

Yaroslav chuckled. "He's not missing anymore," he quipped. "Every newspaper and television station in Eastern Europe is lining up to interview him. I'm sure our own State Security Directorate would like the chance too."

"Seems like the Major's been pretty busy, doesn't it?" Neill asked. "Rounding up terrorists is steady work; might even explain why he's kept such a low profile." When he spoke again, Neill had a faraway look in his eye. "But let's consider another possibility."

"Another possibility?" Yaroslav was puzzled, then noticed the same distant look on Ulyanov's face. "What did you have in mind?"

"You said it yourself, Colonel," Neill began. "The Russians are desperate—and for months now, terrorists have mounted a campaign of fear against the republics, trying to scare them back under Moscow's wing."

"Are you suggesting a connection between the two?" Ulyanov asked with a frown.

"A suggestion, yes. An accusation, no," Neill said. "For that we need more evidence."

"Go on," the Colonel ordered. "Develop your theory a little further."

"Well, for one thing, Russia needs natural resources, something the republics have. Ukraine's a good example; think of everything Moscow lost control over when Ukraine broke away—mineral resources, produce, shipping interests and the like."

"There are a lot of hungry people in the Russian Federation, Michael," Ulyanov said slowly. "But we've always been willing to trade with Russia."

"But that's not the point," Neill replied, shaking his head. "Russia doesn't want to simply pay fair market value for your food and goods; they want it because they think it belongs to them. And they've endured two severe winters—spring's been delayed both times and their crop production has suffered."

"So much for motive," Captain Yaroslav said. "I wouldn't be surprised if they resorted to such tactics."

Neill shrugged. "I'm only saying it's a possibility."

"And what of Malyev and Kobrin?" Ulyanov asked. "I suppose we should take some consolation in the fact they're dead. Do you think Moscow was behind their activities?"

"Somebody had to bankroll this operation." Neill declared. "With all due respect, Colonel, 'misguided patriots' don't operate from a hidden outpost with state-of-the-art weapons; trained terrorists do."

"Trained by who?" Yaroslav asked.

"Pirogov." Ulyanov said, looking up.

"Who better to do the job?" Michael asked. "He's an expert on the subject. It would certainly explain his whereabouts for the past two years."

"And what about Mayakovsky?" Yaroslav was less skeptical with each passing moment, but still not quite convinced. "How was he involved?"

Neill stood to his feet and turned to face a large map of the Commonwealth pinned to the wall.

"That's easy enough," he said. "Kobrin and Malyev would need a contact, someone here in Ukraine who could give them access to nuclear materials. Mayakovsky was the perfect choice."

"But if your theory is correct," Yaroslav protested, "the Russians trained the terrorists to blackmail the republics, then turned around—"

"—and eliminated them." Ulyanov finished for him, nodding his head. "Very neat."

"Exactly." Neill turned to face the Colonel. "It's the perfect plan; the Russian government distances itself from the terrorists and at the same time comes across as the protector of the republics."

"Probably their goal all along," Ulyanov growled. "And with Moscow taking credit, the people have one more reason to cry out for a restored Soviet Union." He pushed aside his teacup and sat back in his chair. For a moment the three men sat without speaking, considering the possibility of what they had discussed.

Finally, Captain Yaroslav stood to his feet. "These matters are for politicians," he stated slowly. "And we are still missing a warhead."

"I'm not so sure you want politicians looking into this." Neill turned again to face the map, tracing a finger from Odessa to Bryansk. "More like a cop. What about the truck Malyev and Kobrin used when they stole the bomb—has it turned up anywhere?"

The Colonel looked up from his desk. "Not yet," he replied in a subdued voice. "The newspaper accounts make no mention of a truck used by the terrorists in Bryansk. In any case, they couldn't have crossed the border in it without the proper papers."

"So it's still here—" Michael said, tapping the map on the Ukrainian side, "—somewhere between Odessa and the Russian border." He had a hunch that finding the truck might point them in the bomb's direction.

Captain Yaroslav whistled softly as the three surveyed the map. "That's a lot of territory, Lieutenant."

Neill nodded in agreement and as he studied the map more closely he realized just how right the Captain was.

"Speaking of newspapers," Michael said slowly. "I met someone yesterday."

Ulyanov sat on the corner of his desk, his eyes narrowing. "Who?"

"Viktoriya Gavrilenko. Ever heard of her?"

The Colonel repeated the name under his breath. "Sounds familiar," he mumbled, then a light went on in his brain. "Yes. Gavrilenko. The journalist." He stared at Michael. "You met her? Where?"

"I ran into her at the hotel," Neill answered. That much was literally true. "She asked a lot of questions."

"I'm sure she did." Ulyanov appeared alarmed by the news. Further complications were the last thing they needed. "What kind of questions?"

Neill leaned against the wall. "She wanted to know who I was, what I was doing here." Michael saw the expression on the Colonel's face. "Don't worry. I didn't tell her anything."

"I'm relieved to hear that, Michael. She is a woman known for getting answers."

"So I hear," Neill replied. "I looked her up online. She's made her career in investigative journalism. Wrote a series of articles on the black market."

"I've read some of them." The frown never left Ulyanov's face. "I wonder what she's doing here."

Neill considered that. "I think we have to assume she's looking for a story. My presence here has probably piqued her interest, but maybe I'm giving myself too much credit. She might be more interested in the facility itself." He looked at the Colonel. "Have you had any requests for interviews by the press?"

"We get them occasionally. All have been denied."

It was Michael's turn to frown. "That might have been a mistake."

Ulyanov nodded. "Agreed. Refusing requests only builds more questions in reporters' minds." He looked thoughtful. "We could alleviate that. Throw the press a bone or two. But I'm not entirely comfortable dealing with this Gavrilenko woman."

"Might be a good idea to give her *something* to chew on—deflect her curiosity a bit. What does the public know about this facility?"

"They've been told that we handle old ordnance. Solid rocket boosters and the like. We don't broadcast the fact that we dismantle nuclear warheads," Ulyanov replied. "That might generate a little too much interest. And with one missing—"

Neill nodded. "Understood. That's definitely not the kind of publicity you need right now. Still, having an ally in the press could work in our favor."

" 'Keep your friends close, and your enemies closer?'" Ulyanov grunted. "Let me know if she contacts you again, Michael. In the meantime, I'll have someone look into her background."

"I'll do that. Do you think she will? Contact me, I mean?"

Michael almost sounded hopeful. The Colonel smiled. "I'm sure you haven't heard the last of her." He recalled some of the articles Viktoriya had written. "She's a very determined woman."

Chapter Sixteen ✳ On the Move

VIKTORIYA GAVRILENKO WAS NOT A WOMAN known to be indecisive. Far from it, forging ahead was her standard operating procedure, but today, at her desk at the newspaper, she was fidgeting and found it difficult to focus. And oddly enough, she was having a hard time making decisions—one in particular.

None of that fit who she was as a journalist and it torqued her mood. In the back of her mind, she knew it had something to do with the appearance of Lieutenant Michael Neill. Quite possibly it was connected to her rather awkward introduction to the young, handsome American. After that encounter, her bruised ego flirted with the idea of forgetting about him altogether; but that certainly didn't sound like the course of action someone with her abilities would take, and after a great deal of consideration, she ruled that out.

No, there was only one path guaranteed to satisfy her professional—and possibly *personal*—curiosity, and that meant following up on the Marine officer's presence in Ukraine. What was he doing here? Did his fluency with the language play a role? She shook her head and frowned. There were simply too many questions about Neill that she didn't have answers for, but having made the decision to dig deeper, she managed to pull herself out of the funk she'd endured since they met.

She picked up her phone and scrolled through her list of

contacts. One name stood out, someone who might be able to provide a clue to Neill's mission in Eastern Europe.

Grigory Valentin stared at his cell phone and frowned. He didn't recognize the number being displayed on the small screen, but decided to answer it anyway. Sorting through some rather mundane paperwork, Grigory needed a break and was pleasantly surprised when he heard the voice of Viktoriya Gavrilenko speaking on the other end of the line.

"I thought you'd forgotten all about me," Grigory said in the deepest voice he could muster. "What can a mere chief of security do for Ukraine's foremost journalist?"

Viktoriya smiled. If he was flirting, he was being very subtle about it. That was refreshing. Many of the men she came into contact with eventually expressed more than just a *professional* interest in her. She had come to expect that type of behavior. While it might have offended her sensibilities as a journalist, on another level—as a *woman*—she never tired of the flattery. "I need a favor."

"Name it."

"Have there been any—*unusual* visitors passing through the terminal recently?"

"Unusual? In what way?"

Viktoriya decided to take a more direct approach. "I'm interested in an American. A military officer. He might have arrived last week," she continued.

Grigory sat back in his chair as his mind went back to the day Neill arrived. "Are you writing a story, Viktoriya?"

"I'm just gathering background," she deflected. "Which may or may not lead to a feature. It just depends on what kind of information I get. Of course, if you don't remember any-thing—"

"No, no. I do recall someone like that," he answered. "A young man, an American—a Marine, I think. Is that who you're referring to?"

Viktoriya pulled out a notepad and got ready to write.

"That's the one. What can you tell me about him?"

He paused and considered how to work this to his advantage, but ultimately Grigory just wasn't that clever. "Not very much. I don't even know his name."

"Surely there's something," Viktoriya pressed. "How did he get here? Did anyone meet him when he arrived?"

Specific questions always helped. "He flew in on an American Air Force jet," Grigory replied. "He was alone. And a delegation of Ukrainian officers were waiting for him."

Viktoriya's pen flew across the pad as she wrote. That made sense. She remembered Neill saying something about security initiatives and being a liaison. "From what base? Did you get their names?"

For anyone else, Grigory wouldn't have been so forthcoming. But she was a reporter. Asking lots of questions came with the territory. He moved across the floor to a cabinet. "Hold on, I have it right here." Opening a drawer, he flipped through several files until he found what he was looking for, an events log from the previous week. "Yes—here it is. Ulyanov, a Colonel. His adjutant was a man named Yaroslav; Captain Yaroslav."

Now she was getting somewhere. "From the squadron at the airfield?"

Grigory shook his head. "That's what I thought at first, too. But none of them looked familiar. And after they met the American, they all got into their cars and drove out the gate."

That surprised Viktoriya. "Is there another military base near here?"

"There's an ordnance station nearby. About six kilometers west. That might be where they were headed."

"Ordnance?"

Valentin smiled. "Weapons, Viktoriya. Explosives. I hear they dismantle old rocket warheads out there. You know, 'Swords into plowshares?'"

The reference was completely lost on the young woman.

"It's from the Bible." Grigory replaced the file and

couldn't resist a gentle dig. "When was the last time you went to church?"

* * * *

"The jacket fits, yes?" the street vendor asked hopefully. He stood to make a good profit on this sale—if the customer agreed to the price—and it wasn't even noon yet.

Ivan Malyev shifted his frame within the heavy wool material, carefully fastening the gold buttons and inspecting the lengths of the sleeves for a proper fit. The rank insignia on the shoulder boards and the ribbons adorning the material over the breast pockets looked brand new. Grunting in satisfaction, Malyev picked up the pair of matching trousers that went with the jacket and held them up to his side.

Perfect, he thought.

"You have a hat to go with it?" Ivan asked coldly.

"Oh, yes, of course." The vendor began shuffling among his wares on the small table he'd set up downtown and produced a visored cap. It bore the markings of a Russian naval officer. He held it up eagerly for Malyev's inspection, who took it and placed it carefully on his head.

The buying and selling of old military uniforms had become quite popular, and this particular vendor had seen his business expand as more and more Western tourists visited Bryansk. It was not as lucrative as selling drugs—which he also did on rare occasions, if a supply came his way. Most of his clientele were souvenir hunters from Europe or the United States, but the man before him now was clearly Russian.

"The uniform—is it for you?" the vendor asked. His customer seemed uninterested in small talk and he regretted the question almost immediately.

Ivan surprised him by smiling back. There was no use in being remembered as a surly client in case someone came looking for him later. "For my brother. A gift," he said. "He lost his uniform after leaving the navy." He could see the curious expression on the vendor's face, then added: "We're the same build. I'm sure he will like it."

The vendor nodded, not really caring who it was for as long as he got his money. Malyev slipped off the jacket, carefully folding it and placing it on the table with the trousers and hat. Then he pulled out his wallet and paid full price for the items without even haggling.

With the folded jacket, trousers and cap bundled underneath his arm, Malyev made his way down the street, then realized his old boots were scuffed far too badly to wear with the uniform. It didn't take him long to find what passed for a department store. Twenty minutes later he'd purchased a brand new pair of black leather shoes.

Ivan emerged from the store and began casually mingling among the shoppers and pedestrians who strolled the busy sidewalks. His success so far today had buoyed his spirits, and the sun felt warm on what would have ordinarily been a cold January afternoon.

The next step in his plan required far more caution, however. His most immediate need was for transportation, and as he continued along he focused his attention on the rows of cars that lined the street.

In due course he found what he was looking for. Parked among several other vehicles, a careless motorist had left his Lada unlocked, giving Ivan all the opportunity a man of his training needed. He paused on the sidewalk in front of the car long enough to light a cigarette, then tossed the spent match aside, stepped off the curb and opened the driver's side door. He shot a casual—although cautious—glance all around, then quickly slid in behind the wheel. He placed his belongings on the passenger seat beside him then ran his hands underneath the dash.

Hot wiring a car was a skill he'd acquired during his training at the camp. His fingers soon found what they were searching for. Within thirty seconds the Lada's engine roared to life. Malyev shifted the gears into reverse and backed carefully into the street. He nudged the car into the flow of traffic and then checked the fuel gauge to find the gas tank half full. His search of the glove box even turned up a highway map.

Ivan smiled at his own ingenuity, then gunned the engine and sped away. By the time the Lada's owner discovered his car had been stolen, Malyev was already far from Bryansk.

* * * *

"I can appreciate the need to be discreet about this," Neill said, entering Ulyanov's office. "But I've got an idea."

It was late afternoon. Since his informal tour of the facility four days earlier Neill had managed to achieve most of his mission objectives. He had documented the station's dismantling and storage procedures with painstaking detail, preoccupied though he was with the news of the missing warhead.

"Just a moment, Michael. There's something I want you to hear." Ulyanov picked up the phone and summoned Captain Yaroslav to join them. He cradled the receiver and gestured toward a chair. Neill had no sooner taken his seat when the Captain walked through the door, holding a printed sheet of paper in one hand.

"I've asked the State Security Directorate to look into your journalist friend," the Colonel announced. He perched casually on the corner of his desk. "I felt it was prudent to have some expectations of her possible motives."

Neill raised an eyebrow as Yaroslav pulled up a chair next to him. "It would appear that we have little to worry about," the Captain announced. "Viktoriya Gavrilenko is, as it turns out, a journalist. We already knew that. But we were concerned she might have been seconded by someone's intelligence bureau—someone from the outside."

"In other words, we were worried she might have been recruited as a spy," Ulyanov explained.

Michael nodded. "Sounds reasonable enough. What did the SSD find out?"

Yaroslav continued. "Miss Gavrilenko has admirable credentials in the field of investigative reporting. She has earned the respect of her peers, and—" he scanned the information in his hand, "—also made a few enemies along the way."

"What kind of enemies?" Michael was now curious.

"Her articles have cast an embarrassing light on quite a few public figures. Politicians, industrialists—even a member of Parliament." He looked up at Neill. "You've read some of her work?"

Again, a nod. "Some of it. And I've skimmed over the rest. Her digging into the black market was pretty extensive." Michael smiled. "One thing's for sure; she has a way with words."

Captain Yaroslav returned to his notes. "And some of those words have had some inflammatory results. About a year ago, she started receiving death threats. Not everyone appreciated her journalistic skills, it would seem."

"So what's she doing here? Most of her stories were centered in Kiev." Neill was still trying to figure that one out. Her presence in Odessa preceded his arrival by several months, but that didn't keep Michael from being just a little suspicious.

"The authorities looked into those threats, but couldn't guarantee her safety there," Yaroslav explained. "They recommended that she either stop writing about the black market, or—"

"—or leave town," Ulyanov quipped. A smile. "I wonder how many of those same authorities were profiting from the underground. Her departure probably made the constabulary in Kiev very happy."

Yaroslav shrugged. "I have no information about that. But it appears that she took their advice. Her employers also own the Odessa Today. She transferred here during the summer of last year."

"The Directorate works fast. Anything else we should know?" Michael asked.

The Captain shook his head. "The SSD conducted a cursory investigation. Their preliminary report didn't turn up any associations or connections—nefarious or otherwise—that raised any flags. 'Viktoriya Gavrilenko is a woman of singular focus, driven by her pursuit of journalistic integrity.'"

Neill peered at the paper in Captain Yaroslav's hand. "Is that what it really says?"

Yaroslav smiled. "The SSD is getting quite flowery with their prose. Perhaps Miss Gavrilenko has inspired them."

"All right, we've settled that," Ulyanov said, taking control of the conversation. "Michael—you said you had an idea. What did you have in mind?" The Colonel got off the desk and stood to his feet. It was almost time to summon Corporal Sevnik to bring the car around for the trip home.

"I'm still convinced that finding the truck is the key." Neill began. "We know the terrorists didn't cross the border with it—the newspaper accounts said they used a small plane to get to Bryansk."

"Where they were promptly blown out of the sky—" Ulyanov grunted, "—while trying to 'escape.'"

Recalling Walter's death, it occurred to Michael that the Russians were making quite a habit of firing on unarmed aircraft. He nursed that thought for a moment, but didn't linger over it.

"Obviously they needed the truck to move the weapon," Neill continued. "It was too big to hide in the trunk of a car—or their aircraft."

"Michael, it's been over three weeks since Malyev and Kobrin stole that truck," the Colonel pointed out. "Plenty of time to disguise its appearance, paint over its markings and switch the plates."

"I know it's a longshot,' Neill conceded.

"Then what do you suggest?"

"Contact the civilian police in every major city between here and the northern border. They had to ditch it somewhere," Neill said. "Maybe the militia has come across something—but do it quietly."

"How?" Ulyanov ushered Neill and Yaroslav out of the office, turning off the light and locking the door behind him.

"Get your adjutant at the airbase in Nikolayev to make some discreet inquiries—that way it doesn't look like the request is coming from the dismantling station." Neill offered. "Have him find out if the district authorities have located any stolen military vehicles within the past two or three weeks."

The Colonel considered Michael's idea as the three men walked down the hall to the security guard's station.

"All right," Ulyanov said approvingly. The Sergeant of the Guard came to attention as Ulyanov signed them out, then activated the door switch which allowed them to exit the building without setting off the alarms. "I'll make a phone call in the morning. Anything else?"

"One more thing," Neill said, pulling on his soft cover as they stepped into the cool evening air. "Tonight after supper, you and I are going to pray for a break in this case."

"Yes," the Colonel murmured softly. He was far more concerned about the bomb than he let on.

"God knows we could use one."

Chapter Seventeen ✳ Apologies

THE LINGERING EFFECTS OF COMMUNISM couldn't completely mar the beauty of Odessa. Her cobble-stone streets and architecture reflected an old world charm that blended both Russian and European influences. In stark contrast to that evocative allure, to the west, on the edge of town, the coastline gave way to a variety of restaurants, cafes and a vibrant nightlife. It was a concession to a new generation of Eastern Europeans, but closer to the city's business district and above the port itself, life was far more sedate.

Neill drank in the beauty of the evening as he walked along the tree-lined boulevards that led back to the hotel. In the distance was the opera house, with its big reflecting pool; then the park, and beyond that the Potemkin Steps. Above him, the limbs of the sycamores had been strung with lights that twinkled in the breeze blowing up from the waterfront. It projected a magical look that had inspired romantics for generations. Michael wasn't the only one enjoying the evening. At one end of the boulevard, he could see a family walking with their children. A little closer, two young lovers walked hand in hand, laughing as they passed the Pushkin memorial, then stopping to share a kiss.

The weather had improved and Michael didn't mind being out in it. The crisp air even felt good as it filled his lungs. It had been a long day, made even more so by having dinner with the Ulyanovs at their apartment. Irina had prepared one of her signature meals and made sure to monitor Neill's progress in consuming it. She wasn't satisfied that he was full until after he'd eaten a slice of cake and drank two cups of tea. Michael didn't mind. It was good to be mothered again.

Neill entered the hotel and nodded to the receptionist behind the desk. The university student who worked the night shift smiled and nodded back.

"Any messages for me, Anton?"

The young man shook his head. "Nothing tonight, Mr. Neill."

Michael bounded up the stairs—the elevator was too slow, and besides, after the heavy meal he felt he could use the exercise—and made his way to his room on the second floor. He let himself in and powered up his laptop, then checked his email. A few came from the IOI office; one was a personal message from Sergeant Arrens, wishing him a pleasant stay while he was in Odessa. He replied to that one first, keeping it brief and then re-reading his response carefully before sending it. His last message came from the office of Willis Avery via the SIPRNet—the Secret Internet Protocol Router. That one was encrypted, as were many classified government communiques, and was filtered through a secure server on Avery's end.

Neill accessed the decryption software that enabled him to open the file. It was a short read—Avery wanted a progress report. Michael filled a glass with ice and poured a ginger ale from the mini-bar, then sat down to compose a reply.

He listed the facts as concisely as he could. Neill had clued Avery in on the missing warhead the same day he'd found out about it. There wasn't much more he could add to that. He did bring him up to speed on their plan to get the district authorities to look for 'misplaced' military vehicles. Neill ended the message by promising to let him know the minute things changed.

Michael shut down the computer and looked at the clock. It was 9:30. He decided to take a shower before turning in and was on his way to the bathroom when the phone on the night stand began to ring.

The digital display told him the call was being routed from the front desk, but nothing more. Despite that, he had a feeling he knew who the caller might be.

"Michael—please, don't hang up." It was Viktoriya. She sounded a little breathless.

Neill smiled to himself. The Colonel had been right—she was a very persistent woman. "Hello, Viktoriya," he answered calmly. "What a surprise. I was just talking about you earlier this afternoon. How are you?"

She wasn't sure how to take that, but on the other end, Viktoriya relaxed a little. "I'm well, thanks. I hope I didn't wake you." His voice sounded so—*pleasant.*

"Not at all. What can I do for you?"

There were a host of answers she would have preferred to that question, but she knew she'd have to respond carefully. She drew in a breath and made herself relax. *Why did she feel so nervous?* She'd done thousands of interviews over the course of her short but meteoric career and rarely felt the sense of anxiety she was experiencing right now. Why was this so different?

"I wanted to apologize, Michael," she said slowly, injecting every bit of the sincerity she felt into her words. "I behaved … well, *arrogantly* when we first met. I disrespected you, and I'm sorry. Truly I am." She was surprised by how much better she felt.

For a fleeting moment, Neill wondered if this was a ploy to get him to let down his guard, then decided to give her the benefit of the doubt. "Apology accepted."

"Perhaps I can make it up to you."

"What did you have in mind?" It occurred to Neill that since the moment they'd met, it had been a continuous—although somewhat playful—exercise in determining Viktoriya's real motives.

"You're a guest in our country," she continued. "You deserve to be treated like one. And besides, I'd like to redeem myself. Prove to you that I'm not a horrible person."

She heard him laugh softly on the other end. "You're hardly that, Viktoriya. You were just doing your job. And as far as being a *guest*, I've always felt more like a native, but I see your point."

"Then maybe you and I could have dinner together. It's the least I could do. And I promise—no interviews." She hoped she was getting through to him. "Are you free tomorrow night?"

"Afraid not," Neill replied. "I have a previous engagement—I'll be attending the opera." Then, after a pause, "How about Friday?

"It's a date. How well do you know Odessa?"

"I've only visited here once before. Can you recommend a good restaurant?"

"Leave that to me," Viktoriya answered. "Six o'clock?"

"Six is fine," Neill replied. He considered giving her his cell number, then decided against it. The resourceful young woman knew how to reach him. "Give me a call in a day or two. We'll iron out the details."

"I'll do that," she promised.

Viktoriya ended the call, then pulled out a notepad and started a list. Friday would be no problem. But tomorrow night—

She looked at her watch. Almost ten o'clock—too late to call about tickets. That annoyed her, but there was nothing she could do about it now so she shook it off. There would be time enough to call in the morning when the box office opened—she hoped.

Viktoriya hurried to her wardrobe and began a quick inventory of everything on the rack. She found the dress she was looking for—and her black clutch would do nicely— then looked for the pearl necklace she kept in the armoire's jewelry box along with a pair of matching earrings. *Perfect,* she thought with a smile.

She gave the dress a once over and then carefully laid it on the bed. She tried to remember the last time she wore it. The gown had been designed with a tasteful but somewhat revealing split that ran up one side, just above the knee. Viktoriya smiled to herself. Elegance and distraction had served her well in the past.

Next, she selected the jewelry and arranged it on the bureau. Then back to the wardrobe, where she bit her lip and frowned when she discovered that not a single pair of shoes matched the ensemble. That simply wouldn't do. She'd need just the right pair, possibly stilettoes, something to give her a little more height without being too ostentatious. And she'd need a wrap, or some kind of jacket or coat that would go with the dress.

It was all coming together, but if Viktoriya Gavrilenko was going to the opera, she'd have to do some shopping first.

Chapter Eighteen ✶ Malyev's Revenge

IVAN SLEPT FITFULLY THAT NIGHT CROUCHED in the back of the car, waking just before dawn with the strongest sensation of hunger he could remember in quite some time. His cold, uncomfortable surroundings might have deprived him of sleep, but they hadn't dulled his appetite.

He sat up and rubbed the fatigue from his eyes, then pulled his tall frame out of the car to stretch his legs. Ivan was far from the main highway, the Lada parked in the tree line next to a winding dirt road that apparently led nowhere. Somehow, that seemed very fitting.

The forest was very quiet. Not even the sounds of the highway two miles distant reached his ears. Malyev retrieved his breakfast from the car, a bottle of water and some cheese and sausage he'd bought at a village during his trip, then built a fire to warm himself. Sparks and flames soon danced skyward, the small twigs and branches crackling as he consumed his meal. Ivan ate in silence, but the scent of burning wood caused a chill to run down his spine. He sat almost trance-like, staring at the flames and recalling the horror of the ambush only four days earlier.

The gentle rush of the wind moving softly through the trees overhead would have been soothing in another time and place. Malyev took no solace in it, nor even noticed. In spite of the sleep deprivation—or maybe because of it—he had tuned out everything until only the sound of Sasha's voice filled his troubled mind.

"Do you realize how easy it would be, Ivan?"

He chewed his food thoughtfully, realizing now that Sasha had had the right idea, but for all the wrong reasons.

Kobrin saw the bomb as the ultimate political weapon, an instrument capable of manipulating entire governments, if properly used. Malyev agreed with that viewpoint but saw something more.

Ivan saw the bomb as a means of achieving not only political goals but personal ones as well. He was a mercenary, but deep down he truly believed that restoring the Soviet Union to its former glory was a worthy cause.

It was at that point that his desire for revenge and the needs of Mother Russia seemed to conflict. He knew that if the bomb was detonated in Odessa, the short term result would be chaos—for the entire Commonwealth. He justified it by taking a much broader perspective.

The Kremlin had seized upon the death of the two terrorists and the capture of their camp by portraying the Russian federation as the savior of the republics. Malyev sneered to himself as he realized that while Major Pirogov was not a politician, his handlers were. Men like General Karpenko—and probably President Murovanka as well, he decided—had manipulated the situation perfectly. Short of some catastrophic event the republics would continue to look toward Moscow for protection.

Let them, Ivan thought.

Major Pirogov didn't know about the bomb. Karpenko and Murovanka didn't either, and everyone thought Malyev was dead.

Put together, the unknown information about the warhead and the false assumptions of his former superiors gave Ivan the edge he needed.

Of course, detonating the bomb would work against reuniting the republics under Moscow's control, but it would make the present government in Russia look powerless to stop the acts of terrorism. Murovanka's administration would suffer politically, and if Ivan were around after the blast to point the finger at Pirogov, his vengeance would be complete.

It was decided, then. Malyev would cross the border into Ukraine, travel back to Odessa and arm the warhead. The detonator he and Sasha had installed in the device had a programmable one-hour delay, which would give him just enough time to escape the blast—if he hurried.

The early morning darkness began to give way to the rising sun and Malyev stood and reached into the car for the map. The border checkpoint—manned by Ukrainian militiamen—lay just two kilometers to the south.

But before traveling back into Ukraine, there was one person he still needed to see—someone who could give him shelter and meals for just a few more days. Besides that, there was something he needed to retrieve. The map told him his next destination wasn't far at all. He would need his wits about him and his current fatigue prevented that. His plan could wait until he got a little more food and rest.

Malyev pulled his pistol, making sure for the hundredth time that the weapon was fully loaded, then got into the car and started the engine. If everything went according to plan, he could be in Odessa in just a few days.

* * * *

"What's next on the agenda?"

Captain Yaroslav stretched as Neill consulted his clipboard. It was nearly lunchtime at the station and the two officers had gotten a late start today. Michael had invited Dmitri to a morning run; the Captain reluctantly agreed—mainly in the interests of furthering 'international relations'—but it was clear he wasn't thrilled by the idea.

Neill and Yaroslav made use of a track that ran along the perimeter of the fence. After the run, Michael was surprised to find that the station had a fully equipped fitness center, complete with showers. The two men got cleaned up and back into uniform, then proceeded to check off more items on Neill's to-do list—which was growing shorter by the day. Making their way through the disassembly bays, Michael couldn't help but notice that the morning run had left the good Captain with a few aches and pains.

"How's the arm?" Michael had almost forgotten the injury inflicted by Mayakovsky. He felt a little guilty about suggesting the morning PT session.

Dmitri rotated his arm and shoulder, but felt no pain. The wound was healing nicely. "It's fine," he answered, then repeated "What's next on your list?"

"Let's go over your safety protocols for lower yield warheads. After that—"

Neill stopped when he saw Colonel Ulyanov stepping into the bay. He found that unusual—the Colonel hadn't been down on this level since he and Yaroslav gave Michael his initial tour of the facility. Clearly something was up.

"Are you two just about finished?" Ulyanov asked.

"Finished?" Neill's curiosity was piqued. The day wasn't even half over. "We still have a few items to go over, but for the most part—"

"Excellent," the Colonel said. "Wrap things up and get ready to go. We're leaving early today."

Even Captain Yaroslav seemed puzzled now. "Early?"

Ulyanov nodded enthusiastically. "Tonight's the Opera. We need to prepare."

Neill looked at his watch. "That's not till later this evening."

"I'm under strict orders, Michael." The Colonel's tone conveyed a sense of exaggerated gravity. "My commanding officer is rather insistent; culture takes precedence over affairs of state." He paused. "At least sometimes."

"Your commanding officer?" Dmitri asked.

Michael recognized Ulyanov's flair for the dramatic. He realized the senior officer was being facetious. "Are you referring to Irina?"

Ulyanov drew himself up to his full height and adopted a rather dignified look. "There are times when they are one and the same, gentlemen." Then he broke into a smile. "And I would never confuse my rank with her authority."

Irina Ulyanov had prepared a light but varied lunch. Her pantry was typically Ukrainian; she had smoked meats and a good supply of vegetables, many of those pickled and sitting on the shelves in jars. Much of the food was salted, or preserved in ways that didn't require refrigeration. Irina had lived long enough to remember the days when markets routinely ran out of food, so she had always relied on produce grown in her own garden.

Many Westerners complained that Ukraine wasn't known for its cuisine. It was true that some of the more common meals tended to be bland, but that only reflected the reality of food shortages and the harsh poverty endured by so many in the country. Most Ukrainian families simply did the best they could with what they had, supplementing their diet with a heavy reliance on dumplings, soups, pastries and bread.

Irina served borscht first, followed by *varenyky* and *perohy*—dumplings filled with cheese; and small pastries stuffed with meat and onions—then a meat goulash was placed before the men to round out the meal. As always, Irina set an exquisite table. The open air market she frequented had been fully stocked that day. While the meal was heavy in carbs and calories, it provided the necessary fuel a body needed.

Michael didn't mind. Like Captain Yaroslav and the Colonel, he'd grown up on meals just like this and came to miss them when he'd left Ukraine eight years earlier. Tasting Irina's cooking brought back fond memories.

"Eat hearty, gentlemen," the Colonel admonished Michael and Dmitri. "Irina has been cooking all morning and warned me that the kitchen will not be open for dinner."

"Where is Irina?" Neill asked. He'd seen her bring the

bowls and plates into the dining room, but she disappeared after that.

"She's making some final adjustments to her dress," Ulyanov answered, then in a quieter voice, "It seems that it's gotten a little smaller with misuse."

Michael and Dmitri nodded knowingly but said nothing. Somehow it just didn't seem appropriate.

"What about you, Michael?" the Colonel asked. "Did you bring your dress uniform?"

Neill swallowed a mouthful of bread before answering. "I did. But I thought I might wear my winter greens tonight. Less showy."

Ulyanov frowned. "The ones you wore on the plane? *Pah!*" Clearly he disapproved. "It's a fine uniform, don't get me wrong. But your dress blues—"

Michael shrugged in surrender. "All right. Dress blues it is." Yaroslav watched the exchange with mild amusement.

The Colonel thumped the table and nodded. "It's settled, then. After lunch, we'll sit down to tea and then later my car will take you back to the hotel so you can change."

The next few hours passed slowly. The three officers cleared away the dishes from the table, then retired to the front room to enjoy tea and coffee. Irina flitted in and out, most of the time carrying her dress, scissors and various other items of evening wear from room to room while directing her husband to give his full attention to a variety of last minute yet completely domestic duties. At least twice Michael heard her ask the Colonel if he still had the tickets for the performance. Yaroslav stepped out to give the security detail instructions regarding the night's itinerary. Neill got up and joined him, deciding it was best to stay out of his hosts' way. After passing the word, Dmitri and Michael went downstairs and exited the building to get some fresh air, while Oleg and Pavel regarded Neill with a suspicious look.

Michael couldn't help but notice. "I don't think they like

me, Dmitri," he remarked in a quiet voice.

Yaroslav chuckled. "We're a cautious people, Michael. And it's not *their* job to trust *anyone*." His expression darkened a little. "If I'd had that same attitude—"

Neill knew where he was going with that. "You blame yourself for the theft of the warhead?"

Dmitri had a faraway look in his eye. "Occasionally. Sometimes more so than others."

Michael shook his head and took in the view of downtown Odessa. The afternoon sun cast a golden hue on the buildings up and down the boulevard. Half a block away, he could see the car with the rest of Ulyanov's security detail.

"That's not your fault, Dmitri. And you did everything you could to stop that from happening."

"I often tell myself the same thing."

Michael suddenly had a stare all his own. "It is odd."

"What's that?" Yaroslav asked.

"We're going to the opera—and somewhere out there is a missing nuke."

"We'll find it, Michael. Put it out of your mind for one evening." The Captain looked at his watch, then turned slowly to re-enter the building. "Let's go back upstairs and give Corporal Sevnik a call. It's time to get you back to your hotel."

The Londonskaya was only a few blocks away. Neill could have walked the distance easily, but Captain Yaroslav insisted he make use of the car. He reluctantly agreed and Dmitri made the call.

Michael left the Ulyanovs apartment on a happy note. Irina was beaming; the alterations to her dress had been successful. The Colonel was also in a jovial mood; he was careful to hide it, but he seemed just as happy about his wife's skills as a seamstress.

Back at the hotel, the desk clerk flagged Michael down as he moved through the lobby on his way to the stairs. As he crossed the floor, he subconsciously looked left and right. He wasn't about to let someone escape his peripheral vision again.

"Message for you, Mr. Neill." Michael stepped up to the desk and Anton handed him an envelope.

"Did you see who left it?"

Anton shook his head. "Came in before my shift." Then he grinned. "You could always open it."

"Brilliant idea," Michael replied.

The back of the envelope wasn't fully sealed, making it easy to open. Inside was a piece of folded stationary, and a fragrance— just a hint of lavender. The words on the page were written in a woman's hand—and the missive was unsigned.

"What does it say?" Anton was the curious type and momentarily forgot his manners.

Neill didn't mind telling him. "It says, *'Enjoy the Opera.'*" He slipped the note into his pocket and headed for the stairwell.

"But who sent it?" Anton wanted details, but Neill had already disappeared.

Once in his room, Michael changed out of his clothes and powered up his laptop. There were a few emails waiting for him, but not one from Avery, and nothing that couldn't wait. He shut down the machine and went to the wardrobe.

Three little words. 'Enjoy the Opera.' Clearly the message had been left by Viktoriya. Was there some veiled significance to what she'd written? Neill considered what he'd read in the note as he pulled a sealed garment bag from the rack. Inside was his dress uniform. He removed it and laid it on the bed, checking the placement of the insignia as well as the ribbon rack over the left breast pocket. Satisfied that everything was in order, he dusted off his patent leather shoes and examined the white officer's cover that rounded out the set of blues.

If there *was* some hidden meaning to the note, Michael couldn't fathom what it might be. He decided to take Dmitri's advice one step further and put the warhead *and* Viktoriya Gavrilenko out of his mind for just one evening.

Chapter Nineteen ✳ Reunion

URING WORLD WAR II THE CITY OF KURSK
had been the location for the largest armored battle
in the history of warfare. Crews manning the famed
T-34 battle tank waged a savage assault against German
troops and thwarted the Nazis in that southern part of Russia.
In modern times, the Soviet Union—and now the Russian
republic—depended on the region for its vast iron ore depos-
its and designated the city as an administrative hub. It was
also home to the Kursk State University and Agricultural
Center.

Ivan Malyev squinted as he drove the Lada west into the
setting sun. He passed the Tuskar River—one of three in
the area, and the site of a new hydroelectric dam—as he approached the old Khalino Air Base. An interceptor squadron
had once been stationed there, but had been disbanded and
replaced by another. Ivan looked out across the open expanse
of the airfield and could make out several MiG-29s parked
on the ramp. He smiled to himself; the area was beginning to
look familiar to him. But while the base was useful as a landmark—it had been a few years since he'd been there—that
was not his destination.

Malyev found the University in short order, then turned
onto a parkway that led to faculty and student housing not far
from the campus. He slowed the car's pace as he compared

the street names to an address he carried on a slip of paper in his wallet. Ivan had arrived just as many of the institute's professors and staff ended their classes and were returning home. They came and went between buildings, bundled against the cold and paying no attention to him.

The car traveled several blocks, chugging exhaust that hung in clouds over the patchy ice on the road. In the heart of the community he found what he was looking for. An incline led up the hill to a four story building and Malyev gunned the motor to get a little traction as he steered the Lada toward it. He found an empty spot on the street, away from the other vehicles, and parked, letting the engine idle. Ivan wanted to keep the heater going for a few more minutes while he decided on his next course of action. A glance at the gas gauge told him it was a luxury he could afford—but only for a brief time.

His timing couldn't have been better. A familiar figure came into view, and even wearing heavy clothing, Ivan recognized his gait. He lit a cigarette and then stepped out of the car and started walking.

By Western standards, the buildings would have been described as urban blight. None of them were really very old; less than twenty years in some cases. But construction in the former Soviet Union rarely stood the test of time—or the elements. Building materials were shoddy at best. With the collapse of communism, not even the government took an interest in maintaining the basic infrastructure. And in a society where the state had provided everything, individual initiative was almost unheard of—if the state didn't care, then who could blame the farmer, the laborer, or the factory worker?

Boris Stefanovich Kobrin was just such a man. He was a soldier once. After leaving the Army he enrolled at the University, getting a two year degree. At graduation, he found a job working in the agricultural department, in the hydroponics wing. And along the way, he managed to keep a few secrets.

Kobrin's gloved hand was clumsy, but he managed to thrust his key into the lock on the front door of his apartment. There he paused. From behind him, he heard the crunch of someone's footsteps in the thin layer of snow. Something about the presence he sensed caused the hairs to stand up on the back of his neck. He stood motionless, then heard a voice call his name.

Boris didn't have to look to know who it was. He recognized the voice immediately, but was surprised to hear it. He turned the key, then withdrew it, gripped the knob and pushed on the door. As it swung open, a wave of sadness welled up inside of him.

He turned to face his visitor. Standing beyond the sidewalk, Ivan looked a little heavier than Boris remembered. He had just a touch of gray at his temples and now wore the beginnings of a beard. Kobrin thought he looked tired.

The two stared at each other for what seemed like a long time. With the wind in his face, Malyev's eyes began to water and he blinked as he sized up his old friend. For his part, Kobrin looked to the left and right, then over Ivan's shoulder. When he did speak, his words seemed to catch in his throat.

"Is my brother here as well?"

Ivan said nothing at first, shifting on his feet. He regarded Boris for a few seconds more, then a softer look spread across his face.

"We should talk."

Boris understood, and then nodded slowly. The news broadcasts were true—about Sasha, at least. He feared as much.

The awkward moment passed and the two old comrades stepped toward each other and embraced.

The water was almost hot enough to pour from the *samovar* into the tea cups. Boris laid bags of black tea into each one. Ivan sat at the kitchen table, rubbing warmth back into his hands, then watched as his host adjusted the furnace.

"How did Sasha die?" Kobrin asked.

Malyev took a deep breath. "It was Pirogov."

There was a pause. "Go on," Boris replied. The news didn't seem to faze him.

"He and his men shot us out of the sky." Ivan winced at the memory. "He died instantly. There was no pain." He thought it best to reassure him; it might lessen the shock.

Boris nodded silently. He took a potholder and poured the steaming water into the cups. "We'll let those steep for a moment." His voice sounded very detached. He pulled out a chair and sat across from Malyev. "And what of you? You were unhurt?"

"Minor cuts and bruises." Truth be told, his ribs were still a little tender.

"I won't ask what you were doing," Kobrin said. "I don't really want to know. But if the Major was involved—"

"Yes," Ivan growled. "The Major was involved. I watched him at his press conference. So smug and righteous."

"I saw it too," Boris replied. "It's been in the papers as well. Which is why I was very surprised to see you."

Malyev wore a sardonic expression. "I can't explain what happened. Why I'm here and Sasha isn't."

"I think I can," Boris said. He got up and retrieved their tea from the counter by the stove. Then he said very simply, "It's Providence."

At first Ivan thought he was just expressing some dark humor. But Kobrin's face betrayed no emotion. He was confused; Boris had never been the type to attribute anything to the actions of the supernatural. He was about to dismiss the comment when Boris continued.

"Clearly it was an act of God." He sat the cups down carefully on the table between them, placing a spoon in each one. "Every man has an appointment with death, Ivan." There was a calm resolve in his voice. "It was Sasha's time."

Malyev watched him curiously as he stirred his tea. He laid the spoon on the table and took a sip. It was still too hot.

"You think God had something to do with Sasha being dead?" Ivan felt something like anger washing over him. "That was Pirogov's doing. And his masters in Moscow. If there is a God, why didn't he save your brother?"

"You misunderstand me, Ivan," Boris said. "It was God's hand that spared you. He could have done the same for Sasha; but *you* were chosen to live."

Was this the same man? "I was 'chosen?'" he repeated. "Chosen for what?"

Boris shook his head. "I can't answer that. All I can tell you is that nothing happens that isn't first sifted through His will."

Ivan was staring again. "What has happened to you?"

"It's a long story." Boris sipped his tea. Maybe later there would be time to talk about the Ukrainian pastor he'd met six months earlier. "There have been many changes since we last spoke, *tavarisch*. And there are some things that I can no longer be a part of."

"Can you be a part of giving me food and shelter?" Ivan sneered. The anger was real now. "There were many times when you helped Sasha and I. Was that God's will, or has that changed too?"

Boris said nothing. Ivan was beginning to think he'd come to the wrong man for help. During the past eighteen months, Boris had been their silent partner; their designated contact in southern Russia. He was of like mind with Ivan and Sasha, with a deep hatred of the West, and disgust in his heart over what his country had become. The three served together in the Army as combat engineers. Pirogov had recruited them for their special skills and training with ordnance. While Sasha and Ivan were the operators, Boris played a more subdued role. He was the one who stayed in the background, channeling funds, information and the occasional weapon needed to pressure whomever their target might happen to be. But as time went by, their dependence on the Major grew and they relied less on Boris for help. Now everything had changed;

Sasha was dead, Ivan was essentially on the run and Boris had apparently experienced some kind of religious epiphany.

For Malyev, the turn of events was frustrating, to say the least. It was time to shift gears.

"All right," Ivan said tiredly. "Forget all of that. I just need rest, and some food, something to take with me." Then, almost as an afterthought, one of the main reasons for his trip there came to mind. "And the package—do you still have it?"

Boris gave a nod. "I can feed you a meal tonight, Ivan. Give you a place to sleep. But that's as far as I go. I can't do it anymore. God has forgotten my past. I'm willing to let it go, too." His voice was quiet and he spoke slowly. His tea cup was empty. "And yes—I still have the package. I must admit, when I heard that you and Sasha were dead, I considered opening it." He stood up from his chair and shuffled through a stack of magazines and papers lying on a shelf above the sink. When he came back to the table, he carried a manila envelope in his hand. He laid it on the table next to Ivan.

Boris had guessed at its contents when he received it in the mail. Ivan had sent it to him for safekeeping. Sasha and Ivan were careful men who watched their backs and planned for unexpected contingencies. Pirogov fell squarely into that category. Malyev had wisely taken every opportunity to document the Major's involvement in their subversive acts—just in case he betrayed them later. As it turned out, his precautions were more than warranted.

"What will you do with it?" Boris asked. "Everyone thinks you're dead. If you come forward now, with this ..." He tapped the envelope with his fingertips. "Then the game will be over. So you have a choice to make, Ivan; do you step out of the shadows, shine a light on Pirogov's actions and risk your life? Or will you continue to let them think they've killed you?" He shook his head again. "Neither prospect guarantees you much of a future."

"And what would you have me do, Boris?" Malyev slid the envelope under his arm as it rested on the table. "Turn myself in? Trust in God to protect me?" He couldn't tell Boris that too much had happened for him to go down that path. And he'd come here for help, not a confessor. "They'd lock me in a cage and throw away the key. Or worse."

This was going nowhere. He stood slowly to his feet. "I won't trouble you any further, old friend. It's quite plain that my presence here has offended your newfound morality." His tone was heavy with sarcasm. "Just give me some food and I'll be on my way."

"And where will you go?"

Ivan considered his words before speaking. "South," he said simply. His answer was obscure enough to give Boris some measure of culpability.

"And don't tell me that you'll pray for me."

It was an awkward goodbye. Boris provided a bag with some bread, cheese, and a few other items he had on hand, then Ivan silently headed for the door. For his trip into Ukraine, sandwiches would have to do. He entertained the idea of stopping at some café or restaurant along the way, but he wanted to reach his destination with a minimum of human contact. Stepping outside, he noticed the weather had turned cold again. Night had fallen, and the faculty campus was now lit intermittently by the street lights that still worked. Ivan started to cross the snow toward the car, then paused and turned.

Boris stood leaning in the doorway, his hands shoved in his pockets. Both men wondered if they would ever see each other again.

"Just remember something, Boris. You may think you've found God, or that He found you. But that doesn't change the past. If you report me to the militia, you'll have some explaining to do of your own."

Ivan expected some kind of reply, but nothing else was said. He walked back to the car with the food under his arm and his breath trailing behind him.

Malyev needed two things. The first was fuel for the Lada. That was easy enough. The next was rest, and if he wanted that he couldn't spend another night in the back seat of the car. He decided to risk checking into a hotel. Those were his short-term plans. Beyond that, he didn't have a clue. Eventually he'd have to formulate a more long-range strategy, but for now he was curiously ambivalent about the future.

There was a gas station on the road leading back to the highway. He checked his wallet, and with plenty of cash, he stopped the car and filled the tank. The station attendant didn't give him a second glance and within minutes he was back on the road again headed south toward the border.

Chapter Twenty ✶ A Night at the Opera

IRINA LOOKED STUNNING IN HER GOWN AND Michael told her so. For most of his life, Neill had known her to be guarded—almost aloof—with her emotions, but on this evening she accepted his compliment with a blush and seemed more relaxed. She struck a regal pose, then stepped forward to squeeze Michael's cheek. The Colonel quietly admired his wife. She seemed as thin as the day they were married, and he had a hard time believing the dress she now wore would have required alterations of any kind.

Michael wore his blues, complete with a boat cloak, which he'd removed and draped across a chair. Ulyanov was decked out in his dress uniform as well. His own waistline had been the benefactor of Irina's cooking through the years, but he still cut a dashing figure. Apart from the array of medals and ribbons dangling from his chest, it was only slightly different from the uniform he wore on a daily basis. Captain Yaroslav was similarly dressed in the garb of the Strategic Rocket Forces, with bright red piping, several medals of his own, and a large visored cap that he held at his side.

"One might think we're stepping out for the evening," Dmitri remarked. "We should take a picture."

Neill fished out his cell phone. "I came prepared."

Apart from the Potemkin Steps, the Opera House was the most well-known landmark in Odessa. The first iteration of the structure had burned to the ground back in the 1870s, but was rebuilt more than a decade later. Its unique architecture and new-baroque look intrigued the eye. Over the years, the theater had received half a dozen renovations to improve its appearance—in addition to shoring up its structural integrity.

Beyond the Italian façade with its colonnades lay the foyer hall. Richly decorated, this part of the building encircled the theater's oval main floor and also housed the box office, cloakroom and a host of uniquely placed exits—with its unfortunate history of fire, and the memory of war still fresh in the minds of the architects, two dozen were placed around the perimeter of the Opera House.

The foyer itself gave theater-goers a hint of its rich past and the promise of a cultural experience that beckoned from the stage. Spaced equal distances apart, and tucked into niches, were busts of famous Russian and Ukrainian playwrights and poets that had shaped Eastern European literature. Gilded figurines and extravagantly rendered oil paintings decorated the rest of the interior.

On this particular evening, the theater was well lit, inside and out. Electric lamps, designed to resemble the gas-lit versions of a previous age, ringed the building's exterior and gave the Opera House an old world glow. The four members of Ulyanov's party arrived just as these were illuminated. Corporal Sevnik drove the group to the foyer's main entrance and slowed to a stop. Neill couldn't tell where they'd appeared from, but suddenly Oleg and Pavel were opening the car doors so the Colonel could exit the vehicle and assist Irina. As she stepped onto the curb, the cold night air caught her breath as much as the beauty of the hall and she clutched the wrap that draped her shoulders a little more tightly.

Michael was also impressed. The whole setting was like a scene out of a movie. They'd arrived early, but several other patrons had begun showing up, dressed to the nines and making their way to the entryway. Neill's impeccably turned out uniform caught the attention of several guests—especially the women.

A doorman in tails greeted them as he ushered the group inside. The foyer was warm and lavishly appointed, trimmed in scarlet and gold—the colors of the Corps, Michael noted—with one of the thickest carpets Neill could ever remember setting foot on. The cloakroom was doing a steady business tonight. The four waited their turn to deposit their uniform caps, Neill's cloak and Irina's shawl. As far as they could tell, the three officers were the only patrons representing the armed forces, a distinction that attracted further regard.

Groups of people gathered in clusters; some in evening dress, but many were more casually attired. It was evident that not everyone attending the evening's performance could be described as being among the very rich; in fact, most were far from it. Michael attributed the variety in turn-out to a dynamic of society that was almost unique to Europeans; tickets were cheap—culture was encouraged, and made easily accessible by its affordability.

"Prepare yourself, Michael," Ulyanov said, leaning in to make himself heard among the din of the growing crowd. "Stepping into the auditorium is like a treat for the soul."

Neill immediately understood what he meant as they moved from the foyer through the hand-carved doors and into the main hall. More of the scarlet and gold motif continued inside, from the plush carpeting to the exquisite mahogany woodwork that ran from floor to ceiling. High above them, the domed ceiling was a canvas of fresco work straight from the world of Louis the XVI. The main chandelier hung directly in the center of the room, with boxes spaced evenly on three floors. The seats on the ground level were upholstered with a fabric that matched the deep scarlet found elsewhere in the theater.

"Breathtaking," Michael announced. "Absolutely breath-taking."

The Colonel took in the view and squeezed Irina's hand. "It's like stepping back in time, don't you think?"

Neill found the analogy an accurate one. "Any spot in this building would seem like the best seat in the house."

Ulyanov pulled the ticket stubs from his pocket. "That's quite true—the acoustics here are spectacular. Of course, it was designed before modern sound systems." He smiled at Irina, a glow in his eye. "We have a Grand Tier box on the second floor, Michael. But I wanted you to see the stage from this level first."

On the way back through the foyer, Captain Yaroslav picked up four programs for the performance. The group had almost arrived at the foot of the staircase when a familiar face caught Neill's eye. He slowed his pace to get a better look.

"Uh-oh," he managed.

Ulyanov saw the odd expression on Michael's face. "Is something wrong?"

"I'm not sure," he answered. "Take a look."

There were few faces that Neill had grown accustomed to during his brief visit in Ukraine, so he was understandably thrown off a bit when he recognized this one. Strolling through the door was Viktoriya Gavrilenko, appearing very stunning in a black dress and heels. Michael couldn't help but take in the view, as did just about every other male in the room. She wore a matching wrap, removing it as she came in from the cold and began to cross the floor to the cloakroom. She smiled at the attendant, trading the garment for a receipt, then turned and pulled a ticket from her clutch. If she'd noticed them, she didn't let on.

"Is that her?" the Colonel asked.

Michael nodded. "That's her."

Dmitri stood at Neill's side. "Did I hear you use the word

'breathtaking' a moment ago?"

"You did indeed," Michael replied. "But I was talking about the theater."

Irina recognized Viktoriya from the papers and was no longer content to remain silent. "Ignoring a woman alone in an opera house is bad manners." She touched Neill's arm. "Be a gentleman and introduce us, Michael."

At that moment Viktoriya glanced up and in their direction. The smile she wore widened, and she waited as Michael walked toward her with the Colonel, Irina and Dmitri following him.

"Viktoriya Gavrilenko," Neill said in greeting. He reached out to take her hand. "May I be the first to say that you look absolutely beautiful tonight?"

The young woman blushed, but kept her eyes on the Marine in a beguiling way. "Thank you, Michael." Viktoriya reached out and ran her fingertips down the sleeve of his uniform. She was reciprocal in her appreciation of Neill's appearance. "You clean up pretty good yourself."

It was Michael's turn to blush. For a moment, the two seemed oblivious to anything else, until the Colonel cleared his throat.

"Forgive me," Neill turned to his friends. "May I present Irina Ulyanov, her husband, Colonel Andrei Ulyanov, and Captain Dmitri Yaroslav." Hopefully, he was following proper etiquette. "This is Viktoriya Gavrilenko."

It was Irina who spoke first. "I've read your articles, Miss Gavrilenko. You're to be congratulated." She smiled warmly and shook Viktoriya's hand, as did Ulyanov and Dmitri.

With the introductions out of the way, Michael continued. "You didn't mention that you'd be here this evening. We could have given you a ride."

"It wasn't a sure thing," Viktoriya explained. "I came by the box office early this morning and caught a break; there were a few cancellations, so I was able to get a voucher."

Neill reached out for her ticket stub. "May I?" He peered at the number, his fingers brushing against hers. "Looks like you have a seat in the main auditorium."

She seemed a little disappointed. "It was short notice; at the time, it was the only thing available."

"Maybe we can help you with an upgrade," the Colonel offered, looking at his wife. Irina appeared to have no objections and nodded in agreement.

"Our gallery box should have room for one more."

Neill liked the idea. "Sound good to you, Viktoriya?"

"That sounds wonderful," she answered, then turned to Ulyanov. "Thank you so much, Colonel." Then, "Your name sounds familiar. Are you based at the weapons station outside of town?"

The words escaped his lips before he even gave them a thought. "That's right; but how did you know—" He caught himself. She *hadn't* known and had used an old journalist's trick—she voiced her suspicion and waited for the Colonel to confirm it. *Very clever*, he mused. *And you fell for it …*

"I got your note," Neill said, his voice nearly a whisper. The group had made their way to the second floor and found their box. "You could have told me in person."

"I wasn't sure I would see you," Viktoriya replied.

Michael took his seat next to her. The little alcove was a bit more crowded with a fifth chair, but no one seemed to mind. "The envelope had a lavender scent. Your perfume?"

Again, her eyes held his and she smiled. "It's my favorite. Do you like it?"

Neill returned her smile but didn't speak. There were some things that didn't need saying.

There were other aspects to her appearance that slowly dawned on Neill as the two talked quietly. Aside from her dress—elegantly paneled in lace, finished with cross-over spaghetti straps in the back, with a bold neckline in the front—her long, dark hair shimmered in waves and framed her face and dark eyes. The pearl choker and other jewelry she wore only added to her beauty. She crossed her legs and introduced yet another distraction.

Dmitri seemed equally enchanted. Even the Colonel seemed slightly out of sorts because of her presence. But not Irina. She was under no pretenses as to Viktoriya's motives. Prodding Michael to introduce them was a concession to her own character as a lady; keeping the journalist close now was simply the reaction of a suspicious woman.

The small group in the box enjoyed several minutes of conversation—Viktoriya made a point of finding something to say to everyone—then the lights in the hall dimmed slightly, signaling the beginning of the performance. The orchestra quietly took their places below the stage and began a final check of their instruments, playing short snippets of music to ensure they were in tune. Neill settled back in the plush surroundings and drew in a deep breath. Attending the theater was just the distraction he needed tonight.

As the hall darkened, Michael turned his attention to the main floor below and watched as the curtains on the stage parted, revealing an elaborate set. The house was nearly full and the patrons in their seats welcomed the beginning of the production with sustained applause.

The opera was a three act performance by Puccini entitled *Turandot*. The story was set in Central Asia, and was based on a fairy tale about a prince named Calaf who falls in love with the title character. The setting made Michael think of Manas, Kyrgyzstan; and he tried to picture the story unfolding there long before the appearance of Soviet and American troops and the succession of wars that had troubled the region for over thirty years.

The *libretto* that accompanied the production was in Italian, a collaboration of several musicians, since Puccini died before the opera could be completed. Much of it was a little too high brow for Neill's tastes, but he found himself thoroughly entertained by the performance and noticed that the rest of the group were enjoying themselves as well—particularly the Colonel and Irina.

"What do you think?" Viktoriya leaned over and spoke into Neill's ear as the patrons stood, giving the cast a standing ovation.

"I think the evening is ending far too early," Neill answered.

Far below, the performers bowed in the face of the audience's adulation. After a few minutes of continued homage, the large, scarlet curtains were slowly drawn across the stage. With the opera's conclusion, the lights were raised and the buoyant crowds began to stir, some forming into groups for conversation, others moving toward the many exits that ringed the hall.

Colonel Ulyanov extended his arm to Irina, helping her up. With a grin on his face, it was obvious his spirits were high. He beamed at the rest of the party. "Shall we?"

The crowds had already thinned as they arrived at the foot of the staircase. Neill led the group, with Viktoriya walking closely at his side, as they passed an original 1926 poster advertising the production. Seeing the artwork gave Irina an idea.

"Time for a picture," she announced. She looked to Neill, who took out his cell phone.

The five took turns staging photos individually and as a group. Dmitri insisted on taking one of just Michael and Viktoriya together. The two were quite photogenic—the Marine in his uniform and she in her gown—and with the unique interior lighting, the images turned out far better than either of them expected.

The officers retrieved their uniform items and the ladies' wraps from the cloakroom. Dmitri called Corporal Sevnik on his cell and directed him to be ready with the car, and with that they strode through the exit and into the night.

Once outside, they huddled together for a little more conversation before the car arrived. When it did, Michael turned to Viktoriya, adjusting the cover on his head. The air was cold, but not bitterly so.

"Allow us to give you a lift," Neill offered.

She glanced at the group, then looked back into his eyes.

"The night is still young, Michael," she said softly. "Why don't we enjoy the evening a little longer?" She turned to the Colonel and Irina. "Please, you've been so kind already. Would you mind if I stole your Lieutenant for a while?"

For the Colonel—and especially Irina—this was not an altogether unexpected turn of events. "Not at all, young lady." Ulyanov gave Neill an expression that spoke volumes. "I'll have Corporal Sevnik pick you up tomorrow morning at the usual time; about six o'clock?" Of course, that was not the usual time at all and both men knew it. Michael smiled wanly and the look in his eye told the older officer that he'd received the intended message.

"We'll be fine," Neill assured him. "I'll see to it Miss Gavrilenko gets back to her—" He paused, then "Where do you live, Viktoriya?"

"I have a flat on the other side of town," she replied. "I'm sure that finding a cab won't be a problem."

"The Colonel was reluctant to leave you," Viktoriya remarked. She and Michael had bid the Ulyanovs and Dmitri good night, and drifted away from the crowds still gathered at the entrance to the opera house. Neill caught a glimpse of Oleg and Pavel shadowing his hosts, far enough away to blend into the background, but close enough to be at hand in a moment's notice. "You two seem like old friends. How long have you known him?"

Neill chuckled softly. "More questions. Always the journalist." They strolled past the reflecting pool by the theater garden, the faux gas-lamps mirrored in the still waters. "As I recall, you said there'd be no interviews tonight."

She was quick to correct him. "No—I said there'd be none for our date on Friday," she said with a smile.

Michael conceded the point. "You're right. And to answer your question, we go way back. The Colonel's an old family friend."

Viktoriya wore a quizzical look. "Then your visit here is personal and professional?"

His eyes met hers. They continued to walk. "That's an added bonus." He could tell there was more she'd like to know. "I'll make a deal with you."

She shivered a little in the cold. "I'm listening." The shawl she wore was fashionable, but did little to keep her warm.

Neill removed his boat cloak and draped it around Viktoriya's shoulders. The heavy garment hung nearly to her calves and was an immediate improvement—although it did obstruct the view.

"You can ask all the questions you want," Michael continued. "And I'll answer the ones that won't get both of us in trouble."

Viktoriya pulled her long hair from beneath the cloak's collar, letting it fall around her shoulders. Michael gave her a lingering look; the glow of the street lamps cast an almost magical aura to the curves of her face, giving her an even more compelling appearance. He found it hard to turn away and she noticed.

"You're staring, Michael," she smiled. "Do I remind you of someone—a woman you're in love with, perhaps?"

Neill raised an eyebrow. That was certainly direct. He could have answered that, but recognized it for what it was— another attempt to throw him off balance and get a response.

He returned her smile. "I'd say *no comment*, but that would be the easy way out."

"And so cliché." She hooked her arm in Michael's, clutching the cloak around her tightly and enjoying the comfort provided by both. "But I accept your terms."

"Good." The two were approaching the park, the Pushkin Memorial coming into view. The lights strung in the trees twinkled overhead. "Maybe we should talk about you for a change."

"I think you're much more interesting," she said softly. "And you haven't answered my question. Is there someone back home waiting for you to return?"

Neill paused to consider his response. "Why do you ask?"

"A woman always likes to know who she may be in competition with." She replied. "And I might add, if there is someone, she's very lucky." Neill caught her eye as she gave him an alluring look.

They took a few more steps before she spoke again. "I've always found American women to be so … *provincial*, wouldn't you say?"

Michael laughed. That was an easy one. "I disagree." He decided to turn the tables a little. "I can think of several who would defy that description. One in particular." He was thinking of his own mother. "Or maybe two," he said, amending his reply. "I think I could arrange for you to interview a few. If nothing else, I'm sure it would generate a healthy debate."

"*Touché,* Lieutenant." Viktoriya pulled Neill a little nearer. The cobble stone road was uneven, and in her heels she found it difficult to keep her balance. Besides that, it was a good reason to get closer. "I didn't mean to give offense."

"None taken," Neill countered. For the moment Viktoriya seemed disarmed.

"Tell me about your parents then," she went on. "Your life *here*; before you left for America. Surely that won't violate national security. " Her interest now seemed truly genuine.

Michael took in a deep breath. "That could take a while." He saw a bistro a few doors down. It was a popular spot for theater-goers after a performance. "Let's get something to eat first; I'm hungry."

She held his arm a little tighter. "So am I."

The little café—Pyotr's Shokolad was the name—had a few booths still available. Michael and Viktoriya sat down to a light, late evening meal. Coffee followed—with tea for her, then Neill paid the tab and they stepped out again to continue their stroll. A light breeze blew and the rustling of the branches above the boulevard ebbed and flowed. After a while, the couple lost all track of time.

They continued to walk and talk until the wind stiffened and the cold, night air became too much to bear, even with Michael's cloak wrapped around Viktoriya's shoulders. They found a cab parked at one end of the boulevard and she gave the driver her address. Neill wasn't comfortable sending her off on her own and offered to ride along to her flat. He wasn't surprised when she gave no resistance.

It was a ten minute trip to her apartment in a rather well to do district. Neill paid the fare and told the cabbie to wait, then escorted Viktoriya up the steps to the building's entryway.

She pulled off the cloak and placed it awkwardly around Neill's shoulders. Michael could see her breath in the air as she tugged on the fabric and worked to attach the clasp in the collar. She seemed to be taking her time. Michael just stared at the beautiful woman standing before him.

"Why don't you come up for a while, Michael?" she breathed, resting her hands on his shoulders. The cold only sharpened the scent of her perfume. She was nearly standing on tiptoe and Neill held her at the waist to steady her. "Send the cab away." Her expression was clearly an open invitation. "You can call another one later."

Michael had never seen a woman look at him quite like that before. This was certainly not how he imagined the night would end. Part of him realized that she was still after a story, but he sensed it was more than just that. Several possible scenarios played out in his head and more than one appealed to the flesh, but those would be out of character for him and might possibly impede his focus. Ultimately, he had a job to do. That had to take priority. He hadn't come to Ukraine to party.

Temptation, thy name is Woman. Neill took her hand and kissed it lightly, then shook his head. He didn't know it, but it was almost midnight. "I have an early morning ahead, Viktoriya." *Was that disappointment he saw in her face?* "But I'll see you on Friday."

She continued looking into his eyes. "I'm counting on it."

Michael gave her one last look, then turned and headed down the steps. He got into the car and glanced back in her direction. She stood on the landing, following his every movement, and then waved to him as the cab rolled away from the curb and back into the street.

The cabbie craned his neck as they pulled away, then smiled and looked at Neill in the rearview mirror. *Lucky man*, he thought. He'd watched them on the steps and saw the look she gave him. He couldn't imagine why this foreigner was back in his taxi. If it had been *him*—

"Where to?"

Neill blinked. "What's that?"

"Where would you like to go?" he repeated.

His passenger seemed distracted and for the briefest of moments, Michael had no idea how to answer him.

Chapter Twenty-One ★ Border Thief

" WHAT TIME DID YOU GET IN LAST NIGHT?"
Ulyanov looked worried as Michael pulled himself
into the seat next to him. Corporal Sevnik had brought
the car around at seven—not six, as the Colonel had stated
the night before. "Did you get any sleep?"

"Yes, *mati*." *Mother*. Neill couldn't resist the gentle rebuff,
but he said it with a smile on his face. He knew what the Colonel
was really asking. "Right after a cold shower." It was intended
as humor, but he wasn't kidding.

Ulyanov grinned knowingly. "I can imagine the reason for
that." Soon the sun would be peeking out over the city. The
Colonel hoped so; a freezing fog had settled over the area during the night. He pulled a small New Testament from his satchel
and flipped through some of the pages. "Have you done your
devotions this morning, Michael?"

"Hebrews. Chapter four. Verse 15. *'For we have not an high
priest which cannot be touched with the feeling of our infirmi-
ties; but was in all points tempted like as we are, yet without
sin.'*" Michael had memorized it as a child.

The Colonel found the passage in the little book.
"Appropriate," he said soberly.

Neill felt it was time to change the subject. "How about you?
Did you get any rest?"

The Colonel nodded. "The Opera always clears my mind

and makes my heart sing. Irina said I snored like a bear."

"So you went from singing to snoring," Michael observed. "Very poetic." In the front seat, Corporal Sevnik suppressed a grin. "Did that keep Irina awake?"

"No, Michael; *you* did that."

"Me?" Neill frowned.

"She was worried about you," Ulyanov explained. "She can be very protective, you know."

Neill was certain of that. Looking out the window, the landscape seemed unfamiliar. Sevnik was taking a different route today. Michael looked at the older officer questioningly.

"I thought we'd stop for breakfast this morning," Ulyanov explained. "We'll go in to the station a little later than usual."

"Really?" Michael found that a little out of the ordinary.

Ulyanov shrugged. "I told Dmitri to sleep in. We were out quite late last night."

"And yet you told me to be ready early," Neill protested. His tone suggested indignance; but this time he was kidding.

Again, a shrug. "I wanted to keep you mindful of your duties." Then he smiled. "Irina reminded me of something after you and Miss Gavrilenko went on your stroll."

"Oh?" Michael said. "And what was that?"

"Last night's production. It was a drama about a determined woman."

"A very strong-willed woman," Neill said, expanding the description. "One whose questions bore serious consequences—for those who answered incorrectly."

"*Ha!* So you *were* paying attention." The Colonel elbowed Neill softly in the ribs. "I told Irina you would figure it out."

Neill watched as the sleepy city rushed by, then yawned. "It did cross my mind."

* * * *

"Still no sign of infection?" She didn't expect any. Dr. Natalya Chekov looked over the patient's chart as the nurse made her report. Natalya was concerned, but no longer worried. She was old enough to remember when antibiotics were a luxury to many patients in Eastern Europe.

"No, Doctor," the nurse replied. She admired the genuine interest Dr. Chekov showed in all her patients. "His vital signs are normal. The wound is healing very nicely—should we continue to restrict his movements?"

Natalya bit her lip and examined his x-rays. A gunshot wound to the chest, especially one that had pierced the lung, was no routine injury. But there was no indication of further damage; the thoracic cavity showed no trauma—save for the bullet's entry point and the path it took into the patient's body. She had checked thoroughly for the presence of a hemo- or pneumothorax, but found none.

She glanced down the hall toward the patient's room. Sergei Goncharov would survive his encounter with Malyev and Kobrin—and the loss of blood he'd suffered.

"Yes. Keep the patient as still as possible," she replied. The patient was a strong young man and Natalya was a skilled physician, but she didn't want to take a chance by relaxing her caution just yet. When it came to gunshot wounds, that could be deadly.

The nurse shook her head. "Sergeant Goncharov won't like that a bit," she declared with mock gravity. "He's ready to go back out on patrol now."

"He will, in time. That's the problem with young people," Dr. Chekov said with a sigh. "You all think you're invincible. Is the good Sergeant unhappy with the care we've given him?"

"It's nothing like that," the nurse smiled. "I'm afraid he's just bored. Any suggestions?"

Natalya handed back the chart. "Give him something to read and tell him to be patient." She saw a folded newspaper lying on the desk at the nurses' station. "The morning edition has another article about those Russian terrorists—that should keep him occupied for a while, don't you think?"

The nurse glanced at the front page with disgust. She felt the media coverage of the incident during the past few days bordered on sensationalism. Nevertheless, this type of reading seemed tailor-made for the police officer in her care.

She picked up the paper and headed down the short hospital wing, looking at her watch as she walked. It was already nine a.m., and she wondered where the morning had gone.

* * * *

The sun was already up when Viktoriya awoke and stumbled out of bed. The events of the night before didn't seem real; then she saw her heels on the floor and her dress lying over the back of a chair and happily realized she hadn't been dreaming.

She moved sleepily to the kitchen and put some water on the stove. Tea was part of her normal morning ritual, but today she changed her mind and pulled a tin of instant coffee from the cupboard. A quick glance at the clock told her she still had more than an hour before she needed to leave for the office.

Despite getting in late, she'd slept surprisingly well. Then she smiled to herself. She would have gladly traded sleep for more time with Michael; but the young Lieutenant was a gentleman and she found him all the more appealing for what *hadn't* happened after he escorted her home. She was really looking forward to Friday now, and for more than just professional reasons.

Viktoriya washed her face and brushed her hair while the water on the stove boiled, then laid out her clothes for the day. A trip back into the kitchen followed, where she doctored her coffee with a little cream and sugar, then to the fridge for a bagel with cream cheese. She was eating her breakfast and watching the morning news when she had an idea.

Her stationery was right where she'd left it on the bureau. She jotted a quick note of thanks on one of the pages, tore out the sheet and scented it lightly with her perfume. Viktoriya folded it and slipped it into an envelope, then wrote Michael's name on the outside and put it into her purse.

The newspaper offices were only a mile or so from his hotel. What she had in mind wasn't in keeping with her style and bordered on being a little too aggressive; but if her schedule permitted, she planned on dropping by around lunch time and leaving the envelope for him at the desk. And as determined as Viktoriya could be, somehow she knew that today's agenda wouldn't prevent that from happening.

"Any word?"

Colonel Ulyanov was surprised to see Michael stick his head into his office so early—Neill usually arrived at his door by noon, but lunch was still hours away. And the young Marine seemed so *spirited* since they'd arrived at the station. Apparently a night of culture had done him some good.

But the Colonel didn't share Neill's mood. Ulyanov looked up from his desk in frustration. "The military is drowning in documentation." He held up a few of the latest forms crying out for attention. "Is it like this in America?"

Neill nodded his head. "I'd rather be deployed than deal with paperwork." He took a chair across from the Colonel's desk. "Have you heard anything?" he repeated.

Ulyanov pulled off his glasses and rubbed his eyes. He'd nearly forgotten about Michael's plan to contact the militias to see if they'd recovered any stolen military vehicles.

"Nothing yet," Ulyanov replied. "The district authorities have been very cooperative, but Major Dobrinskaya reports no new leads." Bogdan Dobrinskaya was the Colonel's adjutant back at the airbase in Nikolayev. "At least nothing substantial," Ulyanov finished, amending his statement.

Neill raised an eyebrow. " *'Nothing substantial'*—what does that mean?"

The Colonel looked a little impatient. "One of the border checkpoints reported an incident early this morning," he explained. "But it had nothing to do with our truck. At lunch we can—"

"What happened?" Neill insisted, taking a seat across from Ulyanov's desk.

The Colonel pushed his chair away from his desk and heaved a heavy sigh. "Someone stole a vehicle just after sunrise this morning, near Shostka, close to the border. The thief approached from the north—driving a stolen Lada—pulled a pistol on two border guards, then took their car."

"Which way was he headed?" Michael knew this was probably an unrelated incident, but something about it tugged at his curiosity in an odd sort of way.

"No one knows," Ulyanov said. "The guards were tied up and blindfolded before the thief left."

"Really?" Neill said. "Sounds like this guy knew what he was doing. What about the Lada?"

Ulyanov blinked. "What about it?"

"He had to leave it behind, right? Where'd he steal it from?"

Ulyanov riffled through some papers, a scowl developing on his face. "I'm not sure ... the report—here it is ..." Suddenly he stopped.

"Well?"

"The car was stolen from Bryansk," the Colonel replied slowly. "... with plenty of fuel left in it when it was recovered."

Now it was Michael's turn to frown. "So why would the thief steal another car? And why tangle with a couple of armed soldiers if you don't have to?"

Ulyanov looked up. Both men were thinking along the same lines now.

"Maybe he didn't have the proper papers to legitimately cross the border."

"Or maybe he needed an official vehicle—so he could travel unchallenged," Neill suggested.

"Or maybe both," they said together.

Their eyes locked as they began to consider what each man thought to be a far-fetched impossibility.

Chapter Twenty-Two ✴ Due South

MALYEV WAS NOW WEARING THE UNI-form he'd bought in Bryansk, driving south in the stolen military staff car as he approached the city of Kirovograd. He still had miles to go before he reached Odessa, but he was making good time and was right on schedule.

The weather had turned unseasonably warm, and the sun that hung high overhead removed the hint of winter's presence. In spite of all that Ivan was disturbed by his own actions back at the checkpoint. For reasons unknown even to himself Malyev had left the two border guards alive—caution advised against it, but he just couldn't bring himself to pull the trigger. He'd tied them up and locked them inside the checkpoint, knowing that it was just a matter of time before someone travelling to or from the Russian frontier found them—

Ivan cursed himself and blamed it on fatigue, then remembered the flood of emotions he'd experienced after shooting that policeman in Odessa. Then there was Boris—maybe his words had somehow snatched away his resolve. They certainly hadn't helped his concentration. The past few days had confused him. Without a renewed commitment to carry out his plan, Ivan worried that some future hesitation might endanger the mission. He reminded himself of all the reasons why he should go forward and held on to them tightly as his justification.

Ivan looked into the rearview mirror, glaring into his own eyes, determined that there could be no turning back now, but not quite realizing that something far more powerful than conscience had begun a work in his heart.

* * * *

His afternoon meal arrived, but Sergei Goncharov ignored it, his attention focused on the newspaper he held in his hand. Staring back at him from the front page were the printed photos of Sasha Kobrin and Ivan Malyev; grainy, but clearly recognizable.

Sergei sat up in his hospital bed, a little too quickly for his own good. The twinge of pain in his chest—and the images of his assailants in the paper—reminded him that he was still a wounded man and he began to move more slowly. He lowered his feet to the cold floor and took a cautious step toward the phone on the bureau next to him.

Goncharov lifted the receiver to his ear and glanced at the photos one more time, feeling somewhat vindicated by the news of Malyev and Kobrin's deaths. No matter how slowly—or swiftly—the wheels of justice turned, it was gratifying for him to realize that law and order usually prevailed.

* * * *

"What you are suggesting is impossible, Michael," Colonel Ulyanov said evenly. "You've read the newspapers—Malyev and Kobrin are dead."

"My head agrees with you, Colonel," Neill replied. "But my gut says otherwise."

By now Dmitri Yaroslav had joined the two men in the Colonel's office, watching the verbal exchange with curiosity. "What's going on?"

Ulyanov handed a copy of the morning paper to Yaroslav, pointing to the photos of the two terrorists printed on the front page. "Michael is convinced that our friends in Bryansk are still alive."

" 'Convinced' is a strong word," Neill said. "But I do believe it's possible one of them survived the assault on the training camp."

Captain Yaroslav frowned. "How is that possible? Their aircraft was blown out of the sky," he said, recalling the media accounts of the incident.

Michael knew there was no getting around that fact. "Granted, a team of crack troops did shoot them down—but mistakes can happen," he replied, defending his theory. "Now, four days later, someone is so desperate to cross the border that he attacks a militia checkpoint and steals a vehicle."

"Michael, that proves nothing," Ulyanov said patiently. "Anyone could have attacked that border station. And even if it was Malyev or Kobrin, why would they come back to Ukraine?" Somehow he knew the answer to that even as he posed the question.

Neill caught the Colonel's eye and paused before answering. "Because this is where the bomb is."

Yaroslav shook his head and sat down. "It's an interesting theory, but you have no proof."

"No, but I know how to get some," Neill said. He was hanging his theory on an awfully thin thread. Michael would be the first to admit his hunch was based on a weak piece of information, but he'd been right before.

"I'll make a deal with you, Colonel. Play along with me on this for the next few minutes. If I'm wrong—and I hope that I am—I'll forget about it." He leaned forward. "But if I'm right—"

"What's your plan?" Ulyanov asked.

* * * *

Ivan continued to follow the route south, passing through the Ukrainian countryside at an unhurried pace. He hoped to attract as little attention as possible. For the most part he was successful, but occasionally he was spotted by patrolling militia officers making their rounds, although few gave him a second glance. It was a common enough sight to see a uniformed military officer travelling in a government vehicle. The district headquarters in Shostka had radioed the outlying areas about the attack on their checkpoint, but the assailant in that incident had worn civilian clothing. With that in mind, the officers who did see Malyev paid him little attention.

Ivan smiled to himself.

His disguise was working perfectly.

* * * *

Neill stood over the fax machine in the facility's administrative building, carefully placing the front page of the newspaper on top of the built-in scanner bed. He punched in a succession of numbers then hit the send button. Within seconds the device hummed to life, scanning the images from the newsprint and sending them electronically to the militia headquarters in Shostka. After confirming that the transmission had been successfully completed, Neill removed the front page and headed back to the Colonel's office.

Dmitri and Ulyanov were waiting for him when he returned, newspaper in hand. "Okay. I've just faxed the photos of Malyev and Kobrin to district headquarters."

"What's next?" Yaroslav asked.

"Next we place a call to Shostka," Colonel Ulyanov explained, picking up the phone. There were times when his mind worked in sync with Michael's. "Hopefully those two border guards got a good look at the man who attacked them." He looked up the number in a phone directory and punched it in.

"And if they did," Neill added, "they should be able to identify him from the pictures we've just sent."

Yaroslav was about to reply when the Colonel raised a hand for silence. He'd reached someone on the other end of the line and began relaying their request to the officer in charge at the northern headquarters. After he finished speaking, Ulyanov cupped the mouthpiece with his hand and glanced at the two younger men.

"We're in luck," he said after a moment. "Our fax just arrived and the two guards are still at the station."

For the next few minutes Yaroslav and Neill sat quietly. Colonel Ulyanov continued to listen, his brows knit together in a look of intense concentration. The serious expression on his face was enough to tell Neill that something was going on, but nothing more. Finally, Ulyanov nodded, thanked the voice on the other end and slowly hung up the phone.

"Well?" Michael asked at last. "Were the guards able to make a positive I.D.?"

Ashen-faced, Ulyanov stared at the wall. That was all the answer Michael needed.

Chapter Twenty-Three ☆ Theories

M ALYEV HAD LEFT THE DNIEPER RIVER
far behind and was rapidly approaching the
city of Berezovka. The increase in traffic flow-
ing along the highway was his chief concern. A convoy of
slower-moving trucks ahead forced him to slow his speed.
Ivan began to worry; the longer he remained in the open, the
greater his chances of being identified by the militia.

It wouldn't do to be caught so close to his objective,
Malyev thought soberly. He checked his map, noting that
Odessa was only about fifty kilometers away, then selected an
alternate—and less travelled—route to his destination. Within
minutes he'd reached an exit and had pulled off the main road,
continuing his journey to the south.

* * * *

The militia commander was out when Sergei called, so
he left a message, hung up the phone and turned his attention back to his untouched lunch. He ate slowly, trying to find
some flavor in the bland meal—hospital food in the former
Soviet Union was as unremarkable as hospital food anywhere
else in the world—and he'd nearly finished eating when
Goncharov's boss returned his call fifteen minutes later.

Captain Yuri Mironov, militia commander in Odessa,

placed the phone back in its cradle and looked across the room. "That was Sergeant Goncharov," he said. "He's just identified the two men who shot him."

The Duty Officer of the Watch could hear the surprise in Mironov's voice and glanced up from his desk. "How?" he asked. "I thought he was still in the hospital."

"He is." Mironov picked up a copy of the newspaper lying on the Watch Officer's desk and scanned the front page. For the next few minutes he repeated everything Goncharov had told him over the phone, occasionally stopping to read aloud details of the secret camp in Bryansk and the two men who'd been killed there. The Watch Officer was surprised to learn that the dead terrorists and the mysterious assailants who had shot the Sergeant were the same men. He wondered what they were doing so far south in Odessa.

Captain Mironov finished his tale, then pushed back his chair and turned to face the window behind his desk. Enclosed by a heavy chain-link fence, the rear parking lot lay just below and Mironov had often joked that his window had the best view of impounded vehicles in the entire building. His eyes narrowed as they swept over the row of cars, then stopped as he focused on a large, green truck parked near the back gate.

"Corporal," he said slowly. "The truck that we found at the waterfront—what do we know about it?"

The Officer of the Watch thought for a moment. "It's clearly a military vehicle—or it was at one time."

Captain Mironov was also sure that the truck had been stolen. It occurred to him that it might be possible to return it to its rightful owner.

"And what about the engine? Has anyone checked it?"

The Corporal blinked. "The engine, sir?"

"Yes," Mironov replied. "The military stamps the serial numbers on the engine blocks of their vehicles; has anyone checked under the hood?"

Mironov wasn't surprised by the blank look on the Corporal's face; the government policy was only about a year old and Mironov had forgotten about it himself until now.

The Corporal stood to his feet and picked up a small pad and a pen. "I'll check it myself, Captain," he said as he headed out the door.

* * * *

"Ivan Malyev?" Dmitri asked in surprise. It was hard for him to accept that the terrorist was still alive. "Is it possible the border guards are mistaken?"

"There's always that chance," Ulyanov said. "But the officer in charge told me they were quite certain."

"Okay," Neill said, turning his attention to the map on the wall. "If we only knew which way he was headed—"

"And why," Captain Yaroslav threw in.

The three had ordered sandwiches from the dining hall and were having lunch in the Colonel's office. "The why is simple," Ulyanov declared. "Malyev is coming back for the warhead. Nothing else is important enough to risk his life for. What he does once he reaches it is the real question."

"It all boils down to that, doesn't it?" Michael picked up a grease pencil from the Colonel's desk and drew a circle around Bryansk. "Let's take this one step at a time," he said. "Malyev stole a Lada here—" He drew a line south into Ukraine, "— then proceeded to the border checkpoint near Shostka. From there it's anybody's guess."

Ulyanov pushed his glasses on for a closer look. "He could have continued on a southerly route," he mused, then shook his head. "Or he might have turned east or west."

Neill looked at his watch. "It's been nearly five hours since the attack at the border," he said. "Plenty of time to get where he's going. And nobody's seen him since dawn."

"He could have made it to Kiev by now," Yaroslav said thoughtfully. "Or perhaps another major city."

Colonel Ulyanov looked at the map and realized just how overwhelming the problem was. They were all but certain Malyev was alive, and they knew where he'd been, but to find him now without a tangible lead to go on seemed impossible. The search area was literally thousands of square kilometers across and time was running out. A dangerous terrorist was loose in Ukraine who knew where to get his hands on a nuclear weapon, and Ulyanov felt powerless to do anything about it.

"If there was ever a time for divine intervention, this is it." The Colonel caught Neill's eye and smiled tiredly. "Michael?"

Neill nodded his head in agreement, then both men bowed in prayer. Captain Yaroslav didn't share their faith, but after a moment's hesitation he quickly and unashamedly joined them by the Colonel's desk.

* * * *

The truck's serial number was right where Captain Mironov said it would be, although it was partially obscured by a thin layer of grease. The Corporal wiped away the grime, wrote the numerals down on his pad then went back inside the station.

The Captain was waiting for him as he re-entered the office. "You have it?"

"6465-03." The Corporal sat down and powered up a small computer that occupied the center of his small desk. The machine hummed to life—it seemed to be operating much more quickly than usual—and soon he had accessed the central militia server in Kiev.

Mironov watched as the Corporal's fingers flew over the keyboard. "Go to the motor registry database," the Captain suggested. "There should be a dedicated site for military vehicles."

The Corporal nodded. He found what he was looking for, then selected a search field and entered the serial number. A simple keystroke after that displayed the entire inventory of military vehicles logged into the system.

"We're in," he said happily, then scrolled down the list to the 6000 series.

"There it is," Mironov said, leaning closer to the monitor.

A column next to the inventory displayed the names of the military installations where each vehicle was assigned.

"Weapons Dismantling Facility," Mironov read aloud.

The Corporal frowned. "There's only one of those in all of Ukraine. And it's right here in Odessa," he said. "The base outside of town."

Mironov stood up and folded his arms across his chest. A vehicle stolen from an airbase or a conventional military post was one thing, but a weapons facility was entirely different. He'd heard rumors about the station and it was unnerving to think that anything could be stolen from such a high security facility. Soon Mironov shared the Corporal's scowl.

He turned away from the computer and retrieved a telephone directory from his own desk. There was a possibility that this was all a big mistake, but just to make sure he picked up the phone and punched in the number for the dismantling facility ten kilometers away.

Chapter Twenty-Four ☆ Breakthrough

THE COLONEL PICKED UP THE PHONE ON THE first ring. "Ulyanov here."

"Sergeant of the Guard, Colonel," a voice on the other end replied. "I have the Odessa militia commander on one. He wishes to speak to the officer in charge; shall I transfer him to your line?"

"The militia commander?" Ulyanov couldn't imagine why he would be calling. "Put him through, Sergeant."

Neill saw fresh concern spread over the Colonel's features, then leaned in as Ulyanov activated the phone's loudspeaker. There was a trace of static, then a click as the Sergeant of the Guard connected the call.

"This is Colonel Ulyanov. How can I help you?"

* * * *

Malyev could now see the edge of the Black Sea as it glittered on the horizon, the road he'd chosen now running parallel to the main highway leading into Odessa. *Finally.* He pulled the pistol from his uniform and laid it on the seat next to him, carefully concealing it under the map.

Next he checked the fuel gauge. The car had been full of fuel when he left the checkpoint and he still had more than a quarter tank of gas; plenty to get him downtown and from there safely away from the blast site. He only hoped that once he reached the maintenance shed the warhead would still be inside. For all he knew, someone might have found it by now, although he considered that to be unlikely. But if that were the case, the authorities might have the area staked out, waiting for whomever left it there to return.

He shrugged off the thought. No sense worrying about what he couldn't control.

* * * *

As Captain Mironov explained the reason for his call, Dmitri Yaroslav became an instant believer in the power of prayer.

"—the truck is in poor shape, Colonel," Mironov was saying, his voice filling the room. "We had to tow it to headquarters."

"I'll make arrangements for its return, Captain," Ulyanov assured him, then shielded the microphone with his hand. "Have Corporal Sevnik bring my car around," he whispered to Yaroslav. Dmitri nodded, bolting from the office as the Colonel continued his discussion with Captain Mironov. "Where did you find the truck?"

"The waterfront," Mironov replied. "At the foot of the Potemkin Steps. The two men who stole it shot one of my officers, then escaped on foot."

"Was it loaded when you found it?" Ulyanov asked.

The question caught the Captain off guard. "No, sir," Mironov said. He grew a little suspicious at the Colonel's remark, then added, "What was it carrying?"

Ulyanov paused, slowly drawing in his breath. He was unwilling to involve the civilian authorities in the search without a better idea of the bomb's whereabouts, but now it seemed he had no choice.

"Captain Mironov," the Colonel said slowly, "the men who stole that truck were transporting a nuclear weapon. We believe they intended to use it to threaten the republics."

"*Bozhe moi.*" *My God.* The Captain realized the seriousness of the situation, then recalled what Sergeant Goncharov had told him earlier. "Those men were the terrorists in this morning's paper." He calmed his fears by reminding himself that both were dead, but still, a missing nuclear weapon could—

"There's more, Captain." Ulyanov's deep voice cut through Mironov's thoughts. "We believe one of the terrorists—a man named Ivan Malyev—is still alive, and has returned to Ukraine to retrieve the warhead."

In the silence that followed, Neill was sure he could have heard a pin drop. Dmitri Yaroslav re-entered the room just as the subdued voice of Captain Mironov again drifted from the telephone loudspeaker.

"What do you want me to do?"

Colonel Ulyanov explained that Malyev and Kobrin had used the truck to transport the weapon, as well as Neill's hunch that finding the vehicle might point the way to where the bomb was hidden. He ordered Mironov to close off both ends of Suvorova Street and Primorsky Boulevard, the two thoroughfares that enclosed the Potemkin Steps and the narrow strip of hillside that faced the harbor.

"My car is waiting, Captain," Ulyanov said. "I'll join you there as soon as I can." Mironov agreed and the line went dead.

Ulyanov had a blank look on his face. "The Potemkin Steps. If it's there—"

"—then it's been under our noses the whole time," Michael finished for him.

The Colonel hung up the phone and began issuing orders to Captain Yaroslav. "We'll need a security detachment—ten men, I should think, standard issue of arms. And a field radio in case we need to communicate with our personnel here. Load the men into a truck—and bring some technicians with you—then meet us at the waterfront." Ulyanov grabbed his hat and headed for the door. "Lieutenant Neill and I will draw two weapons from the armory and go ahead of you in my car. Any questions?"

Everything was moving too fast. "Do you really think he

can detonate the warhead?" Yaroslav asked.

Ulyanov stopped halfway through the door, then turned to face Dmitri. "He used this very facility to modify the weapon; I don't intend to underestimate anything he might be capable of."

Chapter Twenty-Five ☆ Arming Sequence

T HE WARMER WEATHER ENDED ABRUPTLY and another cold front pushed south. From time to time rolling clouds covered the sun, casting a dark canopy over the region. Temperatures along the Black Sea coastal areas began to drop, and the normal flow of visitors to Odessa's scenic waterfront dwindled to only a few.

Malyev drove the stolen military vehicle slowly along Suvorova Street and found he had his choice of parking spaces. Passing the Potemkin Steps, he selected a spot not far from where he and Sasha had left the truck nearly a week earlier, then edged up to the curb and shut off the engine.

There wasn't time to reminisce about the last time he'd been here. Just a few days before, Ivan had been the determined and methodical mercenary, fighting for a cause, and Sasha the wild-eyed revolutionary who threw caution to the wind. Now Ivan's actions were fueled by his emotions and a growing obsession with vengeance, but he could still be objective enough to see something beyond that.

It was pride, one of the strongest of human failings. Major Pirogov's betrayal had stung him deeply and Ivan couldn't let it go. He'd trusted the Major—Karpenko too—and they had rewarded his good faith by trying to kill him. Vengeance was something Ivan held onto very tightly. He justified his passions by reasoning that a wrong had to be set right whether he was personally involved or not, but deep down not even he believed that.

Ivan reached beneath the map on the passenger seat and grabbed his weapon, stuffing it into the belt he wore under his uniform jacket. He had been driving for hours and as he got out of the car his legs felt stiff and sluggish. He patted the padlock key he kept in his trouser pocket and walked casually around to the sidewalk, then made his way toward the maintenance shed hidden at the base of the terraced incline.

Ivan stopped and glanced up and down the street. Curiously, the flow of traffic in both directions seemed to have disappeared. As he ducked into the tree line he could hear the sound of a police siren approaching in the distance ...

* * * *

"Six hours." Neill shook his head as he looked at his watch again. "If Malyev's headed for Odessa he's had plenty of time to get here."

"I don't think there's any question now about where he's headed, Michael." Seated next to Michael in the back seat, Colonel Ulyanov watched out the window as the staff car passed through the outskirts of the city. They were still five minutes away from the waterfront. He mentally urged Corporal Sevnik to drive faster.

"By now Captain Mironov has sealed off the harbor approach," the Colonel replied, praying that it wasn't too late. In a best case scenario, Malyev might not be anywhere near Odessa, but Ulyanov knew that was hoping for too much. He pulled his pistol from the holster at his side and reached for a small box of ammunition placed on the seat between them. Taking his cue from the Colonel, Neill did the same, removing the empty magazine shoved into the handgrip of his own weapon.

By the time Michael had fully loaded the clip with fifteen 9 millimeter rounds they were racing through the streets of downtown Odessa. Up ahead they could see the first of the militia's roadblocks, and as Corporal Sevnik slowed their speed Captain

Mironov himself approached the car.

Colonel Ulyanov rolled down the window and flashed his identification. At a nod from the militia commander Corporal Sevnik parked the car. All three men got out and as they did Neill could see several militia officers quietly urging onlookers to keep their distance as they cordoned off the street.

* * * *

Even with the thick underbrush as a cover, Malyev felt terribly vulnerable. The darkened skies did little to buoy his emotions. He reminded himself that the last time he'd passed this way, it had been a dark, moonless night; and shrugging off the feeling, he continued along the overgrown path that led to the small maintenance shed.

Ivan reached into his pocket and pulled out the key to the padlock that secured the door. He inserted it quickly and with a turn of the wrist the lock came free. He removed it from the rusty metal latch, then swung open the creaking door and stepped inside.

* * * *

"I have men here and here," Captain Mironov was saying. He had unfolded a map of the waterfront and spread it out on the hood of his car. Colonel Ulyanov and Lieutenant Neill flanked him on either side, peering intently over each shoulder as Mironov marked the chart with a felt-tipped pen.

"Do your officers have a description of the man we're after?" Neill asked.

Mironov nodded his head. "I've distributed copies of Malyev's photo from today's paper," he said, regarding Michael with curiosity. Colonel Ulyanov had hastily introduced the young Lieutenant earlier, explaining that Michael was an American officer on special assignment in the Ukraine. Mironov was surprised to hear that Neill spoke fluent Ukrainian; in fact, the Captain could detect no trace of an accent in his voice.

"The force is split into two groups," Mironov continued. "Half are positioned at the roadblocks. The rest are working their way inward, converging on the Steps." He paused and a frown clouded his face. "Unfortunately, I have only a small contingent available for the search."

"That won't be a problem, Captain," Ulyanov said in reply. Mironov had barely finished speaking when a low rumbling sound caused the men to turn and face the street. Beyond the hastily erected barricade, the little group could see one of the Russian Tigers, followed by a large military truck carrying troops in the back. The miniature convoy idled to a halt, the truck belching plumes of black smoke as it stopped, then Neill saw Dmitri Yaroslav as he emerged from the Tiger's cab.

Captain Yaroslav threw a quick salute in the Colonel's direction, then hurried to the rear of the truck and lowered the heavy tailgate. As Neill watched, a security detachment from the weapons facility disembarked and fell into formation on the pavement. The other men got out of the lead vehicle wearing civilian clothing. Michael recognized them as technicians who worked in the dismantling bay.

Ulyanov saw the disturbed look on Captain Mironov's face and quickly explained that the troops were under his command. "With your permission, Captain," Ulyanov said, "my men will begin at the foot of the Steps and work their way outward; is that acceptable to you?" The Colonel phrased his words as diplomatically as possible, hoping not to step on the militia commander's toes; but Mironov was too much of a professional to let his pride interfere with finding Malyev— and the bomb.

"Completely acceptable, Colonel," he said at last.

"One more thing," Ulyanov added quietly. "The local populace should be encouraged to leave the waterfront."

Mironov nodded. A complete evacuation of the city was impossible, but something could be done to lessen casualties—should the worst come to pass.

Turning to his own men, the Captain explained what was

about to happen, then the two groups split up and headed for the slope and the waterfront that lay below.

* * * *

Bleary-eyed already from lack of sleep, Ivan paused in the doorway as his vision adjusted to the darkened interior of the shed. Muted sunlight filtered into the tiny room through small ventilation holes located along the tops of the walls near the ceiling. The narrow, paneless windows allowed just enough light to see that the shed was just as he and Sasha had left it, the tools and equipment stacked in one corner and the steel container that enclosed the warhead against the far wall.

Ivan bent over the device and removed the tarp that concealed the control pad. He flipped the start-up switch and waited as the central processing unit spun up, then read the digital display as the system became active.

INITIALIZATION COMPLETE
SYSTEM READY — ENTER PASSWORD

Swallowing hard, Ivan was aware that he had begun to sweat. He squelched any feelings of nervousness by remembering the anger he felt for Major Pirogov and the others who had betrayed him, then punched in the password and hit the enter key.

PASSWORD ACCEPTED
ENTER FOUR DIGIT START-UP CODE

Once again Malyev tapped on the keys and another message glowed on the readout.

CODE VALID. DO YOU WISH TO
INITIATE ACTIVATION SEQUENCE? Y/N

He hit Y for 'yes.' There was a pause as the unit processed

the information, then the display read:

ACTIVATION SEQUENCE ENGAGED
TIME TO DETONATION: 60 MINUTES
DO YOU WISH TO COMMIT? Y/N

Ivan's hand hesitated, hovering over the keypad. Once the sequence actually engaged, he could terminate it by entering another password, but as he crouched over the coffin-like container he had no intention of turning back.

* * * *

Colonel Ulyanov asked Mironov to show him exactly where the truck had been found. With the security detachment and technicians following them, they hurried down the Potemkin Steps until they reached Suvorova Street. At the foot of the Steps, Captain Yaroslav ordered the troops to begin their search while Neill, Ulyanov and the militia commander headed for the scene of the shooting. As they moved along the sidewalk at a trot, Neill caught sight of something that made him stop in his tracks.

"Lieutenant?" Mironov looked back at Michael as he stared ahead.

"That car," Michael said, stepping forward. "Looks like a government vehicle—"

"Of course," Mironov replied, pulling a folded sheet of paper from his breast pocket. The Captain had received a dispatch from Shostka that included a description of the car Malyev had stolen at the border. He stooped and read the numbers on the license plate then stood erect and shot a look at the Colonel.

"This is the car taken from the checkpoint," he snapped, then twisted his head, looking in every direction. "He's here."

"He's here, all right." Neill's eyes scanned the immediate vicinity, sweeping past the few cars that remained parked along the street and coming to rest on the wooded hillside.

Peering into the tree line, Michael could make out the shape of a small, man-made structure shrouded by foliage.

"Come on," he ordered. "There's something back there at the foot of the hill." Without hesitation Neill headed for the trees, the sound of his boots crashing through the dry brush as he went.

The Colonel followed right behind him, and as the two Captains brought up the rear Ulyanov ordered them all to draw their weapons.

* * * *

Malyev entered the final command and watched the numerical display that appeared next to the alphabetical readout. The countdown began immediately; less than sixty minutes remained until the detonation, giving him plenty of time to escape. As tired as he was, he still felt a rush of adrenaline as the seconds ticked by, then paused to catch his breath before leaving.

Ivan almost hated to go. Crouching in the cool, quiet interior of the darkened shed, hidden from sight and alone, he felt almost at peace, a kind of contentment that the world had denied him at every turn. Ivan knew that the serenity he now felt was only temporary, yet tried to savor the moment nonetheless.

He forced himself to stand to his feet and turned to step out of the shed. As he pulled the door closed one last time he was startled by movement on the path ahead and the sound of running feet. The almost surreal solitude he'd felt only seconds earlier was shattered by the sight of armed and uniformed troops headed in his direction.

Neill was the first to reach him. Coming to a halt only yards away, Michael raised his pistol, taking aim at Malyev's chest as their eyes locked. For a split second, Ivan was confused. The man before him wore a foreign uniform—he appeared to be an American—but the troops running through the bushes to join him were clearly Ukrainian. One of the men he recognized; Captain Yaroslav from the weapons facility, but the other was an officer he'd never seen before.

Ivan took a step back, but then stopped as his retreat was halted by the maintenance shed behind him. The foreign officer—Malyev was sure he was an American now—never wavered, keeping his weapon pointed at chest-level.

"Halt."

Malyev reached into his uniform and pulled out his own weapon. Once it was in clear view Michael fired a round that whizzed past Ivan's ear, shattering a small part of the shed wall and sending chips of concrete flying through the air.

"I said halt." Neill called again.

Ivan knew he could never hope to survive in a fight where he was so hopelessly outnumbered. With more and more weapons being trained in his direction, it became obvious that his bid for freedom was over.

Angrily, he cursed fate for snatching victory away once again. It occurred to him that these troops might want him alive, but the thought of being taken into custody to stand trial for his crimes was too much to bear and he had no intention of allowing that to happen.

There was no escape now. The determined looks he saw on the faces before him told Ivan that it was over. In a space of time too short to measure he remembered how Sasha had died and longed for the same fate. It was then that he realized he had a choice.

Fear, frustration and fatigue took over, and as everyone watched in horror, Ivan placed the muzzle of the small pistol to his temple and squeezed the trigger.

Chapter Twenty-Six ✶ Persuasion

NO ONE WAS MORE SURPRISED THAN IVAN Malyev when the Makarov jammed. For a split second everyone stood rooted to the ground, then Dmitri and Corporal Sevnik lowered their weapons and lunged forward. The two pushed Malyev roughly against the wall of the shed, disarmed him and pinned his arms fast behind his back. Helpless, Malyev sneered at them, but didn't resist. At that point the fight had simply gone out of him.

Several of Captain Mironov's officers heard the report of Neill's weapon and found their way through the bushes to the group clustered around the shed. Mironov nodded to two of them, and soon Ivan was being escorted at gunpoint down the path and out of sight.

Michael holstered his pistol and took hold of the door to the shed. He had barely tugged on the handle and the Colonel was inside, Captain Yaroslav following on his heels. Michael pushed the creaking door all the way open and stepped in after them.

As their vision adjusted to the darkness, Ulyanov's eyes were immediately drawn to the red glow of the control pad's digital readout. He stooped down and ran his hand gingerly over the steel container's surface as Yaroslav knelt beside him.

"This is it, Colonel," Dmitri whispered. "This is the device I saw Malyev and Kobrin loading onto the truck at the station."

The Colonel grunted in acknowledgement, watching as the

numerical display continued its diminishing countdown. "It appears Malyev has activated a sequence of some kind," he said, reading the face of the display. There was no doubt in his mind as to what that countdown was leading to. He ran his fingers over the control console and found it securely attached to the titanium hull of the container.

Yaroslav frowned. "Less than fifty-six minutes to go."

Ulyanov bit his lip and remained calm. "All right," he said at last. "We have to find a way to terminate the countdown and disarm it."

Squinting into the darkness, the Colonel reached into his pocket and pulled out his glasses. As he did so, Captain Yaroslav leaned over the console, but the digital keypad offered few clues.

"None of the control features are labeled," he noted. "Except for the small, individual keys; those are marked with letters of the alphabet." He looked up at the Colonel. "It's a keyboard, not unlike what you would find on any computer."

"Then the commands are relayed to the processing unit by sequenced keystrokes or passwords," Michael interjected.

"Exactly," Yaroslav replied. "And if Malyev can start the sequence—"

"—then he can stop it," Ulyanov finished for him, then turned to Dmitri. "Send a runner back to the top of the Steps. Get the technicians down here. Lieutenant Neill and I will try to persuade Malyev to give us the password."

The three men exited the building and quickly headed back down the path. Mironov eyed them curiously, and as the Colonel stopped to explain what was happening, Michael and Dmitri made their way toward the street. Emerging from the tree line, Yaroslav relayed the Colonel's instructions to a Sergeant from the weapons facility. The young soldier saluted his Captain, then took off for the Steps while Neill's eyes roamed the street in search of the newly captured prisoner.

* * * *

The cab let Viktoriya out in front of the Londonskaya

Hotel and she bounded up the steps to the entrance. Anton had the desk duty and greeted her with a smile as she came in. Viktoriya pulled out the envelope she carried in her purse and handed it to him, with instructions to deliver it to the guest in room 201. The young clerk watched as she turned and exited the foyer and didn't take his eyes away from her until she disappeared again through the double doors. When she was out of view, he brought the envelope up to his nose and gave it a sniff. It might have been his imagination, but even in his distracted state he thought he recognized the scent of lavender.

On Katerynynska Street, a militia car under Captain Mironov's command accelerated to the intersection with Primorsky Boulevard and turned right. It swept past the hotel, its sirens blaring, then navigated a course south toward the port complex. Viktoriya watched as another one followed closely behind. She gestured to the cabbie to wait and walked to the corner, but both vehicles were now out of sight.

Her interest had already waned. She started walking back to the taxi when she heard the sound of Oksana Marpova's voice. She turned to see the older woman headed in her direction—her shift started at noon—and she seemed just a little breathless. In the distance, Viktoriya could hear the sound of more sirens.

"What's that all about, Oksana?"

She shrugged. "The militia is blocking off the roads. And the military is down there, too."

"The military?"

"Two big trucks," she replied. "Green ones."

Oksana had an apartment near the Steps. Most likely it was nothing, but Viktoriya was suddenly intrigued. Navy ships came and went at the port on a regular basis; so the presence of the armed forces probably accounted for what Oksana had seen. But she wasn't aware that the Navy used vehicles like the ones she had described.

They spoke briefly, then Oksana went inside the hotel to start her shift. Viktoriya looked at her watch; her lunch hour

had barely begun. She still had plenty of time before she needed to head back to the paper. After a moment's hesitation, she
got into the cab and decided to indulge her reporter's instincts.
The driver received new instructions, and moments later he
was taking his passenger toward the waterfront.

Malyev had been handcuffed and placed in the back of
a patrol car parked at the foot of the massive staircase. A
squad of four militia officers stood guard, but as Michael approached they stepped aside and allowed him to pass. Under
their watchful eye, Neill bent down and opened the rear door
closest to the sidewalk, pausing momentarily to pray silently
and study the figure hunched over in the back seat. He looked
exhausted and said nothing, his faced expressing a sense of
utter hopelessness.

"You don't have to do this, Ivan," Neill said quietly but
firmly. "We know about Major Pirogov. We know how you
and Kobrin were betrayed." *Grant me the grace to show compassion, Lord.* Malyev remained motionless. "I can understand your desire for revenge, but this is wrong. When that
bomb goes off it'll take a whole lot of people with it." Neill
was well aware of the warhead's yield and began calculating
the death toll.

"Why didn't you kill me back there?" Ivan growled, never
looking up. He was puzzled by the American officer, this
Westerner who spoke Russian and seemed to know a great
deal about him; he felt that he was at a disadvantage as he
tried to sort it all out.

Neill was surprised by the question. "Because I place a
very high value on human life," he answered. "No one's beyond redemption in my book—not even you."

As Michael spoke Colonel Ulyanov joined him and stood
quietly at his side.

"There's a warhead back there on a countdown to destruction," Michael continued. "I'm not sure what your motivation
is; you might be trying to discredit the Russian government—

or maybe you're just mad at the whole world, but if we do this your way, thousands of people die—including yourself—and Major Pirogov and his associates get off scott-free. Is that what you want?"

Malyev didn't answer, but Neill could tell by his expression that he was at least listening to him.

"I've got a plan that makes a whole lot more sense; everybody stays alive, the bomb gets disarmed, and you get a shot at the people who tried to kill you." He paused for effect, then added, "—if you're interested, that is."

Colonel Ulyanov discreetly checked his watch. There were only fifty-two minutes left and he had no idea what Neill was up to. From the corner of his eye he saw movement on the Steps; the Sergeant had returned with the technicians, and as Ulyanov watched the three men disappeared into the tree line.

Ivan considered Michael's words, shifted in his seat and looked up for the first time. He still refused to look directly at him.

"What do you propose?" he said finally.

"You know things that nobody else does, Ivan." Neill leaned forward, hopeful that Malyev might actually cooperate, but more concerned that he wouldn't. "Names, dates, locations. You have contacts in Russia and Ukraine, information that would be very useful in the right hands."

Malyev wasn't particularly shocked. "You want me to betray others like myself," he said simply.

Neill shook his head. "Not quite," he replied. "It's no secret the United States is unhappy with Moscow's current leadership; I could be wrong, but I think you probably share that sentiment."

Ivan closed his eyes. All he wanted to do now was rest. "So what do you suggest? You seem to have all the answers—what do you want me to do?"

"Return with me to America," Michael declared. He expected a reaction from the Colonel; Ulyanov's eyes widened, but he said nothing. "Cooperate with our intelligence agencies, tell them what you know. Give them what they need to build a case against Murovanka—legally. With your help we can put the spotlight on the Kremlin—and the people you implicate will be dealt with fairly, within the law, not ambushed in some clearing."

Ulyanov cleared his throat, somewhat loudly, then tugged at Neill's sleeve, pulling him off to the side and away from the car.

"That's quite a plan, Michael," the Colonel said evenly. "Can you deliver on such a promise?"

Neill remembered the letter Willis Avery had given him— and the authority it contained—and nodded his head. Colonel Ulyanov still wasn't convinced, but he admired Michael's quick thinking. All things considered, the plan had merit, although Ulyanov wasn't comfortable with the idea of Malyev leaving the country.

"Why take him to the United States?" he asked.

Neill stepped farther away from the car to give Ivan a moment to think. "For this to work, everybody has to continue to believe that Ivan Malyev is dead. If the Russians think otherwise, they'll cover their tracks fast and this whole thing collapses. Besides that, Ukraine is too close to the action," he explained. "Murovanka may have spies in your government, people who could blow the whistle on this operation before it even starts."

Ulyanov knew Michael was right and quietly agreed. "Someone will have to know. Several members of the Parliament are friends of mine; good, honest men we can trust."

Neill walked back to the open car door. He had another card to play. "It's up to you, Ivan. Are you ready to hand Pirogov a victory—and accomplish what he wasn't able to do himself?" He lowered his voice. "That's what happens if that warhead goes off. You'll be dead and there won't be anyone left to bring him to justice. And right now you're the only one who can do that." Neill stopped there. He simply couldn't think of anything else to say that might persuade Ivan to reconsider. More than anything, he worried that he might have said too much.

Captain Yaroslav appeared on the path. He stepped up to the Colonel and made his report, the tone of his voice low and guarded. "Danzig has examined the device, Colonel." Otto Danzig was the chief technician, a German nuclear engineer employed by the Ukrainian military. "He can find no way to disengage the destruct sequence externally."

"What does he suggest?" Ulyanov asked.

"He wants to disarm the warhead at the source," Dmitri answered. "If we cut through the container's outer skin, we can get to the control circuitry."

Ulyanov was prepared to defer to Danzig's expertise. There just didn't seem to be any alternative.

"*No.*"

The voice came from the car. The three men turned. Malyev now sat at the edge of the backseat, looking up at them for the first time. A nervous militia officer stepped forward, ready to restrain him.

"The device is tamper-resistant," Ivan told them. "The container is filled with an inert gas; any loss of internal pressure will activate a mechanism that will trigger a chain reaction. It can only be disarmed by keying in the proper password."

Neill took a step toward the car and helped Ivan to his feet. Maybe he'd gotten through to him after all. "How's it been weaponized, Ivan—did you and Sasha rig it as a dirty bomb?"

"A device like that is the trademark of amateurs," Malyev snorted.

Then it *was* a full-fledged nuke. *Dear God*, Michael thought. Overhead the sky had become completely covered by clouds and the sun was nowhere to be seen. A chill wind had begun to blow, whipping dry leaves in every direction.

Ivan leaned back against the car and felt the cold steel of the handcuffs as they gripped his wrists. He was tired and hungry. The American's words before had the weight of logic and had revived his spirit and given him an inkling of hope. Subdued, Ivan Malyev looked quietly at his captors and nodded his head. His resolve had vanished, but in its place was the possibility of a second chance.

"All right," he murmured. "I agree to your terms. Take off these handcuffs and I will disarm the bomb."

* * * *

Captain Yaroslav stepped closer to the Colonel as they stood once more in the cramped quarters of the maintenance shed. Leaning in, he whispered into his ear. "Do you trust him?"

The Colonel shrugged. "Do we have a choice?"

It occurred to him that Ivan might have been playing them. He could just as easily enter a command that would detonate the warhead without delay, and none of them would even know or feel it. Ulyanov forced himself to banish the thought. They were committed now.

Neill watched as Malyev bent over the control console and typed in a four digit number. As the countdown continued another message flashed on the readout:

CODE VALID—DO YOU WISH TO
TERMINATE ACTIVATION SEQUENCE? Y/N

Michael was still tense, but relaxed a little. Once again, Ivan tapped 'y' for yes. The display blinked, then the red glow of the countdown sequence stopped. Time seemed to freeze around them. The group of men huddled in the small room breathed a sigh of relief as the digital display locked at forty-two minutes.

Malyev pulled himself to his feet and looked warily into the Colonel's eyes, but instead of anger he saw only gratitude. He found that odd; he'd never seen that type of expression on Pirogov or anyone else who had trained him in Bryansk. Ulyanov turned and nodded to the troops and militiamen who waited outside. His smile conveyed the best news they'd had all day.

With the danger suddenly over, Neill whispered a prayer of thanksgiving and the group slowly filed out of the shed. Two soldiers from the security detachment took charge of Malyev, but this time Colonel Ulyanov ordered that no handcuffs were to be used. Ivan nodded in thanks and was led away.

Everyone realized that a disaster had been averted. Soon handshakes and congratulations were exchanged between the militia officers and the personnel from the weapons facility. At first, Captain Mironov was not too happy about turning the captured terrorist over to the military, but after Colonel Ulyanov assured him that Malyev was in good hands, he reluctantly agreed.

Only one other detail remained; loading the bomb onto the truck and taking it back to the weapons facility for dismantling. Mironov issued the appropriate orders and soon the truck that had brought the security detachment lumbered through the first roadblock to the foot of the Potemkin Steps. Colonel Ulyanov suggested that the militia keep the streets cordoned off until the bomb was safely—and quietly—removed from the waterfront, then turned to Captain Yaroslav and instructed him to see to the warhead's removal.

Neill faced the sea and drew in a deep breath, the brisk air filling his lungs. The sun broke through the clouds above, spilling shards of light down below and chasing away some of the chill. In the distance he could see an Italian Navy cruiser and some container ships moored at the pier. Beyond that several other vessels were anchored in the harbor.

"Malyev will face some difficult days ahead," Ulyanov was saying. For the first time in hours they were able to relax. "But he's taken a step in the right direction."

"I'm thankful he did," Michael replied. The two had moved

away from the tree line and surveyed the empty street.

"Of course, you're taking a big risk, Michael. I hope you realize that a hundred things could still go wrong."

Neill nodded his head. "Murovanka's a tough cookie. If he's a part of this, I'm sure he's taken steps to conceal it. But with Malyev's help, maybe the CIA can tie enough evidence together to get us close to some real proof."

Michael considered the changes that were about to take place in the terrorist's life, then recalled what Malyev had already been through. He couldn't forget that Ivan had cheated death twice—maybe more—and stood in wonder that God's grace had kept him alive—and unharmed—through it all.

* * * *

The detail of four soldiers, led by Corporal Sevnik, trudged down the path to the maintenance shed. The building was really too small to accommodate all of them, so when the squad reached the door, Sevnik ordered two of the men to wait outside.

Sevnik stepped over the threshold and motioned for one of the soldiers to follow him. The empty shed had been a beehive of activity only moments before; now it was quiet. Standing in the semi-darkened room, he regarded the steel container warily, but the glow of the digital readout remained constant. The Corporal forced himself to accept the fact that there was nothing to fear now. Still, being so close to the powerful weapon made him very nervous.

Sevnik and the other soldier took their positions at each end of the rectangular hull and reached for the handles set into the recessed pockets. The Corporal wanted to be finished with this unpleasant task as quickly as possible. Getting a firm grip, he counted to three, then they heaved the encased warhead up from the dusty floor. It was heavy and awkward in the confined space of the shed's interior, but still light enough to be manageable. Sevnik wondered if the burden would be as great if he were ignorant of what the steel hull contained, then shook his head and dismissed the thought.

The Corporal maneuvered his end through the door first, but nearly lost his step. As he turned to get a better grip, his eye was once again drawn to the readout in the center of the control pad.

The glowing display blinked and then vanished.

Corporal Sevnik stopped in his tracks and waited to see if it would return. He was gripped by an uncertain fear, then noticed that the other soldier was also staring at the display.

After several seconds the numerical readout flashed back on. For the briefest of moments, Sevnik felt relief, but then his fear returned.

With his eyes locked on the keypad, the Corporal watched in horror as the countdown resumed.

Chapter Twenty-Seven ✯ Countdown

THE CAB WENT AS FAR AS IT COULD GO before being stopped by several members of the militia. The roadblock these officers stood behind extended across the entire breadth of Suvorova Street. In the distance, Viktoriya could see several patrol cars and the two military trucks, all parked near the foot of the Steps. She was too far away to be certain, but it looked like most of the activity centered around one of the vehicles positioned between the Steps and the port complex.

One man in what appeared to be a black uniform was being escorted to a militia patrol car. A handful more followed closely behind, wearing different uniforms and carrying what looked like weapons. Viktoriya got out of the cab to get a closer look, moving toward the roadblock. An officer watched her nervously and took a few steps in her direction; the young woman seemed completely engrossed in what was happening farther down the street.

A familiar figure now appeared from the copse of trees at the base of the hill, then another. Viktoriya squinted her eyes and strained to see more clearly. Standing on tiptoe, she leaned against one of the roadblocks to get a better view. She was sure of it now; both men were standing in the open, and there was no denying who they were. One name in particular came to mind and suddenly Viktoriya found her voice.

"Michael?"

She'd barely spoken his name when she heard the sound of someone shouting. The group suddenly turned and headed back into the tree line.

Corporal Sevnik's shouts brought Neill and Ulyanov running, but it was Captain Yaroslav who reached the shed first. Pushing aside the frightened soldiers, Dmitri saw that the steel container that housed the warhead now rested on the path at Sevnik's feet.

The speechless Sevnik could only point at the device. Yaroslav bent to examine it as Michael and the Colonel came to a halt behind them.

"What is it? What's wrong?" Ulyanov hoped for the best, but was in for a rude awakening.

"The destruct sequence has started again," Dmitri replied simply.

"That's impossible," Neill shot back. "Malyev disarmed it."

"That was then. This is now." Yaroslav stood to his feet and gestured to the steel hull on the ground. "See for yourself."

Neill and Ulyanov crouched on the path and examined the control console, but Captain Yaroslav was right. Michael's eyes were glued to the display as he read it aloud:

MOTION SENSORS ACTIVATED
COUNTDOWN RESUMED

A quick glance at the numerical display not only confirmed that the countdown had been resumed, but had reset itself for less than thirty minutes.

"What now?" Michael asked.

"Get Malyev back here," Ulyanov ordered without hesitation. He was at his best in a crisis. "Bring Danzig back with you, too." As Corporal Sevnik nodded and took off through the tree line, the Colonel turned to Yaroslav. "Inform Captain

Mironov that it's not over yet."

Ulyanov and Neill watched helplessly as they crouched under the overhanging branches, each man praying silently but fervently. Within a minute the two men heard the sounds of approaching footsteps and then a mix of soldiers, technicians and policemen streamed down the path to the shed.

Malyev was the last to arrive, escorted by the soldiers with drawn weapons. Colonel Ulyanov waved him forward. As Ivan drew closer to the warhead a look of surprise spread over his face.

Dmitri Yaroslav watched his expression and bristled with anger. He stepped through the crowd and regarded Ivan with rage.

"This is your fault." Dmitri's face was now livid and only inches from Malyev's. There was rage in his eye. He was about to say something else when Neill and the Colonel pushed in and separated the two.

"Now is not the time, Captain," Ulyanov said firmly, then turned to the shocked Malyev. "Can you re-enter the password?"

Ivan's lip trembled as he bent over the control pad. "I can try."

Everyone watched hopefully as Ivan re-entered the password into the keypad. A hush descended on the group as the readout blinked and a new message appeared:

CODE INVALID
COUNTDOWN RESUMES

Fear welled up in Malyev's heart as he read the message. For the first time he no longer felt in control of the powerful weapon before him. He was sure he had keyed in the proper sequence. The mood of the group assembled around him suddenly changed from expectation to open hostility, and Ivan could hear angry threats rippling through the crowd. Without a word, Colonel Ulyanov restored order to the ranks by stepping forward and raising his hands for silence, then knelt at Ivan's side and quietly told him to try again.

Once more, Ivan keyed in the password, but the result was the same:

CODE INVALID
COUNTDOWN RESUMES

"I had no knowledge of this," Ivan snarled angrily. "This is Sasha's doing."

"What do you mean?" Neill asked.

"The motion detectors—" Ivan answered as he made a third, futile attempt at aborting the destruct sequence, "—it's Sasha's trademark. He's entered a sub-routine into the program."

"You mean there's nothing you can do?" Michael was afraid he already knew the answer to that.

Malyev shook his head. "Not without the proper password."

"—which Kobrin took to his grave," Ulyanov added. He set his jaw, drew up to his full height and began to assess the situation, which was getting worse with each passing second. "We still have twenty-eight minutes; Captain Yaroslav?"

Dmitri had calmed down and was thinking more rationally now. In fact, he was quite embarrassed by his outburst moments before. "We already know we can't disarm it here without setting off a chain-reaction," he said. "If we cut through the outer skin, the bomb will explode."

"So where does that leave us?" Neill looked at the Colonel, but as Ulyanov silently considered a reply, it was Dmitri that answered.

"We will load it onto the truck and I will drive it far into the countryside—" It was a noble offer, but Michael and Colonel Ulyanov shook their heads in unison.

"You can't do that, Dmitri," Neill told him. "The motion sensors deleted at least ten minutes from the countdown when the bomb was moved out of the shed. You'd be lucky to get half a mile from here before it detonated."

"It would seem our options are rather limited," the Colonel observed glumly. He turned to Malyev. "Tell me about the motion sensors—can they be disengaged?"

Ivan shrugged. "As I said, Sasha installed them without my knowledge."

"What about the other tamper-resistant devices—the circuitry that monitors the level of inert gas in the chamber—can we bypass those?"

Ivan looked thoughtful. "That circuitry is split into four groups, each wired directly to the warhead. I installed it myself. Each group is mounted internally on the vertical walls of the container—but the circuitry is interconnected."

"What does that mean?" Michael asked.

"All four groups must be deactivated at the same time, or an electrical signal is sent to the warhead," Ivan explained. "Once the signal is received, the chain-reaction begins and the bomb will explode."

"Is there any way to do that?" For the first time, Neill began to see a possible solution. "Deactivate all four groups, I mean."

Malyev frowned as beads of sweat formed on his brow. "That would be the best approach; disabling the circuitry would prevent the warhead's destruction at the end of the countdown."

"But there's no way to get to it," Yaroslav protested. "And we're running out of time."

"And alternatives," Neill threw in. "Any suggestions, Ivan?"

Even with his expertise in munitions and his familiarity with the warhead, Malyev found himself completely at a loss. "I'm afraid I can offer you nothing," he said meekly. "I suppose if you had a large enough hammer, you could smash the container—destroy all four groups simultaneously."

Michael's head came up at that, an odd look spreading

across his face. He caught the Colonel's eye and Ulyanov saw beyond his expression to something much deeper. Their friendship—and shared faith in God—bonded the officers together in a kindred spirit, and once again the same thought flashed through each man's mind.

"A hammer, did you say?" Neill asked.

Malyev shook his head. "An answer borne of desperation. Forget I mentioned it." Ivan tried to dismiss the off-handed remark, but seeing the look on Neill's face made him reconsider. "You don't have such a hammer—do you?"

"No, we don't," Michael replied. "What about the Ukrainian Air Defense Forces, Colonel?"

Ulyanov nodded his head as he considered his young friend's unspoken idea. "It might work."

Yaroslav was clueless. "What might work?"

"And it's not a dirty bomb, so the risk of widespread contamination is much lower. Of course, we'd have to move the warhead out of the trees to get a clear shot," Michael said, thinking out loud. "The motion sensors would pick up on that and delete more time from the countdown."

Now Mironov stepped forward. "A clear shot?" He was now more worried than he had been. "Clear shot at what? From where?"

The Colonel ignored the question. "What about the motion sensors? There's no way to know how much time we'd lose by moving it," he asked, directing his question to Neill.

Michael bit his lip and frowned. "We'll have to take that chance; no way around it." He knelt down and patted the steel container. "Do your pilots have a delivery system that can hit a target this small?"

"Oh, yes," the Colonel answered, then turned to Corporal Sevnik. "Get back to the truck and warm up the field radio—we'll be sending a message to the airbase in Nikolayev." Sevnik was off like a flash. "Dmitri, you and Michael take the warhead to the base of the Steps—it will be out in the open there and clearly visible from the sky."

Neill nodded, taking hold of one end of the titanium container as Yaroslav reached for the other. As they lifted it and began struggling down the path, Ulyanov ran ahead with Captain Mironov at his heels. A procession of soldiers, militiamen and technicians brought up the rear like a strange parade, then the group broke through the tree line and spilled out onto the street by the truck.

"What are you going to do?" Mironov insisted as Corporal Sevnik lowered the bulky radio set from the truck's bed. Colonel Ulyanov dialed in the frequency used by the fighter base at Nikolayev and checked his watch; he had an airstrike to coordinate and didn't have time to discuss his intentions.

"We're going to use a hammer, Captain—" Ulyanov replied at last, "—a Malat air-to-ground missile—to destroy the container, and hopefully the detonation circuitry as well."

"Seriously?" Mironov demanded. "Colonel, you'll destroy the warhead along with it—and spill plutonium into the atmosphere."

"That's a risk we'll have to take," the Colonel conceded. "But the alternative is far worse—and no one seems to have a better idea."

Chapter Twenty-Eight ✯ The Hammer

"YOU HAVE TO LET ME THROUGH," VIKTORIYA ordered the militia officer. "I'm a member of the press—" She pulled her credentials from her purse and waved them in front of his face. "—and I know those men."

The group at the Steps reappeared again from the tree line. There was a hurried sense to their activities now, and she could no longer see Neill. The officer ignored Viktoriya's demands. While the power of the press was growing in the former Soviet Union, it had a long way to go.

"Step back, Miss." He was a professional and had no intention of allowing this woman to get any closer. Someone had fired a shot moments before and that had set the militiamen on edge. Under normal conditions, the officer had an even-keeled temperament, but now he drew his sidearm from its holster. "Please don't interfere." Again, he repeated his request that she take a step back.

Something was happening at the Steps. Viktoriya was certain of that; and it involved the militia and the military. The convergence of both in one place only intensified her interest. This was a story worth finding out about; and that meant it was a story worth telling—and Viktoriya Gavrilenko wasn't about to miss it.

Neill and Captain Yaroslav stopped at the base of the giant staircase and lowered the warhead gently to the ground. Stepping away from the deadly device, both men held their breath as the digital display blinked and a new readout flashed across the face of the display:

MOTION SENSORS ACTIVE—
DEPLETING COUNTDOWN SEQUENCE

The display winked out as the timing device updated itself. The delay was excruciating. Then the clock started running again and Michael could see that the control pad's programming had deleted ten minutes from the sequence. There were now less than twenty minutes left till detonation.

* * * *

The radio crackled and the Colonel heard a reply as he stood at the back of the truck.

"No time for pleasantries, Bogdan," Ulyanov said into the radio handset. "We have an emergency here."

At the other end of the conversation, the Colonel's adjutant, Bogdan Dobrinskaya, was puzzled. He listened as Ulyanov quickly explained what he wanted, stifling his surprise when he heard the reason for his superior's strange request.

"I will see to it personally, Andrei," Bogdan replied once the Colonel had finished. "Which pilot do you prefer for this mission?"

"Our newest," Ulyanov ordered without hesitation. "The exchange pilot from Russia."

"Understood." Major Dobrinskaya frowned. He knew the man to be an excellent pilot, but wondered if he was the best choice.

"Perhaps one of our own would be a better—"

"I don't have time to argue, Major." The Colonel's voice carried a smooth, even tone. "Send Lieutenant Radischev—and his aircraft—but do it now."

* * * *

Viktor Radischev was already on the flight line. When the alarm claxon sounded his heart skipped a beat. He instinctively ran to the air-ops ready room with the rest of the pilots and was surprised to find the base commanding officer and Sergeant Rada waiting specifically for him.

He was confused. Normally, a pre-flight briefing would have followed, but Major Dobrinskaya abruptly dismissed the other flyers. He had a sense of urgency Radischev had never seen before.

There had been no time to prepare handouts or get satellite imagery for this mission. The orders he received were very unusual, to say the least; but they were also very explicit and left no room for interpretation. He was to fly eastward to Odessa, pinpoint a target at the base of the city's most famous landmark and destroy it with a Malat air-to-ground missile.

One issue had not been addressed. Radischev looked uneasily toward the Major and then to Rada. "The plane has sustained stress fractures," Viktor said at last. "It's been grounded. Do you want me to fly something else?"

The Major already knew all about that. Rada had briefed him days before.

"It would take too long to familiarize yourself with our aircraft," Dobrinskaya answered. He looked to the maintenance chief. "How serious is the damage?"

"Enough to cause concern." The chief measured his words carefully. "But you heard the Colonel. It's worth the risk." He turned to Radischev. "Fly your plane, Lieutenant."

That was the answer Viktor wanted to hear. He felt a surge of adrenaline. "I'm on my way, Sergeant. And don't worry—I'll be careful."

Rada stepped forward, shaking his head. "This is not a time for caution, Viktor." Something in Ulyanov's voice told the chief that the danger was very real. "Get in that plane and fly it like the devil himself."

Viktor zipped up his flight suit and grabbed a helmet, then

dashed from the ready room and headed for the massive hangar that dominated the airbase. Major Dobrinskaya watched as Radischev ran to his aircraft, hoping the mission would be successful but wondering if there was enough time.

* * * *

"How long?" Ulyanov asked.

"Fifteen minutes," Neill answered, a little breathlessly. The titanium container was light enough for two strong men to carry, but even over a short distance it could be a tiresome burden. "Did you get through to the airbase?"

The Colonel nodded, still holding the radio microphone as he stood by the back of the truck. "Major Dobrinskaya is scrambling an aircraft now," he said.

"Good," Neill replied, then forced a grin and gestured to the field radio. "What, you couldn't use a cell phone?"

"Too hard to get a signal down here," Ulyanov answered. "Believe me, I've tried."

Captain Mironov stood at the Colonel's side, shaking his head. It was hard for him to believe what was about to happen. Destroying a warhead with another warhead didn't make sense. He wasn't completely sold on the idea by any means, but without a better solution he was reluctantly committed to it.

"How far is the airbase?"

"Less than one hundred kilometers," Captain Yaroslav answered, then asked, "Is there enough time?"

"The weapons will have to be loaded and the pilot briefed …" Ulyanov did some quick arithmetic in his head. "Let's just say it will be close."

* * * *

Lieutenant Radischev strapped in as the fighter's engines spooled up to power. He completed his pre-flight checks just as the ordnance crew finished loading the missiles into the weapons bays and then he released the brakes and rolled the aircraft out of the hangar and onto the flight line. The tower gave him priority for takeoff and minutes later the ground crew watched admiringly as the sleek jet accelerated down the runway and streaked effortlessly into the sky.

* * * *

Neill checked his watch. Time passed quickly, until ten minutes had come and gone, leaving only five to go before the warhead exploded. There was nothing any of them could do now except wait and pray, and a tense silence fell over the group of men as they milled around the truck and looked expectantly overhead.

Neill turned and looked seaward. Aside from a few gulls, he could see nothing in the air.

"Are you worried, Michael?" Ulyanov asked.

Neill smiled. "This is a time for faith, not fear," he replied calmly. "When it's all said and done, this is really about trusting God. We can scheme and plan and try to influence events in our lives, but ultimately we have to leave it in His hands and accept His will." It was a reasoned, mature response; then Neill looked Ulyanov in the eye. "But yeah, I'm a little worried."

Ulyanov nodded in agreement. His young American friend had wisdom beyond his years. The Colonel admired that, but he was also honest enough to express his concern. Standing just a few feet away, Malyev listened intently as Michael's words pierced his heart. The emotions he'd tried to suppress rose up inside of him, but instead of trying to resist them he gave in to his feelings and felt deeply sorry for what he had done. His remorse felt oddly cleansing.

"Captain Yaroslav was right; this is my fault." Ivan's words came out slow. He hung his head, but his voice held the full weight of his shame. "All of us are going to die and there's nothing I can do to stop it."

Michael regarded the subdued terrorist with compassion. "Chin up, Ivan. God spared your life in Bryansk and He protected you from your own hand back at the shed—I don't think He's going to keep you alive through all that just to let you die without hope now. I'd like to believe He's trying to tell you something. I think you'd better listen." His mind raced for a verse of Scripture. He remembered the Old Testament passage he'd quoted at Walter's funeral.

"Acknowledge and take to heart this day that the Lord is God in Heaven above and on the Earth below. There is no other ..."

Neill might have spoken the words, but there was something supernatural about them that shone a light in Malyev's soul. The American might have been right; he'd cheated death more than once. Maybe there was some supernatural force ensuring his survival. Given their current circumstances, he would have liked to think so.

Ivan was about to reply, then looked up as a large, silver shape soared overhead, trailing thunder as it passed.

* * * *

No amount of pleading could convince the officer to let Viktoriya get any closer. She considered breaking through the barricade and running past him, but the militiamen were all holding their weapons now and she didn't want to risk it. The cabbie was growing impatient. She was ready to get back into the taxi and try another route when something roared over the port.

Lieutenant Radischev dialed in a frequency commonly reserved for military operations and keyed his mike. "Ground Control—Shroud One," he said as the jet shot over the harbor. "How do you copy?"

Neill watched in amazement as the fighter banked to the north and began to circle around for another pass and then was lost behind the trees and buildings of the city. The aircraft was clearly designed for stealth and looked just like the plane in the photos Willis Avery had shown him at Arlington.

Ulyanov's eyes followed the jet as it headed out to sea and then began its return. "This is Colonel Ulyanov. We have you in sight, Shroud One. Can you see the target?"

There was a long pause as Radischev brought the front of the plane back around and headed for the waterfront. He raised the darkened visor on his helmet and squinted into the distance.

"Negative, Colonel. I can see the Steps but not the target; switching to infrared scanning." From this distance, the titanium casing was just too small to pick out below.

Viktor's hand glided across the fire control display and activated the aircraft's infrared targeting system. The optical array in the nose of the plane swept across the base of the Steps, scanning until it found the small shape of the container. Sitting in the open and absorbing the sun's rays, the encased warhead showed up as a warm image against the backdrop of the cold granite staircase and the onboard computer locked it in as the primary target. Viktor switched on the laser designator and illuminated the distant case with a beam of high intensity light.

"Target acquired," Radischev said. The computer tied in the data from the optical array and the targeting laser, and with the warhead locked in the crosshairs Viktor turned his attention to warming up the weapons. "Get your people out of there, Colonel."

Ulyanov watched the approaching fighter as the pilot's warning crackled over the speaker. Lifting the heavy radio from the ground, the Colonel ordered the others to take cover.

"You heard the man," Ulyanov barked. "Let's move."

* * * *

Both missiles were now armed tucked away in the missile bays under each wing. Only one thing remained.

Radischev activated the heat-seeking device built into the nose of the first missile and watched as his multi-function display showed all ready for launch. The fighter was now less than a kilometer away from the staircase, and as the jet screamed over the anchored ships Viktor hit the firing switch.

The door of the weapons bay swung inward and the clamps released the missile. As it dropped, the rocket motor ignited and the deadly weapon began streaking ahead of the plane and accelerating quickly. The sleek Malat slipped through the layers of cold air, buffeted slightly by updrafts but never wavering as it sought out its target. Radischev followed it in, watching the weapon's exhaust trail and then veered the jet sharply away as the missile raced in to the target.

Viktoriya had a front row seat. She watched incredulously as the missile streaked in, then ducked down by the taxi as it approached the foot of the Steps, letting out a scream as the weapon found its target nearly a quarter of a mile away.

At twice the speed of sound, the Malat's travel time could be measured in seconds. It struck the target dead center, obliterating the titanium hull in a violent explosion that sent shrapnel, granite and chunks of steel flying at lethal speed in every direction.

The group of militia officers and soldiers had sought cover, but the blast knocked some of the men to their knees. A deafening roar accompanied the shock wave that rippled from the center of the explosion outward. Hundreds of windows in the downtown district were shattered, and Neill and the others covered their heads as a shower of debris rained down around them.

The sound of the exploding missile echoed all around. Instinctively, Colonel Ulyanov braced himself for the flash of a nuclear detonation, but if that had happened no one would have lived long enough to know it. As the smoke and noise of the initial blast faded away, he picked himself up and checked his men as Radischev's aircraft came around for another pass.

From the air, Lieutenant Radischev assessed the blast damage and watched as the ground troops ran to the new crater at the foot of the Potemkin Steps. He winced at the sight of the destruction he'd caused and then keyed the microphone once more.

"Ground; Shroud One," he called. "The target appears to be destroyed—can you confirm?"

There was a brief pause, then the radio crackled again and Colonel Ulyanov's voice filled the cockpit.

"Affirmative, Shroud One." The Colonel's breathless voice carried relief. "The target is destroyed. Nice shooting, Lieutenant."

Viktor Radischev said nothing, but beneath his oxygen mask he wore a thin smile. Passing once more over the troops below, he dipped his wings in salute, then banked the fighter to the north and headed back for the airbase at Nikolayev. It was the second time he'd fired a live Malat missile in recent weeks, but this time he couldn't help but feel a sense of great satisfaction.

Chapter Twenty-Nine ✶ Aftermath

I T DIDN'T TAKE LONG. CAPTAIN YAROSLAV found the stolen warhead, intact and lying on the Steps after being hurled thirty meters above the blast site. Almost no trace of the titanium container could be found, but miraculously, the bullet-shaped casing of the nuclear weapon was virtually unscratched. Leaking radiation was their greatest worry, but after a quick once-over, the technicians pronounced it safe for handling and the deadly device was carted away.

"What a mess." Neill and Colonel Ulyanov stood at the edge of the blast site. The crater wasn't very large, but thousands of pounds of granite and earth had been scooped out by the explosion and cast aside.

"Stone and mortar, Michael. This portion of the staircase can be easily fixed." Ulyanov looked up and beyond the hill to the town above. "A city and its people are not so easily restored."

Both men marveled at the fact that not a single injury had been reported. "What about that fighter?" Neill asked.

Ulyanov chuckled. "What would you like to know?" Once again, it was obvious he was in one of his jubilant moods.

"I saw Russian markings on the tail fin," Michael replied.

"Like I told you before; we've always been willing to trade with Russia," the Colonel answered nonchalantly. "We have an agreement with Moscow to provide us with certain military hardware, in exchange for food and mineral resources."

"Those Russian Tigers," Neill added. "You've been sharing technology. And the plane—is it the same one that—"

The Colonel nodded. "One and the same, Michael. The Russian military moved it here after ..." He didn't finish, and didn't have to. He turned and gave Neill a conspiratorial look. "Would you like to inspect the aircraft?"

"Wouldn't that violate national security?"

"It's a Russian plane, not Ukrainian, although it will be the basis for our own stealth fighter—once certain changes are made to the original design." Ulyanov smiled. "It's a long story, but as I understand it there are a few flaws in the airframe. I think I can arrange a private tour of our hangar at Nikolayev—if you'd like a closer look."

Michael's eyes took in the damage to the Steps as he considered the Colonel's offer.

"What about all this?"

"We'll leave some of our troops here to help Captain Mironov's men."

"That's not what I meant," Neill said. "How are we going to explain what happened here?"

"Oh, yes," Ulyanov had a twinkle in his eye. "In America the public has a right to the truth." He sighed deeply. "But this is not the United States, Michael. Things are somewhat different here."

Mironov's men were busy handling crowd control at the top of the staircase while Captain Yaroslav supervised the loading of the warhead below. That situation was well in hand. Neill's work at the dismantling facility was nearly finished. What Ulyanov offered would give him the opportunity to complete his mission for Willis Avery—an added bonus Michael had almost given up on.

"We need to make a few phone calls," Neill said. "One to your friends in parliament. The other to the American embassy in Kiev."

"If your plan is to succeed, we should act quickly," Ulyanov agreed. He smiled again. "And I think I know of a way that Miss Gavrilenko can help."

Neill had been thinking along those same lines. Everything seemed to be falling into place, but there was still work to be done. The two officers made their way up the Steps and discussed the next phase of their plan.

The militiamen didn't budge. The roadblocks remained in place and the officers refused access to the few brave souls that ventured into the streets to see what all the ruckus was about, Viktoriya included. The cabbie finally gave up in waiting for her and angrily backed his taxi away from the control point, then headed off in hopes of finding another fare.

Viktoriya stuck around long enough to hear the men trading whispered rumors of bombs and terrorists, but they refused to answer specific questions. She walked back and forth, from one end of the roadblock to another, straining to see the area at the base of the Steps; but neither Michael nor Colonel Ulyanov reappeared again. When it was clear she was getting nowhere, she headed back up toward town and caught another taxi to the newspaper.

Nothing but unconfirmed reports swirled there too. Several witnesses had seen the jet streak in from the sea, but details got fuzzy after that. From her vantage point, Viktoriya had seen the plane and the weapon it fired. After the explosion she watched as the aircraft circled back around again before disappearing into the northern sky. Everything had happened so fast that she neglected get a picture with her cell phone.

Viktoriya vowed to find out more. She'd seen Michael and Colonel Ulyanov there, two sources that could give her something; but that might just be wishful thinking. What were they doing there? And why had that jet fired on the Steps? There had to be a connection, but given the Marine's cautious personality, she wasn't too hopeful that he would be forthcoming with any information.

Viktoriya lingered over the thought of Neill. She still didn't know exactly why he'd come to Ukraine, and she might never know. But he'd certainly made her life more exciting since they'd met.

It would be dark in a few hours and the militia would probably be gone from the scene after that. At the very least they would maintain a reduced presence there. The explosion that had scared her out of her wits must have left some kind of tell-tale evidence. She decided her best course of action would be to just play the part of a tourist and visit the Steps during an evening stroll.

One of her colleagues was a photographer. Viktoriya borrowed a camera and began planning her night out. She was familiarizing herself with the camera's features when the phone on her desk rang. The display told her the call was local, with a government agency prefix, but she didn't recognize the number. She picked it up on the second ring.

"Viktoriya," came a familiar voice. She knew who it was right away.

"Michael," she answered. "Where are you? Are you all right?"

A pause. "I'm fine—why shouldn't I be?"

"I was there, Michael," she replied, just a hint of frustration in her voice. "I saw you. *And* the Colonel." She started drumming her fingers on the desk, a nervous habit she resorted to when she was perturbed. "What happened?"

Neill laughed. "Do you follow me *everywhere*, Viktoriya?"

"What *happened*, Michael?" she repeated. The man could be infuriating. Viktoriya could tell he was enjoying this.

"That's a long story. How would you like to take a little drive tomorrow morning?"

That was not a question she expected to hear. "Tomorrow morning?" she stammered.

"I'll have Corporal Sevnik pick you up around eight. Can you be ready by then?"

"Yes. But where will he take me?"

"You'll have to wait and see," Neill replied. "And Viktoriya—"

"I'm here."

"Be prepared to take notes. We've got a lot of work for you to do."

Chapter Thirty ✶ The Exclusive

WESLEY COBB STOOD AND STRETCHED, holding a telephone in one hand and staring out the window of his office overlooking Sikorsky Street. The room occupied the second floor of the American Embassy in Kiev, and Cobb was holding forth on the politics of extradition. It was a rather one-sided conversation, with the Ambassador doing most of the talking, but as a former professor of law, Cobb was thoroughly enjoying himself.

"There's a subtle difference in those terms," he was saying. "What you're talking about is technically rendition; not in the common vernacular, but in the correct definition of the word."

On the other end of the line, Michael Neill was trying to make sense of the terminology. "I'm just concerned with getting this done legally, sir."

Cobb wasn't sure he was making himself understood, which frustrated the teacher in him. "Let me try to clear this up," he answered patiently.

"In basic terms, rendition is simply transferring a person from one area of jurisdiction to another. It's the act itself. Unfortunately, it's come to mean a whole lot more. When you mention rendition to the media, of course, it conjures up images of secret detainees and covert prison sites, among other things."

"Including torture," Neill offered.

"Well, yes," Cobb admitted. "In fact, there are those who

refer to rendition as 'torture by proxy.' And that's unfortunate, because we don't extradite individuals to countries that practice torture. Several years ago, the Secretary of State made it very clear that we don't do that. And the President has signed an executive order that took that off the table.

"You have to be careful when you talk to a journalist about this. Like I said, they immediately go for the more salacious aspects surrounding the subject," he warned.

"I'll keep that in mind." *Because that's exactly what I plan to do,* Neill thought. He was sitting at the desk in Colonel Ulyanov's office. "Do you have an opinion on what I'm proposing?"

"I do." Cobb's legal mind started to work. "And I have to say that I agree with it. It has the virtue of being creative. Very few State Department officials would consider it without running it up and down their chain of command to get approval."

Whereas I'm an amateur, Neill didn't say. Still, he was surprised. He'd expected resistance to his plan, but the Ambassador was being very receptive—for a government bureaucrat.

"Look, we have practices in place that remove suspected terrorists from their areas of operation, so this isn't without precedent." Cobb continued. "In this case, the suspect isn't being turned over to some third world country that may or may not respect his civil rights." He added a thin layer of sarcasm to that last part. "What you're talking about doing is bringing the individual to America—so he can aid our intelligence services. He'll be remanded to the custody of the Central Intelligence Agency. And I can assure you he won't suffer harm on our soil. You did say this man is willing to cooperate, didn't you, Mr. Neill?"

"Lieutenant Neill," Michael corrected.

"Sorry—*Lieutenant* Neill."

"That's correct, sir. He is willing to cooperate."

"Excellent. But it will take more than just his testimony. Our people will want some type of actionable intelligence.

Can he provide any corroborating evidence?"

"He was carrying an envelope stuffed with various documents. Copies of emails, requests for weapons, ledger pages with account numbers—signed by certain individuals, along with several photographs. Some of it appears to be circumstantial, but taken together—" Neill paused. He didn't want to reveal too many details over the phone. Their discussion had purposely omitted names and locations. Both men were speaking on encrypted lines, but operational security habits died hard.

Cobb rubbed his chin. "We'll have to take a look at that. Of course, there are other legal considerations. And you'll need our help to make it happen." Cobb picked up a pen and jotted down a few notes. "I'll have my deputy Chief of Mission start on the documentation you'll require."

"I do have a letter from Willis Avery, giving me some authority for this kind of thing."

The Ambassador wrote that down too. "Good. That could come in handy. I'll give Avery a call later today." He looked at his watch. "It's still early morning in D.C." Cobb thought of one more thing.

"The individual in question—I'm assuming he's in a secure location?"

"Absolutely," Neill answered.

Ironically, Ivan Malyev's criminal activities ended where his most serious offense had begun. He was a guest of the weapons facility, enjoying a room all to himself—with two armed guards just outside his door.

Corporal Sevnik followed the same route to the weapons station as he always did. He had no choice, really. By design, the narrow highway that wound through the forested countryside was the only access road anywhere near the facility.

The view hadn't changed much over the course of the long winter months. The endless sea of trees was still barren, with no hint of spring in sight. To Sevnik, the scenery had the look of a black and white photograph, except for the dull color of a road sign, or the occasional vehicle approaching from the other lane. He'd become very accustomed to the familiar twists and turns of the highway. On one occasion, the Colonel had even joked that he could probably navigate the course with his eyes closed. Sevnik thought he might try that sometime; but that was only boredom provoking him.

The thought of boredom brought a smile to his face—there was certainly none of that the day before. Yesterday's events seemed like a dream. But the role he had played—a *crucial* role, he reminded himself—was one he hoped he could one day share with his grandchildren.

Sevnik was just bursting to talk to someone about it. Today he would have settled for discussing it with Captain Yaroslav, who was seated next to him; but that conversation was off-limits, in deference to the passenger they carried in the back seat.

Viktoriya Gavrilenko had been strangely quiet for most of the ride. Sevnik and the Captain had picked her up at her apartment not long after sunrise. She'd greeted both of them courteously, but said little after that. From time to time the Corporal stole a glance at her in the rearview mirror. She was certainly easy on the eye, he thought. But he did that once too often and when he looked back again, her eyes were on him, and she was smiling. Sevnik was slightly embarrassed. He focused on the road for the rest of the trip.

Neill's call the night before had given hope that she might get answers to her questions. But as the car sped away from town and ventured deeper into the forest she began to feel a little anxious. During the height of the Soviet era, trouble-some people asking too many questions simply disappeared. Viktoriya imagined that might have been her fate if she'd lived before *glasnost* and *perestroika*. Her generation wasn't too far removed from those times—which made her worry.

She banished that thought and assured herself that Michael

and Colonel Ulyanov weren't like that. Both men were far too honest and trustworthy to start suspecting their motives now. And Viktoriya had always liked to think that she was a good judge of character—especially when it came to men.

The car slowed and then edged off the highway onto an even narrower road. A hundred yards from the turn, Viktoriya could see a vast complex of buildings, slightly hidden by trees and surrounded by a tall fence. Troops in uniform milled about inside the perimeter and a sentry checkpoint straddled the road between the gate posts.

Captain Yaroslav and Corporal Sevnik produced their I.D.s to the guard, who looked inquiringly at the woman in the back seat. Sensing he wanted hers as well, Viktoriya retrieved her press credentials from her purse. The sentry took a long look at her photo and bent low to study her face. He finally seemed satisfied and handed them back to her. With a wave of his hand he motioned for Sevnik to proceed through the gate.

Colonel Ulyanov appeared in the hall after the group had cleared the security desk. He seemed to be very pleased to see Viktoriya, smiling broadly and extending his hand. "Thank you for coming," he gushed. Neill was close behind. Suddenly she was much more at ease.

"You two have been busy," she said, returning Ulyanov's grin. "I saw you sight-seeing yesterday." Her statement carried just a hint of sarcasm.

"So I hear." The Colonel's smile continued and he looked at her with a raised eyebrow. "But is there a veiled question in that statement?"

"Probably more than one," Neill quipped. He placed his hand lightly on her shoulder and gestured toward an open door. "Let's step into the conference room.

"I think it's time we had a philosophical discussion."

A tray of tea, sausage, kasha and yogurt—the thick, Russian kind—was brought in, and the assembled group began eating. Viktoriya had been too nervous to have breakfast at her apartment, so the light brunch was especially welcome.

After the meal, the Colonel played host and poured everyone a second cup of tea as Viktoriya pulled out a small tablet computer and laid it on the table. Ordinarily she would have taken notes the old-fashioned way, with a reporter's notepad, but she had begun relying more and more on electronic media.

"We find ourselves in need of assistance," Ulyanov said as he sat down. He sipped his tea before continuing. "Assistance we feel that you can provide."

Viktoriya was intrigued but non-committal as the Colonel set the hook. Even in Eastern Europe there was a level of distrust between the press and the military. It went both ways. "What can I do to help?"

It was Neill's turn. He began by explaining in very general terms why he and the Colonel had visited Odessa the day before. Viktoriya sat spellbound as the two officers took turns relaying what had happened at the waterfront less than twenty-four hours earlier. They were careful not to mention Ivan Malyev by name, or the role he played in the warhead's presence at the Steps. That would come later—after they gauged her reaction and willingness to help.

"There's something you're not telling me." Viktoriya recognized that some details had been left out. She decided to try a little leverage. "And you did say you needed my help. How can I do that if I don't have all the facts?"

The Colonel turned to Neill. "What do you think, Michael? Should we tell her more?"

Neill frowned. "She's been angling for a story for quite some time now. Which one do we give her first?"

"Perhaps the one about Russia's most advanced fighter?"

"The one that has NATO worried?" Michael looked thoughtful. "That wouldn't interest her. I was thinking more about how the bomb got downtown in the first place."

The Colonel shook his head. "Too pedestrian for her tastes. But I think she could work wonders linking Murovanka to the terrorist network the Russians just broke up." He gave the young woman a stony look. "Of course, any information we give her would have to be handled *very* carefully; innocent lives might hang in the balance. Do you understand, Miss Gavrilenko?"

Ulyanov had made his point. Viktoriya was a bit taken aback with the sudden rush of information and wondered if they'd rehearsed their little spiel. But she was clever enough to understand its meaning. She raised a hand to stop them before they could continue.

"I get the picture." She sighed. "Give me your terms. I'm sure we can come to an agreement."

"I've read your columns, Viktoriya." The Colonel was fully engaged now and eager to begin the next phase of the strategy he and Neill had come up with. "You have a gift for uncovering corruption. In fact, it was my wife who suggested that you could help us."

Viktoriya was surprised to hear that. Irina had been polite to her at the opera, but there had been a very real tension between them. She suspected the older woman's maternal feelings for Michael were the reason.

"Like a playwright, we too have a story to tell," Ulyanov continued. "The characters have been assembled and the stage has been set. But the end of the tale still needs to be crafted. That's where you come in."

"We need someone who can connect the dots," Neill explained. "And we're willing to provide key information to help you do that."

"Suppose I help you," Viktoriya replied. "What do I get out of all this?"

"What you've been looking for all along," Ulyanov offered. "A story. And not just one." He paused. "But there is a catch."

"I'm listening," she answered cautiously.

Once again Neill took up the narrative. He started with the reason for his mission in Ukraine and the real purposes of the weapons station. He continued by telling her about the security breach the facility had suffered and the theft of the warhead.

Viktoriya tapped away on the keypad as Ulyanov explained Malyev's role in the plot to steal the weapon. He also elaborated on the evidence they had tying in Pirogov and Murovanka. As he moved through some of the finer points, Viktoriya asked additional questions and recorded the answers on the tablet. Laying out all the details took some time, but by mid-morning the two officers had finished summarizing the facts.

The material was a bit overwhelming, even to a seasoned journalist like Viktoriya. She had enough for several features; and if she read the Colonel right, they were exclusives. But she was also keenly aware that what they'd told her was very sensitive.

"You said there was a catch."

"Explain to me why you got into journalism, Viktoriya," the Colonel prodded gently.

It wasn't the first time someone had posed that question to her. "I believe in telling the truth. Getting the facts is important to me."

"For what reason?"

The answer to that required a more thoughtful response. "Informed decisions demand it. Disinformation and lies can be used for dishonest purposes. Only the truth prevents that."

Ulyanov held his peace for a moment, but he was pleased by her answer. If she truly believed that, then the SSD's assessment of her had been correct. "So ultimately, if the truth isn't handled with care, people can get hurt."

Viktoriya had heard this speech before—Ulyanov was leading her down this path to manipulate her actions. The color in her cheeks darkened a little. "Are you asking me to sit on this?"

Neill worried that she might be resistant to their request, but he answered her honestly. "For the time being, yes. Some of the information you can never reveal. Ivan Malyev is dead to the Russians. He has to stay that way."

"Viktoriya, we've told you everything we know." The Colonel's voice had a subdued tone that softened her temper. "Work with us on this. Cooperate with our intelligence services. When we start getting results, you'll be free to publish whatever you like."

"If you can square up some of the intel we have, then sooner is better—we'd like to start putting pressure on Murovanka immediately," Michael added.

"You want me to work for the SSD?"

"Not *for*—*with*."

"You would be helping your country, Viktoriya," Ulyanov said. "Do you have a problem with that?"

"Of course not."

"Then the decision should be an easy one," the Colonel said. "But it's yours to make."

Even though she was convinced of their integrity, Viktoriya wanted assurances. "And I get exclusive rights to the story?" she asked.

"That's correct," Ulyanov replied. "What do you say?"

She sighed heavily and paused before answering. "I say that it's very hard to refuse a man in uniform." She smiled. "And it's impossible to say no to two of them.

"You have a deal."

Chapter Thirty-One ✶ Pressing an Advantage

C ENTRAL EUROPE SLOWLY GAVE WAY TO THE rural landscape of Ukraine as the Gulfstream banked east. As the plane descended and began its approach into Nikolayev, the pilot dipped the wings a little to take in the view.

The plane had left the sophisticated power stations and in-dustrial plants in places like Austria and Poland far behind. The view changed considerably as the aircraft crossed into Ukrainian airspace. It was easy to distinguish urban centers in the former Soviet empire simply by observing the general state of disrepair that characterized them. What the pilot saw below him now looked very familiar—a lot like the Odessan countryside—but he'd never been to this part of Ukraine be-fore.

He was a little confused. He had dropped off the Marine of-ficer in Odessa, but now had orders to pick up Lieutenant Neill in Nikolayev. No explanation had been given. The change in plans made him a little edgy; the Captain was accustomed to flying in Ukrainian airspace, but this would be his first landing at a military installation.

Once again, the Gulfstream received an escort. Two SU-27 fighters flanked the American aircraft as it made its approach—appearing the moment the jet entered Ukrainian airspace—then broke formation and peeled away as the plane landed. The

Captain watched the two jets disappear from view. He and his co-pilot taxied to the end of the runway and stopped in front of the field's huge hangar. Both men noticed that the doors of the barnlike structure were closed tight.

"Kind of creepy, huh?' the co-pilot observed. The Captain didn't answer, but craned his neck to get a better view of the flight line. The building to their right looked like the air operations office, and as he watched, the pilot saw movement.

"There he is," the Captain said. He unstrapped his restraints and started to climb out of his seat when the co-pilot stopped him. Both men watched as Neill was joined by two enlisted Marines in camouflaged uniforms—undoubtedly members of the security detachment at the embassy in Kiev—each wearing cartridge belts with side arms on their hips. Another man was with them, wearing a simple dark suit and a white, button down shirt. Neill stood with him as the Marines began bringing out a variety of sea bags and luggage.

"That's Neill, all right," the junior officer said with a frown, "—but who's that with him?"

"No idea," the pilot replied. "But I think our passenger list just got longer."

* * * *

Willis Avery flashed his credentials as he entered the CIA building in Langley, Virginia, and was issued a visitor's pass that he clipped to his lapel. Richard Aultman accompanied him and got the same treatment. In short order both men were met by an agency case officer. He introduced himself as Ike Gleeson and escorted the two through the maze of hallways that lead deep into the interior of America's spy headquarters.

They were ushered into a large, non-descript conference room where Lieutenant Michael Neill sat waiting. As the National Security Advisor and his small entourage came in, Neill stood to his feet. The young Marine wore his winter service uniform, as well as a CIA visitor's pass hanging from his front breast pocket.

Avery greeted the Lieutenant warmly and the group delved into small talk for the first few minutes. Neill produced a formal letter from Colonel Ulyanov, which Avery scanned briefly and then handed to Aultman, who filed it away in his satchel. He also had some documentation Wesley Cobb had given him, but Michael decided to hold off on that—it was clear that the National Security Advisor was far more interested in what had been laid out on the conference table in front of them.

Avery lowered his eyes to a series of photographs and sat down. Aultman could tell that his boss was impressed by the pictures he began poring over. The other men took their seats as Avery began reviewing the material.

"Very interesting," Avery muttered. He held up one of the prints so Michael could see. "Clue me in on this feature."

Neill had taken the photos and brought them back from Nikolayev after his 'private tour' of the airbase. "That's the aircraft's fire control data board. Schematics of the circuitry are at the bottom of the stack."

Avery grunted in response then flipped to the next photo. "And this?"

"Forward looking infrared scanner," Michael replied. He didn't have to add that the device had saved his life—and many others—just days before; the National Security Advisor had received Neill's report that morning and had already absorbed most of its content. And he was impressed. Looking first at Aultman, then back to Avery, Neill continued the briefing as the two men listened with great interest.

"Russian advanced aviation is divided into two parts— Shadow and Shroud," Neill explained, beginning to flesh out the details Avery found most compelling. "Shadow is their bomber program. I can't shed any light on that part, but my source tells me that's being developed in the Ural Mountains." He paused and gestured to the pictures on the table. "As for the fighter version—Shroud—well, it's not exactly everything it's cracked up to be."

Avery looked up. "What does that mean?"

"You suspected they'd developed a sixth generation fighter," Neill went on. "What you see there is barely fifth generation—and sometimes it's not even that."

Avery was intrigued. "Go on."

"Apparently the Russians got in a hurry to get to the next stage of aircraft development. They neglected to do their homework and 'borrowed' technology from the Chinese. The fighter they designed suffers from more than a few flaws."

Wow, Aultman thought to himself. The intelligence community would be relieved to hear that; even with their access to resources, this was something they hadn't seen coming. Neill's mission to discover more about the fighter had almost been an afterthought, but he'd already delivered more intel on it than the CIA could provide. And he seemed to know more.

"What about the other aspects of the aircraft?" Avery pressed.

"It has a respectable LPIR—Low Probability of Intercept Radar. But no exotic weapons or stand-off capabilities to disrupt cellular communications. They seem to have perfected a technique for low-observable composites, which they've incorporated into the plane's skin."

Avery's eyes never left the pile of photos. He had hoped that Neill might be able to bring back something useful, but the information the young Marine provided just seemed too good to be true.

"Outstanding, Neill—but how did the Russians manage to develop their stealth capabilities?"

Neill wasn't quite sure how to answer that one. The secrecy surrounding American technology was legendary, even though the general public was quite aware of much of its existence now.

"Word gets around, sir," Michael said casually. "After all, the internet has conquered the world, and they get the Discovery Channel, too—by satellite, of course."

Avery snorted his disapproval. In his opinion, television documentaries that focused on U.S. military technology would one day seriously undermine national security. Still, he had what he wanted and nothing could undo what the Russians had done. 'Red Sky at Morning' had been confirmed and would figure into Western military planning for years to come. The Cold War might be over, but the race went on. It would continue as long as the two countries tried to find new ways of dealing with each other in an ever-changing world.

Neill's voice brought him back around. "It's worth noting that the Russians will be working to correct those design flaws I mentioned."

"Of that I'm sure," Avery grumped. That's what worried him. It might only be a part-time fifth generation fighter. But once they sent it back to the drawing board that could change very quickly.

He pushed his concerns aside and looked up at Neill, a smile spreading slowly across his face. "Well done, Lieutenant," he said, rising to his feet. "Looks like I owe you one. Now let's discuss this other idea of yours."

Neill nodded to the case officer, who got up from his chair and disappeared through a door to the adjoining room.

"Clearly this meeting couldn't take place in my office," Avery intoned. "This is a much more appropriate setting."

"I understand," Neill replied. He was a little more concerned about this part of the discussion. "Bringing our guest to the White House—"

The discussion was cut short as Gleeson came back in, escorting someone known to Neill but unfamiliar to Avery and Aultman.

Freshly-shaven, scrubbed clean and wearing a dark suit, Ivan Malyev stepped cautiously into the room. A visitor's badge like the one Neill wore was clipped to his jacket. He looked at Neill, then hesitantly at Willis Avery. The National Security Advisor was an imposing figure as he stood and Ivan felt somewhat anxious in the awkward silence that followed.

Neill rose slowly to his feet and gripped Malyev's arm reassuringly. "Mr. Avery, I'd like for you to meet a new ally.

This is Ivan Malyev." For Ivan's benefit he repeated the introductions in Russian.

Avery didn't immediately respond, choosing to look over the Russian instead.

"You did say to bring back anything that might tell us what Moscow is up to." Neill paused to gauge Avery's reaction and then spent the next few minutes summarizing what he had in mind. Slowly, the National Security Advisor's features softened as he began to come around to the plan. Michael admitted that Murovanka had probably covered his tracks well, but with Ivan's inside information the charges against the Russian President just might stick.

By the time Michael finished, Avery was genuinely enthused. "It might work," he said softly. "I just hope Murovanka and his cronies don't know that Malyev's still alive, much less here in America."

Avery sat down and then shot a guarded look in Neill's direction. "By the way—how did you get Malyev out of Ukraine without raising a ruckus?"

Michael had wondered when that might come up. "With Colonel Ulyanov's persuasion, select members of the Ukrainian parliament were happy to help; Ambassador Cobb provided the documents that got us past Customs. The Air Force pilot was very reluctant until I showed him this—" he pulled a white envelope from a separate stack of documents on the table. It was stamped with Avery's name and the White House logo. Avery could see that the seal was broken

Avery frowned. "Does Mr. Malyev go along with all this?"

"I'm confident he does," Michael replied. "He's been debriefed extensively by the Ukrainian Security Directorate. Colonel Ulyanov and I brought in a journalist who also interviewed him." Viktoriya had spent several days questioning Ivan as well. "Between the two, we've gathered some promising intelligence." Neill pulled several pages from a folder in front of him. "This is a transcript of the raw data that Ivan's provided. He still faces criminal charges in Ukraine, but if the information proves useful, Pavlovsk has agreed to consider a full presidential pardon."

"But until then, they're more than happy to let us sift through it all," Avery snorted.

"It beats the alternative," Neill was quick to say.

"I suppose so," Avery admitted. "Having the man in our custody is probably the better option." He was still just a little skeptical, but his intuition told him that the Lieutenant's plan was a good one, and if successful it could force a more open and democratic administration in the Kremlin. Putting pressure on Murovanka might make him think twice about using terrorist tactics in the future. In return, the U.S. government would make sure the Ukrainian judicial system knew how helpful Malyev had been in exposing Murovanka.

Avery considered the prospects of the plan and came to a decision. "That's good enough for me," he declared. It was simple to say, but there was still a lot of work to do. "We'll have to integrate Mr. Malyev into our way of doing things; he'll need a new identity, a place to live and round-the-clock security." He looked at Neill. "He trusts you, Lieutenant. I'm counting on you to help him make the transition. Oh, by the way—" Avery pulled a memo from his pocket. "I received a call last night from Ambassador Cobb. The press over there knows about the missile that slammed into the waterfront. The newspaper in Odessa has said very little. They're reporting that the weapon was launched accidentally during an exercise."

Michael wouldn't admit it, but he was the one who had suggested the idea. "Do you think that story will keep?" he asked.

"It should. Emerging technology always has a few bugs that need to be worked out. In any event, the whole thing will probably blow over in a week or so anyway."

As his voice trailed off, Avery stepped around the table and extended his hand. "You've been a great help, Lieutenant," he said. "Now you'll excuse me while I try to figure out a way to sell this plan of yours to the President."

"Just a moment, sir."

Avery stopped and stared. "Is there something else?"

"There is," Neill replied. "Ivan doesn't speak the language. He'll need a tutor." He pulled a slip of paper from his pocket and handed it to Avery.

Avery read the name Neill had written. "We've got plenty of those, Lieutenant. But thanks for the offer." Avery started to hand the paper back to Neill, but the Lieutenant held up his hand.

"Not so fast. You said you owed me one." His tone was very resolute. "Did you mean that or not?"

Richard Aultman cleared his throat and stepped back. Neill was clearly pressing his advantage, and he found the whole scenario amusing.

Avery's eyes narrowed as he regarded Neill. Something told him the bulldog in this Marine wasn't going to let it go. He sighed, but looked ready to deal.

"All right, I'll make this happen." He paused, regarding Neill with even greater respect. "Do you play poker, by any chance?"

"A hand or two," Neill answered. His expression never changed. "My uncle taught me."

* * * *

Avery considered the events of the past few weeks on the drive back to the White House. Once there, he made his way back to his office, sat down and once more looked over Neill's report. He also had the photographs the Marine had provided. He re-read the report and then pulled out a lined pad, occasionally jotting down notes, considering the best way to make use of the information Malyev promised. It seemed like a golden opportunity, but his attention was divided.

Like most days in the White House, this one had been long. Oddly enough, his mind was drawn away by the memory of his grandfather. Avery wasn't sure why, but he had a feeling the young Lieutenant was the reason for that. Something about Neill's bearing reminded him of the way Grandpa Avery had carried himself. As he recalled Neill's words at Arlington, he knew why; separated by a generation of time and worlds apart in their experiences, the country preacher and the Marine officer were nonetheless linked by a common faith.

After twenty minutes, Avery had a rough outline ready to show to the President. He could honestly report that the entire operation had turned out better than anyone expected. He slipped on his coat and gathered up the photographs Neill had brought in, then got up and headed for the door, running a hand through his perpetually tussled hair. As he made his way down the hall, he found himself humming a melody, an old hymn he'd learned as a boy growing up in the hills of Kentucky. He'd long since forgotten the words, but their meaning was something he could never push aside.

Epilogue ✶ The Teacher

S HE SHOULD HAVE TAKEN A CAB. THE BAGS OF groceries were growing heavy in her arms and the weather didn't help, either. Her joints had begun to ache. She attributed that to the cold. Under her feet, the icy sidewalk forced her to take each step with extra care. The wind was blowing in from the north and her coat and scarf now seemed completely inadequate.

She should have taken a cab, but Natasha Lenkov didn't have the money to spare this month. Fuel prices had spiked again. The ripple effect meant higher costs on just about everything linked to transportation—including food. A cab was a luxury she just couldn't afford. Of course, if she had used a taxi, she could have bought more of the things she needed; but as it was, she'd probably need to make another trip to the market by the end of the week. She did a little math in her head; maybe if she did without milk—or by-passed the eggs in the dairy case—she could splurge a bit and have enough for the fare next time.

There was always the bus, but she knew that wouldn't work; manhandling the sacks aboard public transportation was just too cumbersome. Or she could carpool with some of the other ladies from the retirement village; but few of them drove anymore and most had family members who took them where they needed to go.

No, for now she'd just walk and do the best she could. Spring couldn't be far off now. She'd just endure the season a little longer, and once the weather changed, maybe her prospects would, too.

Natasha shook her head. Getting old wasn't easy. Being old *and* alone just made things more difficult. She felt a little moisture in the corners of her eyes, but stubbornly blamed that on the frigid temperatures.

Ike Gleeson knocked on the door again. There was no answer.

"She's not home," he said to Richard Aultman. "Come back tomorrow?"

Aultman shook his head. "Lieutenant Neill was rather insistent. I wouldn't want to disappoint the Marines. And Mr. Avery wants this done today." He shoved his hands into his pockets to keep warm. "Let's go wait in the car."

"Could be a long one."

The two started back toward the street. They'd parked at the end of a cul-de-sac in a modest neighborhood of senior adults. Nothing fancy at all; just row after row of tiny, one story duplexes. Gleeson looked left and right, then stopped as a tiny figure approached from a block away.

"Hold on. I'll bet that's her."

Aultman turned to look, then shook his head. "It's too cold for someone like her to be out in weather like this."

Natasha's arms were locked in a painful embrace as she clutched her groceries. She ignored the discomfort and was silently thankful that her apartment was just a few doors down.

"Mrs. Lenkov?"

The voice startled her. She'd seen the two men in dark suits earlier, but now they were standing only a dozen feet away and blocking her path. She stopped in her tracks and regarded them warily. Neither man looked familiar. She knew most of her neighbors. These two were clearly strangers to her and she wondered how they knew her name.

When she didn't respond, Gleeson repeated her name. "My name is Ike Gleeson," he said. He turned to the other man and they both held up their credentials. "This is Richard Aultman. We work for the federal government." Gleeson wasn't big on people skills, but even he knew that sounded better than blurting out that he worked for the CIA. He softened his voice. "We'd like a little of your time, if you can spare it."

She stepped forward cautiously and examined their endorsements, then winced as the discomfort in her shoulders reminded her that she'd had a long walk.

Aultman was perceptive enough to recognize her pain. "Here, let us help you with those," he said gently, stepping toward her and taking one of the sacks. Gleeson was quick to do the same.

"Thank you—Gleeson, you said?" she asked, speaking for the first time.

Aultman nodded. "Yes, ma'am. And Aultman. Richard Aultman." He stuck out his hand.

Natasha slowly extended a stiff arm, but was frowning. "I'm not in any trouble, am I?" Suddenly she was suspicious.

Aultman laughed. "Not at all, Mrs. Lenkov."

That seemed to please her. "Then let's get inside. I'll fix you gentlemen some tea."

"You come highly recommended to us," Gleeson was saying. The men had shed their heavy coats and laid them over a chair in Natasha's small living room. The apartment had a slightly musty smell and was sparsely furnished, but there were several framed photos on the mantle. Many were very old. Aultman decided that more than a few of them were images of Mrs. Lenkov and her husband.

Natasha seldom had visitors, especially the government variety. The two continued to stand until she told them to sit down. Once she was sure they were comfortable, she busied herself in the kitchen, putting water on the stove and then returned with a tray of crackers. Gleeson was about to wave off the snack until Aultman caught his eye. The old woman was trying to be hospitable, and it wouldn't do to refuse her offer.

"Your tea will be ready in a few minutes," she announced. Her accent was heavy, but she made herself understood quite well. She took a chair between them. "Now what can I help you with?"

"As I mentioned, Mrs. Lenkov, you come highly recommended," Gleeson began. "I understand you're a teacher?"

She nodded. "I was. I'm retired now."

Aultman sampled a cracker. It was a little stale, but he never let on. "Would you consider coming out of retirement?" he asked. "A situation has come up. We have an individual who speaks only Russian. But he works for us now; and being fluent in English would be beneficial not only to him, but to the United States government as well."

"Right now we simply don't have enough tutors to go around," Gleeson said. Aultman knew he was stretching the truth by a wide margin, but it was for a good cause. Neill's gesture was a noble one, and entirely selfless. Aultman admired that. "The American people would be indebted to your service."

"How indebted?" Natasha asked.

Gleeson grinned at that, then got up and retrieved an envelope from his coat pocket on the chair. He removed a single sheet of paper and laid it on the coffee table in front of her. "We're prepared to offer you a generous salary; you'll see it listed here on line twelve."

Her eyes grew wide. "That much? Per *month*?"

Gleeson blinked and looked at Aultman. "Per month?" She'd misunderstood him. "No, Mrs. Lenkov—that figure would be your *weekly* salary."

Generous was an understatement. As she studied the paper, her eyes began to mist slightly. From the kitchen came the sound of the water boiling on the stove.

"A car will pick you up, Tuesday through Friday and bring

you to our offices in Langley. At the end of the day, we'll bring you back home again. You would be a contractor, in the employ of the Central Intelligence Agency."

The second part of what he'd said didn't seem to impress her. "Four days a week?" she asked.

Aultman nodded. "That's right. Eight hours a day."

She paused, considering what they had told her and then left the room for the kitchen without a word. Aultman and Gleeson exchanged puzzled glances. They'd expected her to accept immediately, or even reject the offer outright. Her actions now just confused them.

After a moment she came back in, this time bearing a tray with three cups, along with sugar and milk—and a satisfied expression on her face.

"Tuesday through Thursday would fit my schedule better, Mr. Gleeson—I spend Fridays with my friends at the community center," she said, gingerly handing each man a cup. Then as an afterthought she added, "And let's make it *six* hours a day; I'm not as young as I used to be."

Gleeson was stunned, but he agreed. Aultman broke out in an open grin. The CIA officer did the same. Neither man had expected her to resort to negotiations. Natasha Lenkov had surprised them both and pressed her advantage.

After all, she was old, but certainly not stupid.

Get the next book in

the Michael Neill adventure series.

Tempest of Fire!

Made in the USA
Lexington, KY
09 March 2014